Search Party

○   ○   ○

Valerie Trueblood

SEARCH

STORIES OF RESCUE

PARTY

COUNTERPOINT PRESS

BERKELEY, CALIFORNIA

The author thanks the publications where some of these stories first appeared:
One Story, "The Magic Pebble"; *Wordsmitten*, "Street of Dreams";
Thresholds (UK), "The Llamas"; *Seattle Review*, "The Finding."

Library of Congress Cataloging-in-Publication Data
Trueblood, Valerie.
[Short stories. Selections]
Search party : stories / Valerie Trueblood.
pages cm
"Distributed by Publishers Group West"—T.p. verso.
ISBN 978-1-61902-149-5
I. Title.
PS3620.R84S43 2013
813'.6—dc23   2013002369

Cover design by Faceout Studios
Interior design by David Bullen

Counterpoint Press
1919 Fifth Street
Berkeley, CA 94710
www.counterpointpress.com

Printed in the United States of America
Distributed by Publishers Group West

10 9 8 7 6 5 4 3 2 1

Contents

o   o   o

He said, "If a story begins with finding, it must end with searching."

Penelope Fitzgerald, *The Blue Flower*

SEARCH

STORIES OF RESCUE

PARTY

The Finding

o　o　o

THIS is how my new life came about.

It started with symptoms I thought might be neurological. As a nurse, I was alert to a new unfamiliarity in the way things looked, as if I kept finding myself on the wrong street, or as if I were traveling abroad. The stores of what was ordinary enough to be ignorable seemed to be shrinking. Sometimes I seemed to inhabit my body the way you stand on a foot that has been asleep.

It may be that the organs attempt, in a language we do not know, to give us tidings of their dim world. Or with secret promptings they may impel us to ends of their own.

I had never visited this practice before, but I had worked in the same hospital with the neurologist long ago. He had been someone I knew to say hello to, a well-liked man, a good doctor, married, though without children and said to be unlucky in his home life.

On the morning of my appointment I got up and looked out at the rain. Water was materializing on the windowsill, filmy and soundless. It was December so I put on a red sweater over my uniform. I took a bus from work in the afternoon, and in the neurologist's waiting room, which was empty, I sat up straight to give the nurse the understanding that I was not demoralized by the winter rains of our city, the slow or the steady, or the short daylight. I was not a depressed woman drawing myself up to the radiator of a doctor's attention. If anything I was unnaturally cheerful. I wanted to seize whole tortes from cabinets in the bakery, and bottles of wine from under people's arms, and sofas out of window displays, that I had no room for in my small house.

In the clinic, there was no one in sight except the short young girl with a triangular face at the desk behind the glass, who had slid me a clipboard of forms with her bitten fingernails. When she saw me looking at her half-inch-long hair she turned away and touched it with her fingers. Well, hair is that short! I thought. Where have I been?

After a few minutes she looked up sharply and said, "Just go through the door. Room three."

From the hallway came a heavy sigh, a groan, actually, just before the doctor knocked. Then his voice, very deep — I remembered the voice — sounded from the door. "My nurse is not here," he said. "In a moment Angelique will come in so that I can examine you." He was fifty or so now, with big pale flap ears, and neatly dressed, tall but not erect. He had the stoop of a person with a bad back, and the eyes in folds that I recalled from seeing him in the hospital years ago. Now that I was older I knew these were drinker's eyes. "My nurse called and said she would not be in. She quit. No notice. There are no charts set out, as you see. No X-rays. She simply quit." He appeared only half able to think, like a man who has been up all night.

"I am a nurse," I said, waiting for him to recognize me, although I had been younger and prettier at the time I worked in that hospital.

"I see that," he said, scanning the clipboard.

"I used to work down the hall from you at the university," I said, pointing to my name on the form, and then to my employer's name, to let him know I was not in search of a job.

"Is that so?" he said.

Angelique opened the door without knocking. "What if the phone rings while I'm in here?" she demanded, putting her foot in the wastebasket to stomp down its contents.

"We might empty that," the doctor said, avoiding her gaze.

She ignored him. Hey there! I signaled him with an older-generation smile. Better establish some authority with this girl!

She did get down in front of the examining table and grapple on her knees with a step, which she yanked out for me to mount. I settled myself on the padded table surrounded with metal trees holding instruments. "If you're not going to have her *disrobe*," said Angelique, "I don't need to be here, do I?" and she went out, shutting the door firmly behind her.

The man looked blankly at the ophthalmoscope in his hand. Finally he switched it on and began to peer at my retinas, changing his angle minutely again and again, and breathing as if his belt were too tight. After a while he said, "I am going to have to dilate your eyes. I have not been brought up to date on your problems." He glanced at my forms. "You are a new patient. And you were not referred."

"No," I said. "I came straight to you."

"Headache," he said wearily.

"No," I said. I described my symptoms while he put drops in my eyes. After a while he hunched over them again. At length I submitted half-blind to all the tests with pin and hammer, of reflex, balance, strength, and mentation, naming the year, the city where we lived, the president. It was at the mention of the president that our eyes met. This was some years ago. I could tell we felt the same despairing way about the man. "I am going to ask you to have an MRI. There is only one real finding, and it may be nothing. But we will take a look." He stood up and pressed his wide waist, stifling a deep, trembling yawn.

"I agree," I said. It was not like me not to ask what the finding was.

"Are you planning to stay?" he asked Angelique rather cautiously as we passed her cubicle.

"I have to study my Spanish. You don't remember, but my exam is tonight, so there's no point in going home. So I'll close up!" She swiveled the chair so her back was to us.

"Well, then. I will leave now," he said, "to pick up some things. Good night."

It was dusk but the sun had come out, producing that low-lying light that seems to be coming from below rather than above. The air was full of water. You could hear water slipping over the edges of the grates in the parking lot. On the steps he said, "Now I remember you. Urology."

"Cardiology," I said.

"Well, I have business to attend to." He smiled unpleasantly, as if I had detained him. "My wife, soon to be my ex-wife, has my dog. I am going to get her. The dog." He searched his pockets.

"Where does your wife live?" I said.

"Where indeed. In *her* house by the lake."

"I wonder if you could give me a ride. I can't see. I do have a car, but I came on the bus. I ride the bus when I want to think."

"Well, if you have left off thinking for the day," he said, opening the door of his car. He performed a tight turn to get out of the parking lot, with the tires splashing.

I did not get out at the corner where I could have walked home; I had decided not to. Instead I asked him about the dog. This worked a change in him; his face lit up with malice. He began to talk. His wife was bent, it seemed, on punishing faults in him that he did not name, and would not give him his dog, even though she disliked dogs and had not the slightest notion how to take care of them. She might have changed the locks to keep him out. She thought he wanted to get into the house and make off with things he had bought for her, when in fact he was perfectly happy to have left everything behind; he didn't care even to go near the house again, except for the dog. The dog was his. His deep voice had become a snarl; he shook his shoulders and said, "Where exactly may I drop you off?"

I said, "Oh, we've passed the place." He had been talking, growling, for blocks. "I might as well go with you to pick up the dog, and get out on the way back." He replied with his groaning sigh.

The house was hidden from the street by a dense laurel hedge. It was dark now but not raining, and if you turned back at the top of the steep walk you saw a drop-off with the dark lake spread out below, so unexpected it could have sprung right out of a rock.

A weightless feeling comes over me whenever I look down on water from high up on land. Seeing it I felt a certainty that I was not sick, I was well. Instead of the sensation of being subtly awry I had the feeling I was in the midst of a normal life.

But now I was very hungry. This looked like the sort of house where fruit would be set out in a bowl from which you could help yourself.

The locks had not been changed after all. In the front hall there was no bowl of fruit but a crystal dish of sourballs. I stopped to take a cherry one, and he grimly swept the whole lot into his pocket. I unwrapped mine and dropped the paper on the floor. He offered no apologies for the size of the house or the fussy luxury of its furnishings, but made straight for the kitchen in the back.

Sure enough there was a dog, asleep in the shut-up kitchen without even a rug. It was a damaged version of a collie dog, thin, with an awful coat, and it scrambled up guiltily when we opened the kitchen door, like an old man pretending he hadn't been asleep in his chair. The dog had a smell, a putrid steam, which came up and surrounded us. When it began an agonized wagging and scooting toward him, he fell to his knees.

He knelt and pardoned the dog's appearance and smell and used a voice to convince it it was something besides these things, something an animal might not suspect itself to be. And he picked it up. It should have weighed too much for that but it didn't. Without speaking, he indicated the keys he had put down on the counter. I locked the door behind us, and he lugged the dog down the steps and through the hedge, eased it into the back seat, and got in with it. I thought he was going to get back out but he kept stroking and soothing the dog, which was panting unhealthily.

I had the keys. I got into the driver's seat. Nothing happened so I started the car. I said, "You can't take a dog like that into a downtown hotel, now can you." He didn't answer; he was in a reverie petting the awful-smelling dog, like a schoolboy with his thoughts in his hands. In the rearview mirror I could see them both with their eyes shut.

"So if I took him to my house," I said after a while, "you would have to come every day to take care of him."

"Her. She'll die without me. Look how sick she is now. Good dog. Good dog." He sat for blocks stroking the dog, as the fumes from its coat rose and banked in the car.

"In that case you would have to come with her," I said finally. I had seen the girl tell him what to do. I had seen the whole thing. I pushed all the buttons in the fancy armrest to open the windows. By now it was dark and cold, and the cold air, still wet, whirled in the car. The dog raised its nose to sniff.

He said, "I would have to get my things."

I turned to go downtown, where the hotel was. After a time he said, "Some of my things are at the office. I shuttle back and forth." So I doubled back. When he got out of the car the dog shut its eyes again, hopelessly. We hurried in. Angelique was alone, tilted back in the chair in her cubicle, studying her Spanish book. She had her shoes off and there was a run in her tights.

"Well, look who's here," she said in a lonely voice. "I heard you in the hall. I hoped it was you and not a rapist." I looked down at her. For all her rudeness she was a hopeful girl, thinly dressed below the funny hair, and ill-fed. With some care she could be the daughter I never had.

The Magic Pebble

○   ○   ○

THE flight to Lourdes was open to the whole archdiocese. Huge widebody, full. I was in the middle of coach in a row of five, in the middle seat.

All right, I'll make the best of it. I have my little Sony, I'll turn it on when they say we can and talk to two people, and that will be the program: me, the dressed-up old fellow on my left, and the woman on my right with a nun in charge of stuffing her bag into the overhead bin and getting the seat belt out from under her. At first I thought the woman was blind but she was just slow, in a daze. The nun had a broad pink face, heavily and dramatically wrinkled considering its resigned expression.

I have become aware of resignation in others. By the time you reach the third chemo, one of the things you notice is that the people around you accept death, your death. It happened with my radio show; during my last sick leave, friends from the station kept telling me how well the show was doing on reruns, how I didn't need to feel I had to hurry back to it.

I'm back, though. Now I can ask for anything. My boss Charlie always did give me free rein, but the station manager has taken to sending me complimentary memos not unlike greeting cards. To the manager's way of thinking, according to Charlie, my illness drops a fringed scarf over the rummage-sale nature of the show, lends it a dimly glowing aura of the endangered, the soon-to-be-archival: items veined and burnished and distressed now, like fake antiques, by my attention. As for me, I have finished with the disappearance of the tiger and the frog from the earth, and with the university hospital where patients were secretly injected with plutonium. Away with reproach. On to Inventions and Patents! The Sightings of the Ark! Birds in History!

If you write a noun, any noun, on a piece of paper and slap it down on Charlie's desk he grins, the radio snaps on in his mind. He remembers "satellite" new on everyone's lips. He is happy with his throwback job; he's a gray-haired, loping man who could easily have a beer with the campus agitator he was thirty years ago; he has his own tattered copy of the Port Huron Statement. He remembers "pacification," newborn "fluorocarbon," reborn "terrorist." He charts the passage of world figures in the press, from "madman" to "strongman" to "leader."

"I'm beyond all that. I've given up," I tell Charlie.

"OK," he says.

"I'm going for the fun factual or the seriously miraculous."

"OK."

This trip I am taking springs directly out of *The Song of Bernadette.*

By the time we made our high school graduation retreat the decline in vocations was serious and the hopeful sisters were showing this movie. How beautiful and good the curious tapered face of Jennifer Jones was, so sad-mouthed, in that movie. Even so, we snickered at her dull wits, her inability to speak up for herself when she was the one, after all, to whom Our Lady had stepped out of rock, clothed in white and a blue beyond blue, with yellow roses on her feet—as we seniors of Holy Names knew despite the black-and-white of the movie. No human: a statue come to life, shining with unearthly glamour, melting with bridal politeness. An invisible power filled the air but the girl could not stretch out her hands to determine the source of it. Much was offered, but touch remained in the realm of the unpermitted.

"From the remotest times, out of child-sacrifice to water, out of rainmaking and ceremonial cleansing, from sacred well, holy pool, fountain in oak tree — the *spring* has been thought to possess a miraculous power."

For music maybe somebody blowing into a bottle.

"Unorthodox" — or maybe I should say "orthodox" — "as such a trip seemed when it first occurred to me at the end of chemo, I saw it as something that would perhaps..." "Perhaps" is a little clothespin not really sturdy enough, I'm afraid, for the vast wet sheet of the possible that I have to hang from it. Halfway through I'll break in with passages from novels, pro and con. "That world of hallucinated believers," Zola called Lourdes — which won't be my position; I won't presume to judge. At the station they'll say, "This was her best show, she left her shtick at home, she was honest for a change." Because they know I'm always feigning interest. Even when it's one of my causes, in which I have the most intense interest privately, I slip into this broadminded radio-interest. Whereas the mark of real interest would be silence, like that preserved by my boss Charlie at my bedside. "Saline infusion," I'll read him, "followed by the nitrogen *mustard* . . ." He'll wrinkle his forehead, squint, and then I'll laugh and he'll laugh. I can tell he would like to do a show on chemo.

My husband, with his inborn, unfailing sense of the thing to say to a person in chemo with tufts of her former self in her hands, says irritably, "What's so funny all the time? He's got a crush on you. Charlie. I'm serious, he does."

This trip to Lourdes is the second trip I've taken since then. First we went — the three of us, my husband and I and our son — to Lake Powell.

The hospital doors sighed open and my little boy wheeled me across the rubber divide to the car all packed and waiting. "Southward ho!" my husband said, as I waved up to the smoked glass of Oncology. My son was marching stiff-necked with the thrill of missing a week of kindergarten and Rafe. For him kindergarten has been embodied from the start in the narrow-headed little boy with the buzz cut who glared at him from the next chair. Some of the mothers say the haircut was a practical measure. Rafe's own mother was afraid to wash his hair. She is his stepmother, actually, and she can't stand him, it is said. All she wanted was the father. I don't want to think about this. Stepmothers.

Rafe, a name breathed every night at our dinner table: one of those children who start school already old in the ways of power. After difficulties in another kindergarten he came to St. Joseph's three days into the first week. Not a bully, exactly. His crimes were against property, a dogged wrecking of the bright room, or his part of it, the part where he lurked like a rook—the border, the lanes between respectful groups.

"Rafe," my son ventures, "cut the cat's ear with scissors," looking away in case our faces confirm his suspicions about the place where he lives his days.

At the hospital there was a party for the two of us who had completed our treatment. We were all saying good-bye at the nursing station when a cart rolled down the hall, with an ice swan on a bed of ferns. "From your sweeties!" the nurses chorused, calling the husbands out of hiding in the railed bathroom where so recently my roommate Tracey and I had been sliding down the wall in a sweat.

"She thought you meant *Charlie*," my husband grumbled to the nurses, who had been making much of his jealousy of my boss.

This was the end of chemo for both Tracey and me—whatever happened after this, chemo was, as they said, no longer an option. The swan was in honor of the Birds in History show I had finished taping just before I came in. The nurses ate the delicacies and we all admired the magnificent glistening bird being trundled up and down by Tracey's twins, three-year-olds who got their fingers and tongues stuck on the ice while my son watched.

My husband had gone to a lot of trouble to find a maker of ice swans. It wasn't just a shape, the feathers were etched in perfectly, the eye was an elongated half-closed Buddha-eye, sleepy and benevolent, and the beak had a little nostril. It was a pleasure to see this life-size, realistic bird, after all the angels. Angel cards and angel calendars and angel balloons festooned the whole hospital. When people look back, these huge broody men-women will be the macramé of this period, says Charlie. "Looks like the millennium in here," he says, batting a string of them out of the way. "Never, never will we do a show on angels." Of course there have been requests. He found me Nabokov's story in which a huge moulting angel, all brown fur and steaming chicken-flesh, flies through a window and crashes in a hotel room. To mark its place he stuck in a card showing an angel on a rotisserie. "Like rattlesnake," the man with the baster is saying.

Tracey was way ahead of me in the chemo protocol and that is not good unless you are getting well. When we met we lifted up our gowns and compared our scars. There are good scars and bad scars: hers was bad, formed of shiny blebs as if a red-hot choke-chain had been slung at her chest and fused with the skin. Her disease was bilateral and had reached her bones; she had lost her body fat and was down to membranes and big fruit-bat eyes, a praying, drifting, cloud-woman of the New Age, whose palm was always blossoming open to show me a pink crystal, a vial of aromatic oil, a spirit stone. She was twenty-seven; everybody loved her and her bearded husband and her curly-headed twins, who burst out of the elevator every afternoon and campaigned down our ward scattering action figures and jouncing the vials on trolleys.

The same height at five as they were at three, and rashy, tongue-tied, thin: that was our son, a daydreamer, quietly keyed up at finding himself present at the twins' adventures.

I used to dream our son would fall off something, lose a limb, choke, drown. He had yet to let go of the edge of the pool and swim. Tracey comforted me; she guessed before I said so that the terror of the coming swimming lesson caused his afternoon vomiting. Of course I never told him of what kept befalling him in my dreams, but the psychiatric nurse would say he knew. This woman knew better than to give me *Love, Medicine and Miracles* to read but she did give me a book I couldn't stand, *The Problem of Pain.* Tracey didn't mind her, but the ones I liked brought us *It* and *Pet Sematary* from the nurses' station. "That Tracey is a living doll," my favorite one would say whenever Tracey had been lifted onto the gurney and taken away.

For a while I thought of doing a program on living dolls. "Think of consciousness—" Tracey would pant when she came back, joggled by the burrowing twins so that she had to hold up her arms on the IV boards (she had declined the portacath)—"as a cupboard. All you know and feel is in there!" With Tracey, knowing and feeling had the nature of a bestowal, on the order of musical ability. "But you don't know what else is in there! What I did yesterday"—she showed the twins with a roll of her shoulders—"was I got up onto a different shelf. And I know," she smiled, "I was still way down low!"

There is a tribe that bestows the name "Sky" on a woman who gives birth to twins. She is a blessing to all; her twins are thought to influence the weather.

"Don't forget," Tracey said as she hugged me from her wheelchair. That could have been about the cupboard of consciousness, or it could have been about the Hopi kachina she gave me, Pour-Water-Woman, who waters the heads of children to make them grow, or she could have meant the Chinese grocery where she had her fortifying teas made up.

From our bulletin board with all the angel cards, her husband unpinned only his snapshot of the real Tracey, wearing feather earrings on her trip to blessed ground in Arizona, long-haired and wide-hipped in a pueblo doorway. Shyly he parted the tissue paper to show me his present: the pale pink boa that would float out behind Tracey as her chair skidded to the elevator with a twin pumping on either side.

I had thought I wanted to see what it was like to get behind the wheel again but we agreed I would conserve the energy. Down I-5 we flew, toward Utah.

In all the preparations, we had done something inexcusable: we had forgotten about Lake Powell. My fault; I am supposed to be on top of such things. It's just the kind of program I used to do: environmentocide, the intentional flooding of a proud and ancient desert canyon.

We forgot everything; we only knew we were driving south to get on a houseboat and drift for a few days in the sun. Heal. That's what the ad said, in *Sunset*. "Sunset," my husband said one day in the hospital, absently picking it up in his despair, "the magazine of the radiology waiting room."

I had a mental picture of a houseboat—something between a raft and a gondola, with a deck chair on it, brushing along the reeds. You could pluck a desert bloom with your lazy fingers as you went, in my preview, as you covered over the nasty record of the last year until it was completely crosshatched—the way we used to do segues on TV—obliterated by the new scene of desert sunshine, fish in hazel water, eagles, canyon swifts. It is swifts who are said to sleep in flight, so high in the vault of heaven that if they fall they will have time to wake up. "How would anyone know?" Charlie said.

Charlie found the poem that opened the show: "On a Bird Singing in Its Sleep." *A bird half wakened in the lunar noon / Sang half way through its little inborn tune* ... This bird of Frost's had "the inspiration to desist" when it was fully awake, and that was what Charlie liked, "the inspiration to desist."

The program became a favorite at the station and went into two parts, though I haven't heard how it came out with all the twitters and caws and screeches Charlie dug up, helping me because I don't even like birds.

We began with ancient Rome and the priest-augurs. "Augury was the reading of events in the behavior of birds. In their cloudy retreats, the augurs ..." and so on; we painted them in, hunkering, shy, receptive men, self-trusting as prophets must be, watching the sky. Later I read that half the augury was accomplished on birds heading left instead of right when they scratched in the dirt.

In the course of this show, which had started out with endangered birds as its subject, in particular the little spotted owl of our own woods, we branched out, seduced by the oddness of birds, their dependable, vestigial peculiarity, no more in the reputation for cursing ships and causing headaches (if they weave a hair from your head into their nests) than in any number of real behaviors that must have made for puzzling prophecies: gaping and dancing and chaperoning and adoption and fratricide. We left these subjects to TV, though we interviewed an ornithologist. We'll hear from bird watchers, the kind of call we get after every show no matter how humbly I introduce myself as a dilettante. The auspices are never good when we get into people's hobbies. Auspice means bird observation.

Lake Powell. The "lake" is a vast system of canyons into which river water has been forced by damming: a huge, walled kingdom of rock and sand, first seen by the colonizers in 1776, when two lost Franciscans — Franciscans! — ate their packhorses while exploring it for Spain. The walls of Padres Butte, above the now-submerged Crossing of the Fathers, gaze somberly down upon your water-flea, your "houseboat." This is a camper on pontoons, if a camper responded to your steering late by so many seconds and wide by so many degrees.

Off the main gorge with its massive buttes are an endless number of subsidiary canyons, into which you can "cruise" to "explore," each with its own coves and caverns, and its chimney or arch that you are supposed to look for, sticking up out of the water like the stone arm or leg of its own drowned spirit, not the primary canyon-spirit but some underling, some kitchen girl buried with the pharaoh.

Once, all of this arid land was under water anyway, argued the dammers, who were just people like so many now, "like all of us, perhaps," I'll say if I do the show, people with no inspiration to desist. It was an ocean: sea creatures are embedded in its red walls.

Tour boats the size of ocean liners are afloat on this map of water, these hundreds of miles of "waterway," between the walls of rock with you and your houseboat. One of them meets you, passes, heaves at you a continent of wake. You smack into the wake if you have not swerved into position to "step" your craft across it as the sheet of instructions says to do. Inside or underneath your boat something slides, cracks, makes the noise of a spade pounding. The aft floor with just a railing around it dips under. The rented sleeping bags roll in inches of water.

Imagine you are weak and hairless. You have a taste in your mouth—oh, a diluted chlorine-vapor—and a little hole in your chest like a gas cap for receiving liquids through a hose, and strip-mined patches on your arms where the skin leached chemicals from a puncture. You are an *entity* now. Your husband does not know this, though when your child looks at you, you feel him suspecting it. You have a tape recorder with you, of all things, to record impressions of this vacation for use in a program!

In a bracket on the bow the two of them have installed a little flag they bought in the souvenir shop. All at once you hear the cloth beating, beating. The water is a blackening green. The wind—the wind has kicked up a bit: that's what your husband says, planting his feet wide apart on the deck. Your son is in his arms, thin legs dangling, turning the wheel, but now your husband sets him down. Waves erupt against the sheer walls and toss the whole channel up like water in a tub.

You must have known, and he too—he must have known when he looked up at the disorganized, silently colliding masses of cloud pouring into each other through downspouts and funnels. Now they are coursing heavily west. The water looks exactly like the writhing sea as you once filmed it for a story called "Tender: The Peacetime Navy," safe on a submarine tender in the Pacific.

You are not too disoriented to see that this is not—it is not—in the brochure. To your own surprise and disgust you begin your weak hospital whine. Your husband laughs, with a note of uncertainty that only you can hear, and he and your little chortling son agree to confine you to your quarters so that you will not get in the way of the nautical affairs.

Now the wind seems to have scented something on the floor of the canyon that it once casually uprooted but now cannot reach. As it vacuums furiously along the water the sun goes out, the little hoofbeats of the flag speed up. Your son looks up quickly with his nostrils flared, like an animal. The temperature falls. "The mercury plummeted," you would say, if you could get off the bolted-down bench where you are curled and find the recorder. "The barometer bottomed out so fast our ears popped."

Your husband has given up wrestling the bizarre delayed steering against the wind and has finally run at dusk, disobeying a red buoy, deep into one of the branches of a side canyon and up onto a sandbar. "How will we find our way back?" you whispered as he was wrenching the craft into the first wide turn. "Honey . . ." he said, opening his palm to show a compass.

Some time ago he and your son went over the side and down the ladder and waded onto the beach, where hordes of a dry thorny weed pulled loose by the wind are blowing at a furious rate against their legs. They are in the matching red bathing suits bought for this trip. Long ago in all of your minds there was, incredibly, the idea of going swimming. In a transparent inlet, the two of you demonstrating to your son how it is that lazy circles with the arms easily hold the body up in water.

No one swims here in March. You would have known that if you had been thinking, any of you.

They must make a wide V with the ropes and plant the two anchors in the sand, but they can't get it done. The stern of the flat ungainly vehicle is tossing and dragging too heavily. The engine has stalled twice. "Bring her in if she breaks free!" Could he have yelled that? Each time they stomp one anchor into the sand the other pulls loose, causing the boat to rear back like a horse on one rein.

It is so dark, the air so full of cold, flying sand, that you can hardly see them. You can see your son's white running legs and his arms bent like hospital straws, sticking out of the life preserver that is mandatory for children every minute they spend on this lake. You can't hear them, though once the wind brings you his voice over the sound of your chattering teeth, piping thinly to his father about the stinging weed. He is not crying, though. You are crying.

What are you afraid of? What could possibly frighten you now?

The boat is going to tear loose and spin out of the cove to dash itself to splinters on the red walls of the canyon. Man and boy will be left on this fragment of surviving desert, actually the flank of one of the lower mountains of rock, where the temperature plunges at night in this month, March.

No one told you not to come to this place in March. No one told you not ever, ever to come. You should have known that. Only now do you begin to see it, and only an edge of it, beyond the reach of your trained curiosity, your facts and film and tape— and not just you, *anyone*, anyone who would even listen to you, any tourist of knowledge: *it*, the water-carved, the sheer-walled, ancient grounds, now defiled, of the unpermitted.

In the morning you will be dead, washing along the canyon floor with the Cretaceous sharks and the cacti, your frantic spirit seeking to drag another houseboat off its course into this tiny canyon to rescue your husband and son. One may come, or one may not. There are ninety-six canyons.

I HAVE hair now, very short, chic. With a lot of makeup on I am charming again. Going up and down the aisles I could get twenty good stories if I wanted to, but we like to say three are better than twenty. A good half of the passengers are caretakers, like the nun in our aisle—one of many on this flight, I'm sure, though few others display the little headband scarf and the suit of a vaguely official off-blue—who guards the woman to my right. The nun's liver-spotted, wedding-ringed hand lies ever on the sick woman's coat sleeve.

I came alone. All this has made my husband tired, willing to stay home with our son, who is not allowed to leave kindergarten. His teacher Ms. Lemoine put her foot down: your son has had his special houseboat trip; he must have stability now. He must be provided with structure, continuity. These are the wicks around which candles will form to light his way. Those are not her words; she said, "Let us take care of everything, Mom." Only three of us are Mom to her, the mothers of her favorites. Ms. Lemoine is young, right out of school herself, and a convert; she had two dozen five-year-olds making the sign of the cross and droning the tunes of the St. Louis Jesuits before they could trace their hands. Not that we aren't secretly grateful that she has her clear favorites: the weak ones.

We're in the air. We're going by night, over the pole to Paris. "The Eiffel Tower!" says a little wraith in front of us to her mother.

"Would you consider letting me interview you?" I ask the old man on my left.

"I'll certainly consider it." He winks. He got on late, climbing over the woman on that aisle who had already begun to pray with her eyes closed or else gone to sleep. "Pardon me, pardon me, ladies—!" He bowed to her and then to the rest of us, and smacked his crutches one at a time into the hands of the flight attendant, a slight young man with large ears, who looked familiar to me.

The old man has more hair in his white eyebrows than on his lean crinkled head and he's done up in sharp pleats, heavy cotton, silk. Wingtips. One of those prosperous old guys who genuflect like Fred Astaire. He's ready without any urging and has no idea that despite his promising Chicago accent, on tape he will prove to be what we call a boulder. Boulders are usually men—though a woman can be one—who have sunk into position in themselves, and can never be jostled loose by an interviewer. You may circle and pester them all day, you may scratch your questions on them, they will not budge. They may have sought to be interviewed and looked forward to it, but it turns out they can't explain; they don't intend to.

What is more, the problem with his hip is not intrinsic, not a disease; it is the result of an accident. Someone caused it—kids who knocked him down and robbed him in front of his hotel on a cruise to Mexico. All this he gives out in short puffs of speech with no full stops. "Hip"—prods under jacket—"Pinned twice: replaced the thing: won't heal—" I catch a whiff of cologne. This man would never say, "All of a sudden I was lying on my back looking up at the orange sun, and a voice was speaking, saying '*dolor*,' and the pain was shooting everywhere." On the other hand neither would he say, "I know it's not a matter of deserving or not deserving this but I feel it has made me take a closer look at my life and I see that—" He has a Knights of Columbus monogram on his bag. Of Lourdes he has the businesslike expectation of an appointment to be kept by two. "Crutches: think I'll leave 'em?" he says, nudging me, sensing a doubter. "I hope so," I say. Perhaps there will be a cave-storeroom piled with crutches.

A man across the aisle crossed his legs and poked out a stump with a sock on it. I don't believe one-breasted-ness produces in the viewer the immediate vicarious anguish of one-footed-ness. He licked his finger and flipped the pages of the airline magazine. Of course that man isn't going to Lourdes to pray for a foot. At one time I would have said so, a while back, though that far back I would not have done a program on Lourdes. I would not have wanted to embarrass the good Virgin of my childhood or myself if, dazed with jet lag in the grotto, I heard myself ask for a miracle. But on the trip to Lake Powell I changed my mind. If you ask at all, why not for a miracle. Like the accidentals in music, the notes that are not in the key signature. It might not be the heaving water calmed, or anything so plain.

At Lake Powell we heard about a rabbit that fell out of the sky onto a tent, shook itself, and hopped away. People who had just come in from camping in the desert were telling us about it on the pier as we waited for our boats. An eagle dropped it, they reported. Who knows how many wonders befall animals. An animal would be more accepting, unable to marvel to begin with.

I thank the old man and turn to the woman on my right, the dazed woman. It seems she has been waiting; her cheeks are a hot veiny red. "No, excuse me, the gentleman—!" She leans forward to address him, not me. My boss Charlie calls this dating—as, "You let them date all through the show, you should have taken charge." "Sir—sir? Those boys who robbed you in Mexico were in the wrong. But what if your own son did something like that?"

The old man is not to be ruffled. He stops her with a commanding palm. "Pardon me: this calls for—" The flight attendant has just reached us, that smiling big-eared young man I feel sure I know. We all smile back at him. His face is one of those mysterious human sights that refresh you. After a moment I see what it is, I see he looks like Alfred E. Neuman, if you can imagine that face groomed and somehow *matured*. The old man, who should properly utilize the attendant in the other aisle, calls out, "The burgundy, if you please, sir!" lifting a white eyebrow and holding up his fingers to indicate two. "And—" he rummages briskly—"the ladies." He is going to treat us.

"Wonderful," says the flight attendant—who must have been picked for this particular charter—in a pleased voice fresh as the celery he has ready in a glass of ice. "Sharon," he calls, "I'll take care of the gentleman here. Ladies? Red or white?" and this choice seems, as he offers it, such a pleasant one, so emblematic of all we have to choose from in life, that we sigh one after another, "Red."

The woman won't wait. "My son was responsible for a terrible crime!" On her sleeve the nun's hand begins to pat. I'm ready; I know the way people will sometimes talk when the tape is running, the formal and even pious language they will summon up. *Was responsible*. Like orthodox: it means the same as its opposite. He *was responsible* for it.

"He needed money for speedballs." Ah! Voice of brown permanent, glasses, little parish-council face, saying "speedballs." "He was high. Very high. We don't even know what it means, the rest of us."

Who says we don't? I've had enough Percocet to hurt somebody for fun. Sure. If the nurse with the wrong books had come in at just the right moment . . . when that octane was flowing in . . . who says I wouldn't have drawn my knees up and let fly with both heels at her soft stomach?

I'll do a voiceover on the pause where we let down our trays for plastic glasses and wine, and screw open the little snapping lids. Maybe I will. Let the voice fade into the background noise and come back up farther down the line.

"He didn't know what he was doing. People died. A young couple."

That's enough. I don't want to be told. I don't want the rumors of earth up here, I've left its cities behind, I'm flying to Lourdes. At my most earthbound I don't do crime stories.

"I'm just...I'm just about...because my son..." She groans, loudly enough to make people turn around. "This young couple... and he came through the window. And there, there, there...!" Her hands make that up-held gesture from paintings of the martyrs.

We fill our glasses. The old man keeps sipping and nodding, as if what the woman has said comes as no surprise to him, merely confirms his own experience. The nun is shaking her head. Seeing the woman's distress, and the recorder, the attendant has paused to listen, turning his big semitransparent ear to us.

"So"—she draws a deep breath—"he did that. He did." She squashes the paper-covered pillow to her face and scrubs the skin with it. Then she jams the pillow against her belly and doubles over with another sound, this one harsh, explosive, and absolutely abandoned, more a belch than a groan, a noise a cow or a horse might make in the barn.

I brought this on, with my little mike. I thought she was going to stick with "responsible." It's my fault. After a minute I say, "I'm sorry and I see what you mean about those kids in Mexico. I have a son. I'm sorry."

"Nossir: mama's right there!" The old man hastens to set me right. "Selling trinkets! We're nothing but tourists to them! American tourists! Parents put 'em up to it." Forgetting, because he is old, everything the woman has been saying about her son. She doesn't look at him but her companion does, with a wondering distaste. A deep, surprising rumble, the voice this sister produces at last. "I believe that's a popular myth about crime in poor countries."

The woman has pulled herself erect and allowed the cushion to be slipped behind her, and she rolls her head on it. "You have a son." She's talking to me. "Let me tell you something. If you see drugs you take him to the hospital." Each time she says "you" she points at me, right up near my collarbone. I am sure she was once a woman who would never have pointed. "You make them lock him in. If they won't, you don't leave. Oh, God. No wonder I'm in an institution."

"You're not, you're in Martha House." The nun glares across the thrashing woman at me.

"You *make* them. You don't let them tell you, Go home. You tell them. Or you'll never, never ... you'll be like me. I can't read a book any more. I can't pray the rosary! I can't drive a car." All together we drink, as if there has been a toast.

"Never mind that. Why not tell them a bit about your son," the growl-voice says calmly, with no sentiment at all. "He liked to read, didn't he? He was good at drawing." She's setting up a known routine; she speaks as though the woman's son, long dead, can show himself decently as a child.

"There was a fairy tale he liked," the woman begins obediently, her forehead smoothing out with that look that goes with the repeated, the taken-out-and-unfolded, the *engraved* stories. "A little pig found a marble that turned him into a rock ..."

"*Sylvester and the Magic Pebble!*" But I stop myself; this is no time for yelling out, "That's not a fairy tale, everyone knows that book!" Instead I say quietly, "It was actually a donkey."

"Are you sure?" she says dreamily. "Well, this—donkey's parents went out to look for him. They looked everywhere and years and years went by ..."

I know this story. I have read it to my son, regretting that it is not one of his favorites. It's a book parents read aloud at night with tears in their eyes.

Staring in front of me at the seatback, where there is a phone, I am lost for a minute in missing my son at bedtime, unmoved though he has always been by the boy turned into a rock and, worse, by the parents—who are somehow *old* in the illustrations—as they search and search. Unmoved by any of it. The despair of it. The hopeless decision the parents make one spring day to go on a picnic.

Unmoved. It is good that he is so. A sign, a small sign, of strength. I say to myself, there's a phone right here, I can call him.

The woman's son had another reaction altogether. "Every

time I would read it, he would *hum*. He couldn't stand to hear it! You see? This was a boy they said was heartless. Heartless, they said, at the trial. He'd put his hands over his ears and hum the whole time the pig was a rock."

"And then he's released!" I say. Uh-oh. The nun has a repertoire of black looks. She thinks I mean the son. The woman knows, though. Surely she remembers the ecstatic ending of this story. She must remember that. I remind her, I urge her on: "They spread the tablecloth on him! They find the pebble and put it on him by chance while he's wishing!"

"Never was he heartless," she replies in a dry, tearless whisper.

"No, no," the nun, who seems blessed with no skill but patting with her hand, concludes the matter with a last scowl at me.

I can't do anything with this anyway; I'll have to start all over again in another direction when we get to Lourdes. The woman squeezes her eyes tightly shut when I thank her, and weakly waves me away as she lets her head fall on the nun's shoulder.

I switch off the recorder and lean back. There in the seatback in front of me—the sight of it filling me with an almost intolerable desire to wake my son up so that he can speak to me—is the phone.

I didn't want to think, on this trip. It's as simple as that. But it's too late. My mind, steered by force away from my son's sleeping form in the dark bedroom where my husband must have finished reading to him hours ago, wanders and fidgets over his routines, and alights on his school. *I can't stand his teacher.* I say this to myself with deep, poisonous pleasure, up here in the sky. Not just because of her "Mom," her "Let us take care of everything." She's the only teacher, so who is this *us*? The living? The little Flores boy, this snub-nosed young woman says with an apologetic grimace, just pollutes the classroom. That's her word, *pollutes*. I wonder if she would say it on tape.

It's Rafe, the boy my son is afraid of, of course. Ms. Lemoine is recommending that Rafe be steered to a more suitable school, where there are other children with a similar learning style.

"That's *Rafe*," my son says with pride, indicating with his shoulder, afraid to point at him. No one plays near Rafe. He kicks over the Lego buildings, pees in the sand pile. Of course he does. Tortures the cat saved from the pound to show the kindergarten birth.

He is heading for major trouble. He's heading for the pound himself.

Under the shadow hairline the little beast-face. Poor little devil. An idea rises in me rather grandly and stupidly, unsure it has been untied, like a hot-air balloon. One of those large ideas that sometimes exert a force on you in an airplane. Ah. No. Not at all what it says in *The Problem of Pain*! It says, if I remember . . . that the pain of animals, their tearing each other to ribbons, their *dying*, does not figure into the equation. But if anything is left out . . . if pain . . . or rather evil, if they are not the same thing . . . if anything is left out . . . But it's no use. As fast as it came to me the whole contraption bobs and drifts away. I can't get it back.

FIRST there was the head appearing, coming up the ladder. My husband carrying something under his arm like a bedroll. Bringing it up from the dark beach.

It was our son. The sight copied itself on the way to me, coming by degrees as if I were blinking. This is the way the lightning of reason blinks through the mind, too swift, too hot for one steady cut. He was dead, drowned, and I would soon be dead! With an awful thrill, I inhaled the cold green air and held it. In a rigor of pity for my husband I dragged my eyes to his. But he knew our son was not dead.

A sound echoed out over the wind. I reached up. My boy was ice cold, wet, laughing. "I went swimming! I got my head wet! Dad didn't but I did!" He shook his wet hair onto me. I reached up. His cold skin sanded my palms as he planted his freezing kiss on me. "I swam!"

In the middle of the night the boat yawed, bumped—what were these intermittent thuds coming from the underside of it, like a huge stymied heartbeat?—and strained at the ropes. We were all three frozen in the wet sleeping bags. Miraculously, two had gone to sleep.

I did not notice right away that the wind had stopped and that I was hearing the water lap against the hollow pontoons with a chop-licking sound. I had pulled way back, up into the night, and was looking down at a walled ocean with tiny rocking huts sheltered in every inlet.

I unfolded my sour limbs and got up unsteadily, my bare soles squishing on the indoor-outdoor carpet, to rummage for the tape recorder. In the dark I whispered the date to it. I was ready to continue but nothing came to me. I sat there, sliding against the wall and slumping forward, back and forth, with the boat's movements. I sat there for a long time, maybe an hour.

It was then I received the augury. I saw birds, four of them, long-billed shorebirds of a tawny pink color, and transparent, like tinted cellophane. A foamy tide ran in and out around their feet. One, slender and high-stepping, stretched its neck and flapped its wings. All of this with no sound. That one was young and was, I knew as you do in dreams, my son. About the others—the adult ones, the *three* adult ones—something could not be put into words at all, but I knew it. That I passed over, in the dream.

So my son would make it through adolescence, into a long-legged, proud stage. He would get that far.

Off to one side and above the beautiful, backlit sandy reach on which these birds were stepping, hovered, or actually sat in midair—its wings were folded—an owl. It was smaller than a spotted owl. It did not really have the implacable eyes of owls, but half-closed, rather sleepy, childish eyes. Words came from it. I saw, or read, or almost heard them, words of the deepest comfort. Not the words themselves but a hum, a bird-signification. Some note at a very low frequency was aimed toward me and meant . . . I don't know what it meant.

I knew at the time but I lost it when I woke up. I felt wonderful. I was at home. I thought, I'll call Tracey, she'll love this, and I did, but she had died. Then I really woke up, and saw that I was on the houseboat.

It was palest morning. Not a single bird. Orange-tinted boas of cloud were lying on nothing, above the water and halfway up the stone chimneys. All around us the air had a faint tremble and a taste, like air in a room where the TV has blown out. The thorny weeds had exhausted themselves against a shelf of rock; the sky was a swept-clean floor.

THE sister sighs. She is too old, older than the old man; she has worn herself out in Martha House, cleaning up after sick, messy, dislocated women with somber grievances. The old man is even now—accepting no rebuff, squinting out of one eye in the quickly achieved tipsiness of age—making an effort to bring things to a satisfactory conclusion. "Now, sacrifice . . . Now, the Blessed Mother . . ." I know this old man; he is a lordly old Midwestern tithing Catholic of a disappearing kind, apt to fall into teasing reference to saints and sacraments on the golf course or at the dinner table. He's the type, with his expensive shoes, his "if you please," to have some right-wing justification for capital punishment in the back of his mind, that he's too chicken to mention openly to the mother of a criminal son.

On the other hand he could be simply comparing the confused grieving woman to the Blessed Mother.

I don't know. There's no way to know.

I won't ask anybody anything for the rest of the flight. Why do I have to? I don't have to. I'm going to make a telephone call and then I'll rest. I'll go to sleep.

We bank sharply, perhaps avoiding something, some unimaginable night-sky traffic, and for a time I can see the crescent moon gliding from window to window as the plane slowly rights itself.

Someday my son's kindergarten class will laugh at the elephantine maneuvers of jets. They will have their own wonders, as I have lived to see the day when a telephone call can be made from an airplane.

In India the face you see immediately after looking at the new moon—is this the new moon or the old? I have forgotten how to tell. How few I have actually stored, of these alchemical facts! If the face you see is the face of a good man, it will bring you luck the whole year. Don't look down on luck, bedraggled though it may be when you pull it up out of the jumble and see it is yours, all tangled with planets, clouds, wind, inventions, dolls, pebbles, birds going left or right.

The face of a good man. Oh, where is the flight attendant with his tender smile? But it's too late, I've glanced at the old man, who has gained no satisfaction from the sister and is opening his third burgundy. All right. So be it.

I excuse myself in a businesslike way, and pull my card through the slot. I know the number. I have something to say to that young woman, my boy's teacher, advocate of stability, of security, that she is. Take back what you said. *Pollutes* is a serious word, at St. Joseph's school. You can't expel that boy, the Flores boy! His name is Rafe. You have a lot to learn.

No one answers at the school, because it is night.

Please leave a message. I will. I'll leave a message.

Not so long ago the answering machine, "machine" now everywhere on earth, belonged to very few. All that was required was the assembly of separate inventions to call it into existence, and already it is giving place to something else. Soon if you are not there, there will be a hologram of yourself to deliver your messages, simple enough for a child to operate, and even if he stretches his hands right through it, it will not go away.

Downward Dog

o   o   o

DOOLEY had to keep the session with Vo and Jackson short because it was midmorning and he had to get back out in the halls before classes changed. He was in a new life. He was off the force; he was doing security. Working with the young, as his social worker put it. He was the owner of a new dog, a big dog, when for his wife's sake he had always had little dogs.

At the pound they had said the dog was as friendly as any animal they had on board, but this was the last extension of his stay and on the weekend he would be put down. Because frankly people didn't want a dog that big unless it was a purebred. Keeping a heavy paw on his knot of rawhide, the dog had smiled at Dooley.

When Dooley hauled a kid in by the shirt and sat him down, the dog's head stayed on his paws and his eyes stayed on Dooley. Always. These two faced the desk, with the dog at their feet on a blue mat that had been Dooley's wife's yoga. "Dog bother you?" he said, because maybe half the kids were scared of a dog.

"What's his name?" It was the Vietnamese kid, Vo, who asked, which surprised him since Jackson was the one in real trouble, the one he was aiming at.

"Bruno," he said. "Great Pyrenees plus Malamute." In the tiny room the words had the sweep of a map, but it would be lost on these two, Vo and Jackson. The dog took up so much room in the office both boys had to sit sideways. Before Dooley came on board there had been no office. This was a supply closet with a stenciled sign on the door, SECURITY OFFICER. The sign was the principal's doing. She had given him the go-ahead for the dog. "It's your deal," she said. "It's Dooley's deal," she told the office staff.

She knew he had beaten up a guy in an arrest. She had the report on her desk; the school district did a background check, even on a cop. He had been exonerated but they had made him do anger management and see a social worker at his own expense and he had quit. Quit the force. He was in a new life.

On the desk he had a jar of pepperoni sticks. Sometimes he offered one, but the kids didn't take them so he ate them himself. "They're worried about their breath," the principal told him. He tipped the chair back so far laughing he cracked his head on the wall. On an empty shelf he had placed his wife's Mr. Coffee. A few of them drank coffee if it had sugar and creamer, though there were drawbacks: a kid had thrown a full cup at the wall. Kid who liked the dog. Hot coffee had splashed on the dog and the dog had done nothing more than shake his ears and thump his tail. So Dooley had fought down the urge to put a real scare into the kid. He had made him swab down the wall and eight shelves with the dust of sixty school years on them. While the kid was doing it Dooley talked. He couldn't believe he was repeating stuff from anger management.

Both his sons were on the force by the time of his administrative leave and they had stood by him. But he could tell they weren't sure about him any more, and their wives weren't, and their mother wasn't there any more to explain him to them and to himself. All he had was the dog.

If gangs were involved, he wouldn't find out from Vo. The Asians kept quiet. Vo was a little guy, but Jackson—tall as he was he should have been playing JV—was the one with the eye swollen shut. He should have been able to fight; he was the one with the scars and the record at fifteen. Both of them were going out—automatic three days for fighting in the halls—but Jackson was heading for juvie or worse even though he was the loser in this and his previous fight on school grounds.

"Are you surprised? You raised kids." That was the principal's response to any comment he might make about what went on. It seemed to him now that his wife must have done most of the raising of their boys. He couldn't say he liked the kids in the halls and johns and parking lots of this particular school. Maybe he didn't like kids. "That isn't what matters," his social worker said. She was a girl some years younger than his sons. She used the same voice with him, a kind of purr, that the female wardens used to soothe a nut case.

But if not that, what? What mattered?

When Dooley said "OK, Bruno," the dog would lumber up, wave his tail. Until then he just lay there. Vo had faced forward but Jackson still had his long legs pointed at the door and his eyes on the dog. Vo saw that, and let his fingers drop to the top of the dog's head and give it a casual but showy caress. The dog shifted on the mat, Jackson shrank back in his chair. Vo's phone went off.

"OK, Mr. Grant Vo. You put this on your little screen you got there and send it to yourself: 'Think jail.' You read that. You come in here again, I'll be unhappy." Dooley knew not to make a real threat. The bulk of him was the threat, the uniform, even one he paid for and ironed himself. "I'll be unhappy, you'll be unhappy. Now go see Mrs. G. in her office and then go see how they like you at home." He waved Vo out.

"Not you, Mr. Temp Jackson. See your name's Temple. Momma named you Temple." He smiled a smile he knew was mean. The dog was smiling a real dog-smile at Jackson.

Slowly, through stiff lips, Jackson said to the dog, "Don't you get near me."

"He's friendly," Dooley said. "Most of the time." A bit of a scare wouldn't hurt this kid. "OK, Bruno." The dog got up.

"Don't get near me!"

Jackson jumped up, reached down the front of his sweats and pulled out a gun. It was so small in his palm that for an instant Dooley thought it was a cell phone. A make Dooley didn't even recognize, though he recognized the moment. A moment both fast and slow, well known to him in dreams. What he did was what he did in dreams: he waited. He wished his sons were there to see him so composed. He waited to die.

The boy shot the dog. All this took three seconds. The dog just stood there. Then he sank into the position Dooley's wife, when she was doing her cancer yoga, had taught Dooley was Downward Dog. Then he rolled over like he was just going to show his belly to be scratched. On the floor he panted with a tongue-out smile.

Dooley had his own weapon in his hand. At anger management they had a woman up there telling you anger was grief and you had to list everything bad that ever happened to you. Hours of that. Nobody defended anger or said you'd better have some so you could die for your buddies on the force or your dog.

But the boy Jackson had more going on than Dooley or anybody screaming in the outer office knew about, because what he did in the next second was point the gun at his own head. And that was when Dooley did the job the girl social worker had pretended all along to think was his. Arguments came to his tongue. He talked the kid out of putting a bullet in his own head.

The dog bled all over the mat but he lived too. He dragged a foreleg but he was a young dog with a trusting nature and he was going to go on for years doing his part of the job.

The Llamas

o o o

Ann told her friends she was nowhere. What was ahead? She didn't love her boyfriend. He accused her of not liking him but he thought the love part could survive that. He didn't like her, either, even though they maintained a truce over their differing views of the world. Ann's had always been that where the world was not cruel, it was treacherous, even though many advantages surrounded and secured her, including a job several rungs above his in the same company. His view was that the world didn't matter if you were having a good time.

When Casey Clare's brother died, Ann had to attend the funeral because she was Casey's boss. She felt the obligation even though Casey had been her assistant for only a few months. Todd, her boyfriend, said the obligations she felt were imaginary half the time and they did nothing but add random pressure to her crowded life. Her friends said the same thing. They didn't press the point that she often shirked these responsibilities after getting herself into a state about them. But she had said she would go to Casey's brother's funeral, and she did.

As an assistant—Ann had known it within a week of hiring her—Casey was not working out. She could spend half a morning being reassured and primed by Ann to get down to jobs that weren't all that complicated or taxing. Every day, she presented herself anew with her blunt inquiries into Ann's affairs, and then a rundown of things seen and done between close of business the day before and the reopening of the office doors.

Ann had to sit turned away from her computer at an awkward angle, looking up at Casey with an expression of commiseration, gradually picturing how it would be to lean over the in-basket and slap the girl into action. Girl—Casey was thirty-three, two years older than Ann. But her big smiling face and her packed lunch and her blouses a little too tight, as if she had just grown those breasts, made Ann think of an overgrown schoolgirl turned loose in the workplace and fending for herself. Or not entirely for herself: Casey did have a large family, a whole phone book of relatives advising, making demands, dropping in with food, all comically devoted to each other. Not to mention the dozens from her church who prayed at the unconscious brother's bedside.

He was in the University Hospital. Every day, Casey urged Ann to visit him, as if the problem Ann had was simply getting up the nerve. Casey said, "Yeah, why not this Sunday? Just stop by, come up to the floor. After you get done with the vigil." She knew Ann attended the Green Lake peace vigil—not that far from the hospital—any Sunday that she could make it. She had done that since before the beginning of the war in Iraq.

"Come on," Todd said. "Let's get out of town."

"The vigil is all I do and I have to do it or I'll go crazy."

"That's crazy," he said. He didn't go out of town without her; he didn't have the focus to plan a trip and get in the car all by himself and stay with it, and she didn't say it but that was why he wasn't getting anywhere in his job.

The peace vigil: that was no problem for Casey. God wasn't on either side; how could he be? Almost every day, Casey had a question about God for Ann, and not trying to smoke her out as an atheist, either, but simply assuming that the matter of what God would think or do would interest anybody. "I mean, you wonder," Casey would say. September 11, war, and the accident that had befallen Randy—an angel to all who knew him, a fireman, minding his own business and raising llamas. "You wonder how these things can happen." Ann would agree, clicking her nails on the keyboard as she appeared to give thought to the conundrum. Eventually Casey would go sighing back to her desk, where she would pick up the phone and call whoever was sitting with Randy in the ICU. She herself began and ended each day with a visit to the hospital where he had been lying in a coma since before she started working for Ann.

"I admire that about her," Ann said to Todd, who was telling her that if she couldn't face firing Casey she ought to get her transferred out of the office right that minute, before she wormed her way in any further. Ann thought about that and because it raised the question of exactly where, at work, her obligations lay, she said, "I think she'll get down to work when her brother gets out of the hospital." But the day after they had that talk, Randy Clare sank deeper and died of his injuries.

HALF the people who had arrived from the funeral were standing in the rain, mud oozing into their shoes. They were smoking, drinking wine from plastic cups, and watching two llamas.

They had trooped out of the house where the wake was going on—or not wake, reception, or whatever the church the Clares belonged to called such a gathering—off the sagging porch and down the path, really a pair of ruts, to see Randy's much-loved pets. Two wet animals as tall as camels stood by the fence. One of them, head high, had apparently walked as far forward on its front legs as the back legs, stationary in the mud, would allow. The other stood with its four feet—pads with toenails were not hooves, were they?—close together. That one was almost tipping over, like a tied bouquet. Then the stretched-out one raised a delicate bony leg and then another, and stepped a few paces away from its mate—if it was a mate—and the mate sprang loose and planted its feet on a wider base in the mud.

Ann said, "Does it seem to you like they're posing?" All the while a soaking rain fell on their thick, wormy-looking coats and on the long faces both supercilious and gentle. One of the women said, "Those poor things aren't rainproof like sheep, did you know that?" and people answered her, as they had not answered Ann. Some of them knew that piece of information and some didn't.

The eyes of the llamas were glazed and gentle. But the heads were poised atop those haughty necks. A face came vaguely to mind, someone looking around with a sad hauteur. Who? An actor. Somebody gay.

The woman, an older woman with a smoker's voice, knew something about llamas, though no one, she said, could hold a candle to Randy Clare on the subject. Randy had explained to her, as he would to anyone with an interest, the spitting behavior of llamas. Llamas spat when they were annoyed and what they spat was chewed grass, a kind of grass slop brought up from the gut and carrying the smell of that region.

"See the pile of dung over there? That's their bathroom. They all use it. They don't just go any old place."

A wet dog trotted up and crouched, head down, licking its lips and yawning with eagerness as it peered under the fence. Ann thought it might suddenly slip under and give chase, but it did not.

Even so, the two heads of the llamas swung around and the big dark wet eyes rested on the dog and then moved back to the group at the fence. Certainly there was some emotion there, in those eyes. Did the llamas know they were bereaved?

"All right," Casey said. "You've seen 'em. Bootsy and Baby. His darlings, except for Baby isn't so darling. Let's get back inside and get dry and get drunk."

They waded back to the house. Nobody said anything about caked shoes and muddy pant legs, though the women fussed with their dripping, flat hair. They piled their wet raincoats onto a top-loading freezer in a room off the kitchen just big enough to hold it and leave space to pass through the back door. "Deer meat?" Ann asked Casey, indicating the freezer, proud of herself for recalling that Casey and her brothers hunted deer. "No way, not now," Casey said, closing herself into a tiny bathroom off the kitchen. "Donna's catering stuff," she yelled from inside. One of the sisters had her own business; she had done the rolled meats and the trays of vegetables and dips in the dining room, and the laurel leaves on the tablecloth, which were actually sober and pretty, Ann thought, with white candles at either end.

Around Casey's desk, and at the copier too, the sagas of her sister Donna's business could be heard any day: the crushed cake boxes, the tiny refrigerators some people made her manage with, the cucumbers leaching dye from beets.

At the table sat the not-very-old mother, wearing big tinted glasses. Three of her grown children had lived in this small house with her. Two now. Why didn't they leave home? "You're all together, that says so much about your family," Ann said to Casey through the bathroom wall, hearing the sugary tone in her own voice.

"There were seven of us." Casey came out waving her hands behind her and saying, "Don't go in there just yet." Her eyes were extraordinarily red; they looked the way Ann's had long ago, in college, on weekends when she smoked too much weed. It occurred to her that this might be what Casey had been doing in the bathroom. "Rocky and I are the last ones, and who knows when we'll get kicked out."

"Watch yourself," the mother called out from her chair in the dining room, pointing with the cigarette, taking a deep draw, and coughing with her mouth closed.

Casey grabbed a framed photograph from among the cakes and pies on the shelf of the cut-away window to the kitchen, and held it out to Ann. "This is him. Randy." The picture was of a very young man with a florid, heavy, smiling face. He had the fireman's neat mustache.

Half the city fire department was in the house. They had all driven to and from the cemetery in a caravan with little flags flying from their windows, though Randy had not died in the line of duty but in a freak crash on a secondary road in the eastern part of the state, where he had gone in his truck to pick up a variety of hay the llamas liked to eat.

The firemen all seemed to belong to the same church the

Clares did or to be familiar with its terms. "Prayer partner." Ann heard that one twice as she moved from one spot to another with her wine. She was on her third full cup. "Randy Clare. Casey Clare," Todd had said. "Shouldn't they be Catholics?"

The rambling service, with its speakers standing up for the mike to be passed their way and its sudden calls to prayer, had had an air of unfinality to it, like a wedding where the vows had been written by the bride and groom when they had had a few too many. In the huge, carpeted sanctuary, light poured through skylights onto a botanical garden. The music for the funeral was piped in, but sound equipment hung from the ceiling, along with banners and American flags, and the plants rose in tiers to a band-stand with keyboards and a drum set.

Years ago, Casey told her, the founder of the church had gone around the state preaching against war. That was in the eighties, when there was no war going on. He was a young man and he was preaching against nuclear war. Being attacked on our own soil had washed all that stuff out the window. This afternoon in the hot, crowded house Anne had heard several restatements of this position, from people steaming, as she was, in their damp clothes. The firemen seemed to scent her politics—whatever her politics actually were.

She poured herself more wine. There was ample wine. The massed bottles were positively Irish. Ann's own heritage was Irish. That was why she had to be careful, as Todd would have reminded her if he had been there.

As far as she could tell, there was no one in the crowd with whom to be ironic. She had to answer, "I'm sorry," when a broad-chested man blocked her way and said, "Casey tells me that's your car with the NO WAR sign. Well, I sure wish there was no war, too. And not only that, ma'am, you're gonna need a winch to get you out, where you parked." She had felt the car settle into mud. There had seemed nowhere else, by the time she got there. She gave a shamed, appeasing laugh. Fortunately Casey appeared and said, "Sam, you leave her alone. That's my boss."

"I know that. That's why I'm talking to her. I'm making a good impression."

"This is my big brother, Sam," Casey said, flashing her red eyes. "Come in here, I'll show you Randy and Rocky's room," she went on, taking Ann's free hand and pulling her. By the laden table Ann pulled up short and set down her cup to refill it. She had come, she had done her duty, but she had to protect herself. Casey kept hold of Ann's hand and held her own cup out to be filled too. "You haven't actually met Mom," she said. "This is my boss, Ann," she called to her mother across the table, waving Ann's hand at her. Her mother was talking to several people sitting up close to her chair or bending around her, but at the sound of her daughter's voice she looked up and smiled, wreathing her forehead with the smoke she was blowing straight upward into her own nose, away from the faces of her listeners.

"How do you do?" she said. Behind her frames her eyes were the same blue as Casey's, though their red seemed more like that of normal weeping.

"I'm so sorry," Ann crooned to her across the laurel leaves. "I'm just . . . I'm so sorry."

"Oh," said Casey's mother, waving her fingers through the smoke, "we all are. Did you know Randy?" It rushed into Ann's mind that it was Vincent Price. The llamas. Their expression. Vincent Price.

"No, but I feel as if I did. I've heard so much about him from Casey."

"Randy," said the mother. "Randy was the one."

"He was," the group around her said in unison.

"Donna, you get Ann something to eat," the mother said, and a blonder version of Casey stood up and began forking sliced meats onto a plate. "Kendra honey, would you just get me a little more coffee. Right there, the decaf. That's something you could do for me. Donna, you don't need to make her sick."

"I get to decide," Donna said, winking at Ann and kissing the top of her mother's head. She added baby carrots and cherry tomatoes and leaned her big breasts across the table to hand the plate to Ann. She fluffed out one of the little napkins and handed that over too.

"Oh, thank you," Ann said, immediately starting to eat. She

wiped her mouth. Her impulse was to go around and seize the winking, sensible, food-providing Donna with a hug of sympathy, but Donna had already sat down again beside her mother.

"Come," Casey said. She was leading Ann by the edge of her full plate. "You need anything else?"

"No," said Ann, eating as she followed, popping a log of rolled-up ham into her mouth and glancing up insolently at the firemen they were bumping into. They had to let her pass, with Casey in the lead. She sank against the doorframe, once they were in Randy's room. But of course it wasn't only Randy's; there were twin beds in the dim, close room. The other brother, Rocky, was in the service. He had been at the bedside as much as he could be, but then he had been flown somewhere he couldn't get back from in time for the funeral. "He'll never get over it," Casey said. "Not being here." He was stationed at McChord getting his training in something to do with cargo aircraft. Something Casey kept saying the name of, day after day.

Todd would say she had let herself be lured into this room where Casey had the advantage and would talk her ear off and somehow get something out of her that she would be responsible for remembering when they got to work on Monday. Not only that, she had drunk too much, too fast, and she wasn't used to it because of her regimen of abstaining except on weekends. She wobbled off the door. Her limbs were heavy. "Oh Casey. I ate too fast and I've had too much to drink." Now she'd done it. This would be something they had between them, on Monday.

"So?" Casey said.

"I think I should just go outside. The cold air's good."

"Go ahead," Casey said, sitting down on the bed.

"Are you all right?"

"I'll never be all right," Casey said, swilling her own wine. "But I think of all the people who've had someone die."

"That's true," Ann said, letting her eyes fall shut.

"My father died, but I was too young. I didn't have to really go through that. The older ones did. Mom did."

"My father died," Ann said in self-defense, looking into the dark red-brown of her own lids until that too began to swarm and she had to open her eyes. That was better.

"I know," Casey said. "I know that." Ann could remember getting up abruptly and leaving for the ladies room, after Casey had somehow tapped into the story of her father, at the office. "You were ten, I was six," Casey said. "I wasn't the youngest, Donna was. Well. What can you do." She lay back on the bed with the cup in her hand. "Oops, spilled. I hoped you'd come today. And Jesus told me that you would."

Ann had stayed close to the door, but she couldn't turn tail and make her way to the sanctuary of the little bathroom, leaving Casey lying there. She said, "Your brother. Tell me about him."

"Nothing to tell," said Casey. But she drew a long sobbing breath of preparation.

"Oh," Ann said. "I don't feel well. I'm sorry."

"You could lie down," said Casey, without moving.

"I think I need to get outdoors into the air. I'll just be a minute." The crowd from the dining room had filled the hall, so that she would have to push even to get out of the room. "Uh-oh," she said. "Do you have—is there a wastebasket?"

"Here, just hang your head out," Casey said, rolling off the bed and yanking the window open. Ann got there and fell to her knees, thrust her head out into the cold air and let it hang down over the cracked, mossy sill. "Or, you can climb all the way out," Casey said. "That's how we used to always do it." She pushed the window up all the way. "There's no drop. It's low. Just put your leg over. Oops, yeah, it's sorta rotted out. There."

Ann climbed out the window, threw up a small amount, and felt immediately better. The rain had stopped and the flowerbed gave out a powerful earthen smell. The dirt was wet and black but not mud. Leaving footprints in it, she stepped carefully over the tips of crocuses and the puddle of chewed meats she had left. "I'm sorry," she said to Casey, who was kneeling at the window just as Ann had been a moment before, except that now Casey was praying. She had her face raised to the sky, her hands on the windowsill with the palms turned up, and her eyes closed.

"Well, hello there," said a man's voice. It was Sam, the brother, out in the yard. He saw his sister in the window and said no more until she opened her eyes. "Hmm," Sam said. "Case, you're stoned. And your boss . . . I wonder if she might be a little smashed."

"I am not," said Ann. "Or if I am, I am."

Casey hoisted herself through the window and fell out onto the dirt and the crocuses. She held out her arms like a child. "I was asking Jesus to come and be with us."

"He's in there with Mom," said Sam, picking her up.

"I'll go back in and sit with her," Casey said. "We were just getting some fresh air. Oh, I wish this whole thing was for something else. Oh, if only Randy was here."

Sam did not answer but took a bandana out of his pocket and with uncommon tenderness, Ann thought, wiped his sister's smeared arms.

"I'll change, I'll get this off, don't worry," Casey said. "Now on Monday, this won't have happened. I won't have fell out the window. Fallen."

"And I won't have barfed," said Ann, surprising herself.

"Don't worry," said Sam. "You're not the first."

"Everybody does it. Not only that, everybody falls out the window," Ann said. Ordinarily she could find a note of bored flirtatiousness at parties and get through a whole evening on it. But this wasn't exactly a party and how could she talk to him in that or any other way? For one thing she would have to brush her teeth. She'd go straight to the little bathroom—would there be toothpaste she could put on her finger?

It was no longer raining but it was getting dark. How to get out of there. There was no way she could drive, even if she could get her car out of the mud and around the other parked cars. Casey was pulling on her, hanging from her arm for balance, using the wet grass to scrape the soil off her shoes.

"Seen Randy's llamas?" Sam said.

"I did. They're something."

"See the baby?"

"No, I did not." She was forming her words with care. "See a baby."

"The cria. The baby llama."

"No. No baby. Not when I was out there."

"She's in the barn. Born Saturday. Day Randy died. Shoot, what he woulda given. We told him, but . . ."

"He heard us," said Casey. "The nurse said they hear."

"Maybe," Sam said. His eyes on Ann said he knew her skepticism about that, about everything. "Come on, Boss, have a look."

"I'm . . . I think I should just go in and sit down."

"You'll be fine." He looked her over. "The walk will help. Come on, Casey."

"Except you think Mom needs me?"

"Nope. Donna's in there."

The baby llama lay on a bed of straw in the dark little barn. Its forelegs were tucked under its . . . was it chest? Breast? Nothing so softly narrow could support either name, with a thin column rising from it, pale as mist, to hold a flower. On either side of the flower glowed a giant infant's eye, in an aged, creased lid. Ann caught her breath as a bottomless innocent darkness took her in. The petals of the forehead narrowed to a small black rose. The nostrils flinched. Did it smell her? Its coat was white, spotted with a pale brown, and it wore a little canvas jacket.

"You can sit down if you need to," Casey said. "Straw's clean."

"Better not," Sam said. "Hey, Case," he said, grabbing Casey's arm as she got ready to plunk herself down. "Come on. Stand up."

Ann said, "Why isn't the mother in here with it?"

"That's Baby. She wants to think about it. She's not real sure about her baby. We're feeding this little girl. Every couple hours since Saturday. She got her colostrum from the vet."

"Randy would have a fit," Casey said. "I'm glad he can't see how Baby's acting."

"If he was here, who knows. Everything would be different," Sam said. "Baby was hand-raised herself," he explained to Ann. "That makes them cantankerous."

"Could I . . . does it mind if we touch it?"

"Her. No, that's not the problem, she doesn't mind. See, she wants to nurse off you."

"Off your finger," Casey said. The baby did seem to be feeling for Ann's hanging fingers with its divided lip.

"But no, don't pet her," Sam said. "All we do is feed her. It's them she has to be with, not us. She does fine with her daddy and there's still a chance with the mom. Whatever, it's them she has to pattern after. Too much is going on, when you're this size. You can get so turned around you don't grow up right."

Ann felt like crying. Her mother came into her mind, the still, listening look she would get on her face when Ann was mean, in middle school and high school and even after that, and the unanswerable thing she would say every time, "You used to be such a happy child." And before that her father and his cancer and his long-drawn-out unfriendly death. Oh, no, don't let me get started, she thought as she began to cry. Neither of the others noticed for a minute, and then Casey saw and moved to circle her shoulders with an arm and pull her off balance again. Casey began to cry too, while Sam simply looked away and shook his head. He was not the crying type, Ann could tell. At least the tears had a cleansing effect on her mouth and throat, if she had to kiss him. This barn. The rain, the mud. Llamas. Firemen. She was going to have to stay the night. She wanted to. It would be like running away with the circus. They would put her in that little room, Randy's room. The hell with Todd. The hell with her car in the mud and her life. It was llamas she loved.

Think Not Bitterly of Me

○　○　○

WHEN she was a little girl in the thirties Abby had an experience that got into the newspapers.

At the beginning she was on the front page of half a dozen papers in Virginia, amid the stories of bank failures and foreclosures, and at the end, more than six years later, the story ran again in the whole tri-state area. A story like that, with a happy ending, got passed around, read aloud, pinned up in social halls, because it was the thirties and by then the rest of the news was bad, news of farmers burning their corn for fuel, and coal miners in West Virginia who had to have the Quakers come in to feed them.

If it had happened today, her story would have been explored in a different way, Jake Seligman told her when he was making his film. Certainly it would not have been allowed to fade, go unsolved, and reemerge only by happenstance. Abby said, "Well now, the Lindbergh baby got plenty of attention, and where was the benefit?"

As it was, Abby had the single envelope of clippings, all bearing the same bleached photograph of two little girls standing on either side of a wagon with a baby in it. The smaller, prettier girl, a five-year-old in a smocked dress too large for her, with her hand on the back of a long-bodied dog, was Abby.

Because the film took a number of years to come out, Abby had a hazy memory at best of the weeks Jake Seligman spent interviewing her, and her memories of the events themselves, as she was the first to acknowledge, were not sharp.

"I know a good bit of this is what I was told," she said to Jake the first time they met. He was a man from Hollywood who had called her up because he had once lived in the town of McBride, her home. He had lived there for one year, "long ago," as he put it, in the fifties, a time when their paths would never have crossed because she was a grown woman raising daughters and working nights and he was a kid in high school.

He had seen her picture, the little girls with wagon and baby and dog, in his senior year in high school, when he was looking up the Depression in the library. The Depression had remained his interest, always. Probably Abby had not run across his documentary about the WPA? His first film. It did play here and there in theaters, though not in towns the size of McBride, no. "I don't go to movies myself," Abby said. To her surprise, when he got back to California Seligman sent it to her on video. Next time she saw him she apologized. "My daughters gave me a VCR but I don't work it unless they're over, it's not worth it. I'll just look at the ones on TV."

That was early in their acquaintance, before Abby felt any embarrassment at his knowing the amount of time she spent in front of the TV, sometimes asleep there.

Each time Jake was in town he put a tape recorder no bigger than his hand on the table and had Abby say whatever came to her while they sat at her dining room table drinking coffee and smoking cigarettes. She remembered that distinctly: days on end of having someone to smoke with, so that if her older daughter visited after Jake had been there she would step into the house waving both hands in front of her nose.

"Now don't you blame me," Abby told her daughters. "He was pumping me. You say *something* when somebody's after you."

Both of her daughters, however scarce they made themselves most of the year, had been planning to be in town to attend the premiere of the movie of Abby's experience. But the daughter in Richmond went in early to have her third baby and her sister decided to go to the hospital instead. "I hate to miss your movie, but I just think at forty, when it's a C-section, you want family with you." It was the kind of thing that daughter did, the older one, to show Abby. So Abby would think, oh, she's a sight more helpful than I am. Because as a mother Abby never did come up to the standard of her daughters, shockingly insistent and painful as her feeling about the two of them had been at one time, awake in her bed at night worrying and planning because of no one to ask. No man. Or at least no husband. The first one had cleared out; the second, who looked like Gary Cooper, was not Gary at all, not a force held in by fairness and gallantry, but a mess, so shiftless he might as well have been one of her children. She thought about her second husband with the same feeling of commiseration with her old self that she had when her best friend Darla, who was younger, described the hopeless men she had to choose from in McBride.

For Abby there had never been a shortage of men, in days past, though few of them the father type. In her years away from the town of McBride she had been one of those said to go through men.

While she was getting dressed she got the call saying the C-section had been accomplished, a boy had been delivered. "They just lifted him out, like a jar out of the canner! Your last grandchild," her daughter added, in the way she had of catching at you before hanging up.

So Abby was going with Jake. He was picking her up in the Mercedes he rented when he flew in. He was in town to answer questions after the show and he was the mayor's guest.

"I think Mr. Mayor expects your movie to be about him," Abby said. "He's got a girl from the Washington paper coming in." She never could separate one mayor from another by name but she knew this one to be a grandstander.

"I heard that," Jake said, laughing and almost winking through the phone from the mayor's house. Jake was a sad, stooped, Jewish man, handsome in a way Abby had thought, at first, that nobody other than herself would take any notice of. He laughed at everything she said, until she really settled in to talk. Then he leaned on his elbows with his hands in a tent over his forehead, and once that happened he would get wrapped up in it and take off his glasses to clear the steam if she so much as said the dog died.

With her daughters not coming he had said to invite anybody else she wanted. So they had had dinner with Darla ahead of time. By now Abby knew more about Jake; she had seen him with her own girls. She knew and she should have known all along from her own experience that the way some men looked at you was a language, spoken in ways you thought were private, but they were not private, not reserved for you. Darla had fallen under the spell of Jake's eyes with their dark circles, and his accent that made her think of Joan Rivers, and the jokes. And certain qualities abnormal in a male—an interest in any confession, a tenderness for mistakes when they were made by women—qualities made known to Abby only gradually, in private.

Darla had taken trouble with her face and her big auburn permanent and was wearing her long green chiffon skirt, the same lop-hemmed style of skirt that Abby's own granddaughter had in her closet, as her daughter had pointed out to her after Darla sat by them at the *Messiah*. Darla had the skirt on with boots, and a new blouse of thin white material, not real silk, opened low and straining a little at the first buttonholes, and she was going to town with her impersonation of a woman a good bit younger than herself. Several times Abby had had to cut in on the storytelling and loud laughter Jake and Darla got going between them in the quiet restaurant. They were in the Hilltop Room in the old grange hall that had become the inn.

When Darla got up to go to the ladies room Jake stopped laughing long enough to watch the green chiffon drift across the lobby. A coldness passed over Abby, coupled with a mental picture of Jake in his open overcoat hurrying back into that same lobby after he had taken her home, and Darla waving her fingers at him from a table in the corner.

"Your friend is something," Jake said, with a lingering and

almost spiteful note in his voice, she thought, and one finger absently stroking away the grin he had been wearing through dinner. He filled his glass to the brim with the rest of the wine.

Normally Abby could have thought of a remark that would give Darla her due as a good person to whom nothing much had ever happened, a flirt. But Abby was not as springy as usual. All evening she had been slowed by the effort of thinking what subject she might raise now that would have anything like the hypnotizing effect her words had had on Jake five years ago, when their acquaintance was new and it was all he could do to push himself back from her table after the windowpanes had gone dark and they had eaten up all of her lunchmeat and cottage cheese, and take the dishes into the kitchen the way he did and rinse them off for her, still putting questions to her over his shoulder while he emptied the ashtrays.

"Darla wanted to come so much I called her up and said I didn't think you'd mind," Abby said. "She does my hair."

"So she said." He was stroking his sad mouth.

Abby did notice he was not nervous, or no more so than usual. He was always high-strung, ready to laugh or groan, or even shed tears, or go into one of his long-drawn-out explanations, looking straight into your eyes to convince you—and this too had had its effect on Darla, whom Abby could picture right now in the ladies room going round and round her mouth with the pearlized lipstick and powdering her hot cheeks—when you had forgotten what you had said in the first place to get him started.

Half the town was in the theater. People who had not called in years but who knew Abby's story had been calling up, assuming she'd seen the movie and cleared it. "Nope," she said. "I told him I'd see it when it was done. And if I hate it I can stand up and say, Lord, he's lying. I can stop it in the middle. I can do whatever I want." "Oh, but won't you be embarrassed?" Darla had said, and then answered herself, "No, you won't." For Abby was tough, and known to be. "I'd be more embarrassed if it was about me in my twenties!" Abby said. "There you'd have something to make a movie out of."

"If you take me to the movies, you have to hold my hand,"

she told Jake. Their roped-off seats were past the middle and she was going to have to look straight up at the screen. "Oh, but who's going to hold mine?" cried Darla, sending a smile across Abby and getting out of her best coat with a shrug of her bosom.

o o o

A WINDOW with a blowing curtain, with clouds visible outside it. The clouds were flying and the trees were bowing. Two trees. So it was going to be in black and white. Well, why not? The time was fall, from the look of the sky. Birds on the wind. Too blustery for summer, though the big oak tree was in full leaf, in a corner yard with patchy grass that sloped to a flowerbed full of weeds.

But that's not right, there wasn't a yard. No yard, the house right on the edge of the road at a crossroads, where there was a plank sidewalk. Hills behind, grown up and strong-smelling with the wild onions they called ramps. She had learned to eat them. Coal cars sliding by.

But no. This wouldn't be the West Virginia house at all, it would be the other one. It would have to begin in that house, the one where she was born. *That* house. Those two trees: a tall, straight tree and a sobbing tree.

You could see that house today, the real one, though the town had closed around it and Wilson's Barbecue Pit stood next door, with parking where the big trees had been. For that reason, when he was filming Jake couldn't use the actual house; he had to find an old-fashioned place that looked right to him. When he found it, it was in a town in South Carolina, leaving him obliged to make it up to the mayor of McBride with plane tickets and studio passes, because he had promised the filming would be in McBride. So the mayor and his wife had gone around L.A. in a car with a driver, and tonight they had both strolled down the aisle of the theater with offhand smiles as if they too were guests in the town.

The girl, Abby, was not going to be found at the window with the blowing curtain, looking out, as you expected. In fact your eye passed through the window into the yard, where you lost your balance cruising unsteadily around the huge low-branching tree. The white oak. Twice around it, dizzyingly, and there was the girl, sitting in the branches with her light hair blowing. She was a pretty little thing. That was part of it, of course, a big part. It always is. The beautiful blondes.

The title jumped onto the screen: THE SOBBING TREE.

She had tried to get the title out of him and he wouldn't tell her, he said, "Wait and see."

The girl in the tree was eleven or twelve. The whole thing was over by then, Abby's experience. So they would be looking back over the whole thing. You didn't have to go to the movies to know the story was going to go backwards, the same thing was on TV.

The girl was humming to herself. She could carry a tune but she wasn't humming happily, you could tell that. Her small, bony fingers picked the bark. Out of the tune she was humming, music commenced, a guitar being played while the tree limbs, which arched downward of their own weight, swept and lifted and sagged in the wind.

A piano would have been the suitable thing. Either that or an orchestra, not this slow picking, though Jake could not necessarily be blamed for not asking her what music she liked. He did know she had almost married a music professor. At sixteen she had moved away and found herself a job at a state college, landing it for the simple reason that she had written down the word *music*. Not only could you get work by then, but you could call attention to your hobbies and interests on the application forms.

She had gotten a kick out of telling Jake about the music professor. By that time Jake knew she wouldn't have been a professor's type.

The letters of Jake's name materialized on the screen, grew a shadow, and sank away. Another name appeared. At that point the camera lunged as though it had to swing across miles of the world, and without any warning at all a woman filled the screen. She was putting on lipstick in a car mirror. Nervous. A nice two-piece outfit with black frog buttons up to the little flat lapels, and a tight skirt.

She was unusually pretty, with a hairdo that gave Abby a stab of regret that time could not be reversed so that her own blonde could have lain on her shoulders in just that silken way when she bent her head getting out of a car. It had been pretty hair all right, but not like that, not perfect. When the girl drew her legs out of the car she had on the wartime nylon stockings with seams, and ankle-strap shoes. A man held the door for her, followed her up a flight of stairs and unlocked an apartment, carrying sheet music under his arm.

Abby sank back in her seat. Bowen. This was not any part of the experience and it would have been the considerate thing to let her know it was going to be in the movie.

She would not have spelled out the details to Jake, she felt sure. In fact she could remember Jake saying the later years did not concern him.

Bowen Gray. As soon as ever they got behind a closed door they would fall kissing onto the bed and kissing get back up to pull their clothes off. And Abby was well aware that movies felt free to show that, all the way to the clear indication of just where a body sank itself in another.

But as it turned out nothing happened, it was just a brief scene, puzzlingly there for a minute or two and then over when the last of the opening credits faded from the screen. Abby was amazed, when the scene was over, at how much could happen or seem to happen in that amount of time, with a woman doing nothing but strolling around a man's room, wearing only his half-unbuttoned shirt and touching the things he had, with a cigarette in her fingers.

The girl glanced over her shoulder at the man, who lay on a Murphy bed watching her with narrowed, critical eyes. Against one wall of the room was a piano. That was what appealed to me, Abby thought. I always liked somebody who could sit down and play the piano. Piles of music on the rack and the bench, and along another wall a phonograph cabinet and an entire bookcase

of records. The girl went over and pulled out records, pretending they impressed her, while the ash from her cigarette dropped
on them.

She held on to her arms, the ash dusting her own skin while
her thumbnail flicked the cigarette. She had on a dark nail polish
and heavy lipstick, garish in black and white. But she didn't look
hard; she looked too young to be smoking and to be engaging
in an affair like this one, full of accusation and disrespect. You
wouldn't have to know a thing about it to know that was what
it was. A stupid girl. Of course Jake would go to some trouble
to make exactly this kind of an impression on you; that was the
business he was in.

Abby looked over at Darla, who was watching the screen
exactly the way she watched *Another World* in the mirror while
she was coloring your hair, with her lips pursed and her eyebrows
pulled together.

The woman leaned on the windowsill, with an expression on
her face that made it clear she was just barely keeping herself in
hand. She had it in her to do something unexpected and possibly
awful. Her dark lips were moving but the music drowned out
her words, and the man was not listening anyway. The camera
came close and the angle made her whole face slope back from
the mouth opening for the cigarette.

Again there was a tree outside the window and as the branches
tossed, the girl, propped on her elbows, stared and stared at them.
She had stopped talking and the cigarette burned down in her
fingers, and you could follow the pretty line of her back and neck
to the eyes fixed on a tree.

What was coming? Jake couldn't have the girl jump out the
high window because she, Abby, was alive, she was here in the
theater.

Jake had been rubbing her hand all during this scene as if to
warm her knuckles, until she became conscious of the thin skin
pleating under his thumb, and put a stop to it by balling up her
hand. He was a devilish man, under the sad, half-old mask he
wore. Abby couldn't believe she was going to have to watch

this part, the trouble with Bowen Gray when she was still in her teens. And then what, her husbands?

It had never occurred to her that anything any later than her coming back home in the police car in 1937 would show up in the movie. Not that she was ashamed of any of it. Half the women in the auditorium with them—half the women in town—were divorced, so she had been ahead of her time.

She braced herself to head into it, but the movie didn't do that. Jake simply went back and started at the beginning. He might get to it again, but when you came right down to it what difference did it make anyway, if Abby had a wild time and the whole town saw it? Let them, let them see exactly what went on.

o   o   o

NEXT the girl who had been in the tree was down out of it and she was much younger, a little girl with scuffed knees, loose socks riding down in the shoes. Towheaded. Dress much too big for her.

A man and woman walked into the yard where two big trees made a noontime shade, and talked to the little girl. Her plain big sister was with her at the swing and they had the baby in the wagon, just like in the picture, though everything looked completely different from the way it was supposed to.

Abby was not ready to think about this yet. She was still turning over in her mind the picture of the man playing Bowen, on the bed, straight hair fallen across his forehead. She was surprised by this evidence that Bowen must have been a boy in his twenties. And not a professor, no. Not at that age. An instructor, sauntering by her desk every day with his remarks, a kid. When Abby had always said professor to herself.

The big dog didn't even bark at the couple coming into the yard. Roamer. The couple's car was parked at the curb; you saw it from the girls' height past the red and yellow zinnias—somewhere along the line the thing had switched to color, the way they did in commercials, and zinnias now grew thickly in rows in the weeded flowerbed—a big car with a running board and brass handles by which to pull yourself up out of the deep back seat. It was their car, but these two weren't rich. If anything they were poorer than Abby's family had been at that time.

She remembered telling Jake about this car, and the Oakland that he had up there on the screen could have been the same car. A 1926 Oakland Landau, with a sunshade on the front window. This was 1931. The couple had come down from the days when they had bought this car. Jake had done a good job with that. You could sense a lot about this couple. The man squatted down to pet the big dog, which allowed him to crumple its long ears in his hands.

Roamer. Somebody shot Roamer when he killed a chicken. But of course this dog was not Roamer. With a picture to go by, it would have been easy for Jake to get his hands on a dog like Roamer, just like he did with the car.

He couldn't get the people right, though. Abby was disappointed to have no personal feeling about the actors, even the little girl, beyond a vague recognition of certain things they had on, and even those things were a little off, as clothes in the movies always were, too neat or too messy, too evenly bleached, instead of faded with color still showing at the seams.

The man was good-looking, just a bit hefty the way men were then—or the way trousers made them seem, work pants or old slacks. He was in shirtsleeves, with no job to go to. He was the kind of man who would get into a fight over the woman. He had his hand on her waist in that way, looking around at everything as if he expected a challenge.

But the man he was playing had died just like anybody, after an accident on a tractor, one of those old contraption-tractors that got you tangled up in them, when they had the big mean metal wheels without any rubber on them. He had died not of the injury itself but of infection, due to mistakes made in the hospital. Abby did not remember that. She knew it from being told, not from memory, though she remembered voices whispering above her head, and the violent soap smell of the bathroom down the hall from his bed.

That was the only trip to the hospital she was ever going to make. Her own girls knew not to expect her there when they had their babies and they knew not to take her into a hospital unless she was already dead and they wanted to give her body to science.

The man didn't know machinery because before they settled in this town in West Virginia where nobody could find them he had been a horse trainer in Florida. The woman had been a singer, and for a few years they had had a wild life. During Prohibition, that was. She had reformed; she was on the Narrow Path, she liked to say. *Wild life*. Those were words that ever after lifted the hair on Abby's arms.

And so . . . the woman knew how to sing, but nobody paid you any money to sing any more and she had given up the kind of singing she had done for her living anyway. The man knew how to take a racehorse and get the devil out of its eye but he didn't know how to keep a sleeve out of a PTO shaft. He had had a job selling stock powders to the farmers before he tried harvesting oats. Not the coal mines; that, he wouldn't do.

Oh, he was on his way out of the whole thing even if he looked, with his black hair and bright eyes, as if it was just beginning. He was not going to be the one who went through the entire experience. There was not really room for him in it. Maybe that was why Abby had as good as forgotten him. You could almost tell in the way the camera flickered past the face with the soft moustache that he was going to die.

She wasn't ready to look, really look, at the woman Jake had cast as the mother, other than to notice the long blonde hair. But she could tell the woman was not secretive or anxious, was not wondering whether she was doing right. Jake had the woman smiling at the little girl, the prettier of the two little girls playing on the rope swing in the straight tree, the locust, not the oak that swept the dirt. Not the sobbing tree. The woman was smiling with tenderness and joy.

Next thing the girl was in the car with them and gone.

o   o   o

"I DON'T know, I only know they had me six years. Don't ask me how you convince a five-year-old you're her parents. Don't ask me. My own girls say they would have known a lot more about who had them at that age. I was different, that's all I can tell you."

"I expect it took a while for you to think they were your parents. But children adapt."

"They do but you have to wonder," she said, though she herself did not wonder.

"All the better," Jake said, speaking from under his hands.

"Why do you want to make it into a movie?" She liked to keep after Jake. Usually this provoked a long-winded answer having to do with the Depression, and the interest he had taken in it since high school, which had brought its reward, finally, in a prize for his documentary. "A substantial prize." He put that in every time, as if money would be the thing that would interest Abby.

The fact was—as she told him herself into the tape recorder—he was nosy. Most of his questions were about *people*. People who went all out, who were desperate. Those were the ones he was after. Smart desperate or crazy desperate, he didn't care.

He laughed. He said that was close. He made her admit they were talking about a period that had lured people into doing things they would never have dreamed of before, because—and he was right, she supposed, though it was not really her time, the forties had been her time—because of the way, in the Depression, everything shifted and slid downward, important people lost their importance, ordinary people slid into being no-account. Long, hopeless fury at the president, government, law, caused the whole outfit finally to fade from the average person's mind, and out came the thin dogs, women who might have taught you in school stepping up for their box of beans and flour from the church, cars with furniture strapped on, the hopeless sharing, the sudden, reckless seizing.

It was, Jake said, an atmosphere of suspended regularity. It was the nearest thing to a home front that you could have, without a war.

He said, "How old do you think I am?"

"Oh, forty," Abby said to flatter him.

"Ha. I was born in nineteen forty-two. Where do you think I was born?"

Of course she said, "New York."

"I was born in Poland. So tell me, nobody has any pictures of you from that period. Six years. They were afraid to take any?" This was a couple of years into their acquaintance, when the filming was under way and he was in town double-checking everything.

"Might be," she told him, "and might be it was just their way, not to take a picture of everything." Jake liked to have several explanations to choose from, she knew that.

"But those two . . . I can't help thinking somewhere there might be one. Because if they really believed they should have you, and you belonged with them . . . Jesus, what did they believe?" Abby didn't have to answer. Jake had states in which his features sagged and he splayed his fingers on his chest and stopped taking notes or lecturing her, stopped everything and just sat, dissatisfied, even disgusted with her, it seemed, and with himself. Now he said bleakly, "But of course to have pictures they would have had to own a camera."

So far not a word had been spoken on the screen. Just as she was going to ask him if he had made a silent movie, someone, a woman, began to talk.

"In nineteen thirty-one, when I was five years old, I was taken from my front yard by a man and woman I had never seen before. I went to live with them. He had different jobs he would get and on one of them he died. A farm accident. I don't know just when that was but I had turned seven by then, I'd say. I remember the funeral. It was in our church."

This was put together from her own words, because Jake had them on the tape, but the voice was a surprise and an unpleasant one. It was not her voice at all. He had an actress doing it. It was much older, it was the voice of an old woman. And the accent was the wrong part of Virginia—more like Tidewater, with that throaty ladylike sound. A quavery, pretty, old-teacherish voice, soft, so that Abby could hardly catch it with the hearing aid turned down the way it had to be in crowds. Although she was not yet seventy she was hard of hearing, and Darla told her her voice was loud.

She was sensitive about her voice because although she could sing, it was fair to say her speaking voice had always been higher than average, with what the daughter who went to college called a twang. A man had said her voice surprised him. Because, he had said without any apology, her beauty had led him to expect a different sort of voice. Bowen. He had had a fund of such remarks. It didn't matter. She had survived it. He ought to see her now, at this premiere—skinny and her hair still blonde, and young-looking, so that people thought she wasn't all that much older than Darla, who was forty-six, or they thought at least that she was in her fifties and were shocked to find out her real age, to find out that what had happened to make her famous had happened in the Depression.

The movie was all cut up, with some scenes taking place twice, the second time a little different from the first, and the music was cut up in the same way. Now a banjo took over with a song they used to hear on the radio every day, "This World Is Not My Home."

The couple and the little girl came out of a little broken-down house, more like a sharecropper's place than a house in town. Way worse off than the house Abby remembered, even though on the inside that one had had missing floorboards and doors blocked with towels at the bottom. But she was not criticizing. No, she could go along with how everything had to be exaggerated. The house had had one nice feature and Jake had remembered to put it in, a front door with a big oval glass pane in it, a door that looked as if it had been taken off another house.

They got in the car. Sitting between the talking man and woman as they rode along, the girl began to smile. Out the window was a long coal-train they were outdistancing. She leaned her head back on the high seat. You could see now how pretty she was, how the mother had put her hair up in pins just long enough to give it waves.

The girl had a Bible in her lap, and gloves on, so they were going to church.

Abby thought, I did have gloves like that. If they got a hole in the finger, she sewed it. She did mine and then hers. She washed them in an enamel basin in the kitchen. She did everything for me. You wanted to do everything for your daughter if you had one.

When we stood and looked at ourselves in the glass door with our church outfits on we looked alike. The beautiful blondes, he said.

"They were churchgoers, you see. But not the pious type. She played the piano at church. Oh, she could play! Play and sing! They had an old upright in the sanctuary with a good tone. She always said one night we were going to go and steal it," the woman went on with a ladylike chuckle. "And the two of us would push that thing on its casters down the aisle and out the door, and down the street without making any noise, under the moon. Well, now, we didn't, of course, because of course they would have caught us, in a place that size." Nevertheless the scene was taking place on the screen, the piano rolling and jolting and the moon huge, with the icy look it had in movies.

"Now, what did she sing. She sang 'Balm in Gilead' and all the Methodist hymns. She sang 'Bury Me Not.' 'Just a Song at Twilight.' And 'In the Gloaming'! That was her favorite. We could harmonize." And just as Abby recalled her own effort, with Jake joining in, on the first afternoon they had brought out the gin, the ladylike old voice began to sing,

> *In the gloaming, oh my darling!*
> *Think not bitterly of me!*
> *Though I passed away in silence*
> *Left you lonely, set you free.*

The woman doing the voice kept to the tune, that was about all you could say. She took a deep shaky breath and finished up:

For my heart was crushed with longing.
What had been could never be.
It was best to leave you thus, dear,
Best for you and best for me.
It was best to leave you thus, dear.
Best for you and best for me.

Then the guitar—this time with some backup music—took it up and went on for some time.

The part in the tree, when the girl was back where she had started, at the first house, was black and white; the other part was color. That was it.

The real parents did not appear. A little boy in short pants could be seen slipping through the door onto the unlighted porch while the girl was up in the tree, and down into the yard in the near dark with bats in the air, and turning tail and running inside, letting the screen door slam. And then creeping back out to be with her. Jerry. Her real brother, the one boy in the family, poor kid. Always crying his eyes out about something. Cheeks permanently chapped. Begging every night to have the lamp left on. And she, at the top of her voice, "Why don't you leave it on for him?" Having a fit. She didn't care if it cost money to burn a light in a bedroom. No, she couldn't get along for a minute with this family they had dropped her back into. Except for Jerry none of them knew how to treat her. And if they had wanted her so bad all the time she was gone, it must have been for the work she could do.

Jerry. Weak-kneed as he was, he got out of there, he joined up and got himself killed in Korea before he turned twenty. Abby was long gone by then, but his letters, when they finally came, were all to her, nobody else.

The boy was the one calling her when she was in the tree, calling her by the name Amelia.

He brought her hard candy he had stolen out of the bin at the mercantile and she reached down for it. This ran several times, with her arm hanging down and Jerry on tiptoe closing her fingers around the candy.

All right, Abby thought. Get down from there.

Color bloomed on the screen again but now the girl was much older; she was the same age as she was in the black-and-white part when she was back home. She was walking very slowly along a corridor, with a fat-rumped woman in a uniform who reached back for her hand so that she would speed up, but she wasn't going to. She sat down at a table and pretended to play the piano on it until a woman was brought into the room. It was the blonde woman who had been her mother, long hair cut short. At the sight of her the girl jumped up sobbing and threw herself on her, grabbing her loose dress savagely and knocking her off balance.

Wait. She sat in her chair and let the woman come slowly into the room in an awful dress with no belt. She let the woman come up to her where she was sitting and kiss her cheek. The woman sat down on a chair after kissing her and they talked in very low voices, or the woman talked and the girl sulked and swung her feet. Abby couldn't hear this part. The girl would not even look at the woman. The woman actually — speaking, taking hold of the girl's hand with both of hers — actually knelt beside the chair. The girl looked down on the clipped head and made no sign she heard.

It wasn't right. No, no. It was the first way.

But then they back up and do the whole thing again, the second way, only this time the warden gives an order at the end and the woman gives the warden a slap — the slap *the girl* deserves for being so cold and cruel to her. The woman just slaps the warden's face, because although it is a jail and not the asylum, the woman is, after all, in a certain way, crazy.

The woman is in a small pen, like a dog run. She is yelling, at such a high pitch it affects Abby's hearing aid unpleasantly. This is a dream, because while the woman is hollering, her hair is growing back very fast, just pouring out of her head.

Then the girl is in bed. She has been having a dream. She shouts, sits up with her face pinched and wild, holding her pillow with her chin hooked over it. She is in a room with another girl, her sister Martha. She looks with the wild face at her sister for so long that you can't tell if she is going to get up and smother

her just to get the wildness of the dream out of herself. The hair growing like that, pouring out of the woman's head.

No one comes into the bedroom to check on the girl after she shouts. She is back where she belongs, in her own home. Where are the real parents?

When the dream scene was over with, Darla on the other side of her said, "Whooee."

Abby pressed Jake's hand. He was watching with a frozen squint. "Oh, now," she whispered to him, "did I ever say it was that bad?"

He pressed back and smiled at the screen. The girl was in the tree, with the same circuit of the camera allowing only glimpses of her while the watery old voice said, "Six years after I left, I was returned to my home." We already know that, Abby thought. We just saw you in your bed.

The picture steadied itself and the girl's face filled the screen, a face pointy and sour, and at the same time, with its big gloomy mouth, even prettier than the face of the woman in the first scene, in the apartment. It was a beautiful face, really, that the young actress had. Looking at it Abby thought she could see why people made such a fuss about pretty versus beautiful, and she knew suddenly that no matter what she had been told, in reality she had only been pretty. What if she really had looked like this girl?

"Everyone was there to greet me when I got out of the car, only the baby was in the first grade and there was a different baby, a girl. The man and woman who said they were my parents were very nice to me. For that first little while they were especially nice. People came out to celebrate. The house was a ways out of town then. They grew their potatoes and corn and beans. They say things were in short supply there too . . . but I had been over in West Virginia in a little coal town in the middle of nowhere, where you noticed it more. Not even a town, really. A crossroads. That was it . . . that was all it was. We had chickens at first, there. Tramps would come up on the porch and ask a setting of eggs. But by the time I left, the chickens had all been put on the table."

Suddenly, out of nowhere and more or less under the music, which had left off its picking on the guitar and become regular movie music, a male voice spoke. It was not Jake's voice, it was deeper and smoother. "Did you think about your parents, your real parents." Not a question really.

"Can't say I did or didn't. Oh, I must have . . ." The camera stuck on the beautiful face of the girl, as she hummed to herself in the tree. The eyes went back and forth, back and forth. They lit on what must have been the front porch down below. An older girl had come out holding a baby. Dark braids, plain. Square jaw and small gentle mouth. "Amelia," this girl called out timidly. In the tree Amelia drew back under the leaves and clamped her full lips tight. Made a mean, savage face. Oh, Abby thought. A nasty thing.

The older girl jogged the baby on her hip. She did not have the breasts you could see on her younger sister in the tree.

"Oh, the trouble I caused," the old voice said. "Took away every boyfriend my sister had. Wasn't a week before Harry who was her little shadow was eating out of my hand. He was eight and they're little men by then, you know." Harry. Amelia and Harry, instead of Abby and Jerry. It made a difference, the names being wrong. And her plain sister Martha—but no one called Martha by name at all.

"No," said the man's voice. "If he was the baby in the wagon, Harry must have been six when you came back."

"Well, he liked to play doctor, I know that much."

"What about the new baby?"

"She and I never hit it off. A crier. I never did let my own daughters get away with whining. That sister doesn't live here in town, nor the older one either. They got away."

All the while the voices were going back and forth, the story was proceeding. The talk among them was so faint you couldn't make it out. There was music swelling over it. The two girls were pulling wash off the line, and standing on chairs to lift dripping quart jars out of the canner, and spreading squash seeds out to dry, and when you saw the boy he was drilling holes in a cigar box so he could string it to make an instrument. Jerry wouldn't have thought to do that, though. Jake had it wrong there, so she must not have said much about Jerry, poor kid. He wouldn't have been making himself anything to play with, he would have been right there in the way for everybody to trip over, helpless. And then the older girl, not so plain as the real Martha, buttoning dresses onto the baby.

Martha put her nose down and smelled deeply against the baby's neck, and came up smiling. The baby girl was dark-haired, closer to Martha's looks than to Abby's, though everybody pretended it was a pretty baby. The baby Jake had put in the movie looked about right, it was stout and had a spoiled, milk-fed look and one of those squashed-in, satisfied baby faces.

The baby didn't even know Abby had been gone. It didn't know she had ever been born.

You could tell everything had gone back to normal in the house by the time this baby was born, to make it fat and satisfied and getting the fuss made over it that Jerry missed out on, being the baby at the time Abby was stolen.

Everything was too clean, but Jake had the general idea.

Where were the real parents?

o o o

THIS time the girl was straddling the branch with her cheek against it and her legs and arms hanging down on either side as if she had been dropped from a height. Nothing happened at all on the screen, they just kept on showing her lying there like a dead thing all during the dialogue that was taking place offscreen. It was easier to hear because the music had come to a stop for the time being. The music was bothering Abby anyway. No piano, in the whole movie, when it was the piano she loved, the sound of a woman at the piano playing songs.

"Your real mother. Did you ask her about those six years with you gone?"

"Well sir, I remember her telling about one thing: somebody

shot the dog. Dogs were in for it, then, if they got after the chickens. Shot. Spine-shot and crippled, so they had to get rid of him. Happened a while before I got back. After they kept him fed one way or another all that time. She told me about it. The only time I knew her to cry. Cried like she lost . . . lost everything. She kept saying, 'You remember him, don't you? Roamer?' as if I would have been thinking about a *dog* for six years."

Abby turned up her hearing aid, dissatisfied with the manner in which the woman made her replies.

"But if you had forgotten everything . . . I expect she wanted you to know what had happened to everybody. I expect she kept trying to tell you about it."

The "research" they were all talking about, that was it. Jake could have gone and seen anybody. Got them talking. Given them that look that said he could see exactly what they meant, exactly what their point of view would have been, the ones who would say, "That child when she came back didn't have a kind word to say to her own mother."

And where was the woman who was supposed to be her mother, anyway, in the movie, if Jake cared about her so much? Where was either one of them?

"What do you remember about her?"

"Well . . . let's see . . ."

She must have said *something* about her that Jake could put in, about the two of them, her original parents. Even though she got away in her teens and didn't look back for quite some time. She wouldn't have just left them out of the whole experience.

That's the tree your mama called the sobbing tree out there, see it?

That was something said to her while she sat uncomfortably on somebody's lap. Of course that would have lodged in her memory, because it was awkward to be taken onto someone's lap when you were eleven years old. Somebody from town, some visitor come by to celebrate? A man. Men liked to get her close to them. She always listened more to men.

Perhaps it was her father. How was it she had no memory at all of her father?

It didn't matter who it was. The words were being said by the old woman, with a troubling pulsation as if the mute pedal was being pushed and released on a piano.

He said, That's the tree your mama called the sobbing tree out there, see it?

My sister said, That's the tree I used to climb up and look for you.

My little brother Harry said, Roamer looked for you. We went down by the grange every day because they seen a stranger there. Roamer snuffed all over.

It was mama went down there every day, and how do you know that, you were a baby, my sister said. But not meanly, she was good to him. Good to everybody. Not like me. How do you know he snuffed all over? my sister said to him.

I know it, my brother said.

He said it to me not her.

I know it.

Jerry, Abby thought. Nothing went right for that boy, did it. Nor for Martha either, nor any of them, never mind that they weren't the ones that had the experience.

She had left out a lot with Jake that she couldn't put in now. All that trouble. But it wasn't her fault. It isn't your fault if people want you. And it was not looks that did it, as people would say to her when she had her looks. It couldn't have been. No, it must have been . . . what? Fate? But how did one person's fate get separated out from another's? How could anything happen to any one person that didn't pull in everybody else and their fate, and the world, for that matter, and the universe, how could it all be sorted out, if any one of them had a fate? And if they didn't, what made you go through what you went through? If your life was just any old thing, what made you keep at it?

There was a long silence and then the old woman resumed answering the question in her flat, maddening way. "I guess—oh, of course she did, she missed me—I guess after all that time we couldn't, we just couldn't get used to each other. Oh, she always said we were poor and there were so many mouths to feed, and I knew we weren't poor, for one thing, compared to what poor was in the other place. Oh, not that she didn't want me back. Both of them. They got the money together to hire a detective from Winchester. But you may know this, a good many detective agencies then were just men who had lost their farm or their store. It was just a fluke I was ever found. Somebody traveling, like they did in those days, selling galvanized buckets. Drove across the line, into West Virginia. Somebody from the town of McBride."

WHEN the screen finally went blank Abby sat back out of breath, as if she had climbed the stairs to the Hilltop Room for a second time. She looked around in the hazy light that had flooded the theater like an unwished-for morning. The whole thing had been like crossing a floor in the dark not knowing which boards were going to sink in. She was not quite steady, and sat with her knees apart feeling the slant of the floor under her feet. Her upper arms ached.

The mayor stood up clapping forcefully, and then everybody stood and clapped while Jake was letting go of Abby's cramped hand so he could get up. He jumped up onto the platform, rubbing his eyes in the light. He got his tie loosened and with his hands on his hips he shifted from foot to foot, pleased with himself and shyly sociable, grinning as if he had done every one of them a good turn, like changing a tire or moving something heavy, that had left him flushed and out of breath.

So there was more to come, and Abby could not go home, she had to stay in her seat.

It was going to be a big surprise to her if he got a question out of this audience.

But she had reckoned without teenagers, girls as well as boys, who wanted to know how you got the camera up into the tree, and how you got it into the car, and whether the women really had no clothes on underneath if you showed them in a bedroom in a man's shirt, or in other movies where they showed them with nothing on, who all was there on the set? One of them in this group that raised their hands had a mother in the audience who covered her face, but Jake let her know it didn't bother him. "That's exactly what I used to wonder," he said, taking the microphone off the stand and swirling the cord, and he told them what they wanted to know.

The kids liked him because of his messy hair, which Abby happened to know he struggled over with the comb, and his New York accent that caused them to snicker with delight as if he were putting it on, and because of the strong charm important people gave off, when they answered questions as if they would be just as happy to know you as all the rich people they did know. Darla had shown at dinner that she did not recognize this, but Abby knew it from way back, from the faculty dining room, after Bowen finished improving her manners.

Then an older woman asked Jake how he did his research. He said he had done it over years, in this town and towns like it, and mentioned his documentary, but she flapped her hand right back up to know how he got the little girl's story.

"I copied it out by hand from an old newspaper, and many years later I found she had been here all along—or rather come back with her children—and was a lady gracious enough to give me many hours of her time. I didn't want to keep strictly to the experience she had, but I wanted to preserve it as the core of a film about a period of American history. As it happened I became interested in the individual. But of course I departed from the facts she gave me. Something else happens, or you hope it will, when you work in film." He bowed to Abby, who was paying attention to her pulse, which had given over to heavy and uncomfortable rocking while he was speaking of her, as it had not throughout the movie. At some point Darla had placed her arm around Abby's shoulders and now she snuggled her a little as if she were an old grandma, and glanced around possessively.

The audience would have let the subject rest, but the next question came from the same persistent woman. Abby decided she was the new librarian, intent on showing off some information she must have up her sleeve. Turning around to see, she had a side view of a woman with long gray hair held off her face with a barrette, wearing a fringed blanket with a hole cut in the middle for her head to come through. It was not any librarian from McBride and not the well-dressed girl from Washington, the reporter; that one was writing in her notebook but not asking any questions.

The woman stayed on her feet, egging Jake on with the mention of other directors and their movies, repeating "film" and "your film" until you could slap her. She knew something about the movies, it was clear—she knew about Jake and she had made the trip from somewhere—but now she had changed the subject. She had him talking about the war. Talking about himself, as any man would sooner or later, while Darla yawned and signaled disgust with her darkened eyebrows, and the mayor, who had a speech in his pocket he was going to pretend he made up on the spot, started fidgeting for it to be his turn.

But Jake had dropped his guard now, along with the casual act, and was pacing with his hands clasped to his chest with the microphone between them, and talking the way he liked to, as if everything that happened had three or four explanations. All about how he had come to this country from Poland. Somebody had unearthed distant relatives for him, an older man and wife who had no children and who, when he was finally at home there and had almost finished high school and had perfected the accent—that brought the house down—moved away from New Jersey. His foster parents moved. He struck himself in the forehead. First to McBride, when he was in high school, where there were no Jews in school except him—and to this day he did not know why they had conceived the idea of retiring here, he said apologetically, passing his hands through his wayward hair in a way that made Abby think of several women of her acquaintance in the room, in addition to Darla, who would be trying hard to remember a Jewish family that ever had lived in town, in order to have an opening to introduce themselves afterwards. But despite the beauty and hospitality of the town, his guardians soon picked up and moved on once more, to Florida.

Abby snapped open her change purse to see if she had any of her relaxant pills in there. She had been made almost ill at the start by having to crane her neck to see the screen, and by the dizzying shots of the girl in the tree, and then put through the Depression in some infernal way—after being made to look like a hussy at the outset, if you thought about it, although the audience, thank God, never saw anything but the one scene.

"I think my parents stayed with a couple who agreed to hide them if they would—in the event their capture became inevitable —if they would leave, and leave me behind. Now, this is what I never could put together. There are two theories. One, that my parents agreed to this and the couple saved me although they could not save my parents. The other, that they turned my parents in so that they could keep me." He looked up at the ceiling. "So they could keep me!" he repeated, or really wailed, like a woman, in a kind of shrill comical disbelief.

Abby thought for a minute Jake was going to fall into one of his old-man states. He had stopped his energetic pacing, and stood with the microphone dangling from his hand. She thought he might be going to lose his hold on the audience. To her dismay he pulled a handkerchief out of his pocket. He unfolded it carefully but did not use it.

"And so how did you end up in this country?"

"Someone got out. Got away. He made it his business to find me. Someone very tenacious. He had known my mother. I believe her grief—even there, in the camp—had made an impression on him."

Abby had lost all patience with the woman who had changed the subject and with Jake himself, who in his excitability had forgotten, apparently, after his first success with the kids' questions, that the only thing people in the room really wanted to hear about was Hollywood.

Without trying to hide what she was doing Abby reached up and pried out her hearing aid. She wanted to get home and Jake had to come with her. He owed it to her not to go back to the inn and meet Darla but to come in, sit down on the couch and let her pour him, and herself, some gin out of the refrigerator.

She had a grandson born today and at the very least she

deserved a toast. Furthermore she deserved a chance to have her say about her own life.

He might think she had told everybody here what she had told him but she had done no such thing. She never talked about her experience. Even though everybody professed interest in it, the interest had really died away long ago. He ought to hear her own daughters if she ever brought it up.

Something had come between her and her daughters, the way mold can get between the layers of an onion that looks fine on the outside, and she could not identify it to this day, something that made it so that once they had their own children, her daughters started in telling them things that were not true.

"Nobody thought to tell me this at your age," the older one in particular would say to her own daughter, in Abby's hearing, "nobody taught *me*, but I want to make sure *you* know . . ." With that one, who had gone to college, the problem was clearer: college had changed her. She had come home the first two or three times with a lot of mean energy in her and the makeup scrubbed off, and a way of retelling events to make them unpleasant. "So you were such a big deal that you got stolen, and then stolen back. And why was that, in your opinion?" Though there had been a time when she and her sister could never hear the story enough, and crowded against Abby, their little-girl scalps sending up a sweat of suspense through the fair hair. *Stolen* from your *mother*. Unthinkable.

It was too late to go into it and clear everything up with her own daughters. But with Jake it wasn't. Sitting across from him in her own house with a shot of gin warming her — the thought joined the sensation the movie had left in her sinuses, the hot-cold you would get smelling ammonia. But at the same time pleasant. Of course it was neither thing; it was her imagination, not an actual sharp breath, as it seemed, of tree bark and ramps and coal, or of the washed blonde hair of the one she loved best.

The only one she loved, ever.

To whom she had done that terrible thing. Not spoken to her, not said a word, when she came into the room of the jail in the jail dress.

Abby almost moaned. Her whole body had gone sore and stiff. If and when she was given the chance, she was not at all sure she was going to be able to get up. With difficulty she uncrossed her legs and crossed them again. She must have done it a time or two, because Darla got a sympathetic look and patted her knee and whispered something to her that she couldn't catch without the hearing aid.

"What do you know about it?" she said to Darla, more viciously than she meant to.

Darla sat back and Abby tried to soften what she had said by picking something off Darla's chiffon skirt and buffing the cloth with her fingers. But Darla's lip had begun to tremble. She laid her palm on her see-through blouse where the bra was visible, and pressed her heart.

"Oh, for God's sake, Darla," Abby began.

"It's not you," Darla said, the first tears dropping out and sticking the blouse to the skin of her breasts. "Everything's not you. Aren't you listening to what he had happen to him?"

Abby looked straight at Jake, and that was when she saw, in the smile that came to his bitter mouth at the sight of Darla crying, a smile with a little down-turned corner of pleasure craving and determination, that this tear-stained cheek of Darla's would most certainly be laid, tonight, on his bare skin. It couldn't be stopped. It was like a film that was going to run until it was over. It was too late. Abby could not start to cry herself, she was beyond such an outlet. She could not make clear all that Darla needed to know about the matter of being chosen, and what it got you, and what it got anybody who had to be left out of it.

The girl in the tree certainly did not know what was coming, did she? She thought all the trouble that could come to her would come from too many people wanting her, and she welcomed it, the cruel, stupid girl.

If those people, if *a single one* of those people wanted anything the way Abby had wanted the wrong mother, every day of her life since the day at the jail, she hadn't met them. And Jake hadn't met them, either. But he had met Abby and he knew.

Jake went looking for the people who wanted a thing they

were not going to get. He knew them when he met them and that was what interested him and he would put it into any movie he made.

She felt a shiver. She remembered something. She remembered thinking, when Jake first told her about the movie, that he meant she was going to be in it. That he wanted her—impossible as that was when you thought about it—to be in the movie of her experience. To play herself. Of course she realized. She never said anything.

She turned herself in the seat and found a smile for Darla.

∘   ∘   ∘

NEAR the end of the movie a point had come when she shook herself back to attention and it seemed to her that she had been in the theater, trapped in the low seat, for days. She wished she could go to the bathroom but she thought about crawling over everybody in the dark and gave up the idea.

She had decided sometime earlier in the evening that by "docudrama" Jake had meant that he was not going to make a movie at all but something more on the order of a slide show, if slides could move, and having once decided that this was what his movie was, she had found it easy, as she always did when anybody showed slides, to close her eyes.

A long time elapsed and when she took notice of the progress of things again the girl had her hair in a ponytail and the mother had a bandeau around hers and they were washing windows. They were on the porch, dipping rags into a brand-new, shiny bucket. You could tell the water had vinegar and ammonia in it because when they wrung the rags out they made faces. They were washing the front window and the big oval pane in the door. It was spring.

Then there was a scene she almost couldn't look at.

The camera circled the mother as if to trip her. The girl, tall and developed as she was by then, was lifted like a child and placed in the back seat of a car, and when she unlocked the door a man leaned on it to keep it shut, so she rolled across to the other side, seeing the mother trip on the plank sidewalk and totter on the arm of a uniformed woman to the other car, the one that belonged to the two men who were now holding both doors shut on Abby. These men would not have had the strength between them to force her mother if she had been herself and fended them off. But she went; she didn't even make the two men leave off holding the car doors to put handcuffs on her, when you would have thought she'd have been ready to die for Abby, and might have on another day, with time to plan—though why was the plan not made and agreed on between them, why not agreed on a hundred times?

But she didn't fight or die; she got into the car without looking back at the unpainted house where they had been washing windows because spring had come and she and Abby were alike in their love of clean windowpanes and swept floors, as in everything. She got in without even looking to see where Abby was, and put her head back on the high seat, and shut her eyes.

"Do you think she told him?"

"Told who?"

"The man from McBride, when he came through. The bucket salesman."

"*Told* him?"

"Did she have any way to make a living when her husband got killed?"

"Nobody did, did they? Nobody did."

"Yet they had to. Didn't they?"

"She worked at every kind of thing. For instance she made candy at home and I wrapped it up in papers I cut out of a catalog and she sold it. She sewed aprons and dishtowels for different places . . . the school, I think, the church."

"But it didn't make money. Not a living for two people. And if she was sick, and knew she . . ."

"She was fine. She was never sick."

"Well, no matter," the man went on, in the voice quite a bit deeper and more confidently soothing than Jake's. That was why

Abby had a hard time remembering being asked any of this by Jake. That and the old woman's voice and her impossible attitude. Her bragging how she wrapped candy. "No matter. What happened to her?"

There was a long silence. "Oh ... all right. I'll tell you. We had a reunion! Years later. Or not so long as all that. When she got out of jail ... oh, they didn't keep her but a little while, no, they would have seen how she didn't belong there ... It must have been after the war was over."

"That would have been almost ten years."

"Oh. Well then, let me see. Well ... but my land, we went over all our memories. I do believe we sang a couple of songs."

For a horrible moment Abby thought the old voice was going to sing again. But it just said dreamily, "We would've sat there and cried our eyes out. You know. Just thinking about ... how poor we must have been."

The picture changed, in one of those maneuvers of the camera lens that let you know something that looks the same is different now.

"But now tell me, why don't you, what really happened." You could do it with a voice too. Move in closer.

After a silence the voice whispered, "I saw her that one time. The day they took me over to the jail. She must have been sick. She died in jail. It was that same year, the year I turned twelve. She died. She died."

It was then the camera began its final sweep around the tree. Not that again, Abby thought, catching hold of the chair arms. This girl was not the one a brother had climbed a tree to wait for. She was not sister and daughter to them, or anyone. Right there you could see what was happening. Right there—she was going to look out for herself, cause some people a lot of trouble, kill the love of her own children. The guitar kept on with the one chord. The little girl stared out. She was not little, though, she was almost grown. She was ready for the life nobody could alter any more by what they did to her, because it was hers.

The Mouse

○   ○   ○

THE critic Lindenbaum had been a handsome man when young, large-eyed behind his glasses and wearing his dark hair in thick waves. "Dark one," Sofya Lindenbaum called him in her book of love poems.

Dark one, today my heart is light,
because today you are coming back from the dead.

With his money, Lindenbaum would have been a contented dilettante if he had not become a literary critic. But he gave his heart to the profession. His claim was always that it existed in defense of art. Though he never wrote a political sentence, the poet he married, Sofya, from a Russian émigré family, ranked him with Belinsky—the idealist Belinsky, with his belief in the saintly individual. "But even Belinsky, of the warm heart, the soulful eyes—though blue, not your glamorous color—could wield the knife."

Ungrounded in a university and lacking theory or any instinct to criticize, Lindenbaum wrote only one book, a thin volume about the Symbolists, begun in his days as a French major and finished in his fifties. The rest of the time he wrote, and gradually published in the newspaper book reviews of the time, approving essays about an assortment of books, most of them novels and biographies. At this work he had a prolonged if minor success.

It was of little consequence to him either that his essays and reviews had loyal readers or that his book did not. He quoted Sainte-Beuve: Being a critic is saying whatever comes into your head. Like many wealthy eccentrics he was an admirer of technology, but he lagged decades behind it, peppering his writings with "transistors," and "remote control" and "the hydrofoil," interspersed with "the flesh" and "the soul." He did not ally himself with any school of thought. He would take off the shelf a writer long and firmly retired by serious critics and end a rambling essay with "but we must wait and see." "What is this 'wait and see'?" said Sofya. "What do you wait for, from this man who is beneath your notice? They will put it on your stone. 'Wait and see.'"

Lindenbaum had fallen into his profession after leisurely years of study in two or three universities. His time was his own. He didn't have to teach, or champion his own book, or sustain the competitive spirit or the straining after novelty or even the fastidious labor expected of the academic critic. He could take his time, raise his dogs, tend his difficult wife, a poet originally admired by only a small group of readers who with their devotion to poetry lived worlds away from any poet, let alone one with the bitter nature of Sofya Lindenbaum. He could make his undercover attempts—"I beg you to consider what she has gone through!"—to pacify Sofya's literary enemies, as well as people she had insulted or sued, driven out of her house or reported to the police. There is no hint that he ever longed for a more agreeable companion. A man ambling along the lakeshore in Chicago, following his beagle, one beagle after another, dogs whose inbred hearts gave out and broke his own, Lindenbaum could dream the afternoons away.

Some said he could afford, literally, to be kind. At any rate he was soon old. He had reached the age of struggling to rise from the armchair where he napped at the bay window. "Come now, stand up, my Ivanov!" Sofya would say, pinching his thigh

muscle. Ivanov was a Russian strongman who had believed in
ice-cold baths and loving his fellow man.

"Unless we consider being a sweet guy a profession," said one
of Lindenbaum's eulogists, "we will have to concede that our
dear Lindenbaum was lazy. Yet driven, in a lazy way. Driven to
defend those whom few extol or even remember . . ."

"That awful woman." This was heard in more than one row
at Lindenbaum's memorial, as Sofya was taken out on the arms
of two of his friends, like a bride with two grooms though with
a shout of grief, a theatrical stagger, a savage backward look. To
meet her requirements the memorial had been postponed and
postponed until finally at his friends' insistence it took place
almost a year after his death.

Lindenbaum was the only child of a pair of philanthropists
who had made a fortune in business. The material good fortune
kept on with his own marriage to Sofya, from a family similarly
well placed if not as openhanded. He owned buildings, including
the one he and Sofya lived in overlooking Lake Michigan, where
he forgot to raise the rents and allowed the tenants pets. They
feared she did not cook, and brought him cake. His own door
opened on a household of pets, birds as well as dogs, and even
white mice for a number of years until the short life span of the
mouse began to wear on him.

He was twenty-some years older than his Sofya. Some vague
scandal was attached to their union, but there was no call to
remember it except among a few old people, Russians clustered
in New York. Sofya's poems were devoted to the period before
that, to her own wrathful self and to the parents born for some
destiny that had been left behind in Russia and was not parent-
hood. The parents had agreed with each other's impulses; they
were united in starving their maids and in thinking a violent and
uncontrollable child would mend her ways if she stayed long and
often enough in a closet, deprived of water so she would not have
to go to the bathroom.

In this closet, where she could do nothing but think, her first
poems came to her. The door was cut high for a sill that had been

removed to allow air to pass, and she would lie among the shoes with her cheek on the floor, waiting for the sun to reach a line of red diamond-shapes in the border of the Persian rug visible under the door.

One day, she saw a mouse. It didn't approach the closet, though the bread she kept there for her captivity might have drawn it to the bedroom. But the vast old apartments with their glass doorknobs and loose floors had harbored generations of mice, so the sight of one—even in the daytime, when in a house they are night-going creatures—was not the shock it might have been to another child.

On this day, at the same time the sun arrived, and out of the same silence, a mouse appeared on the red wool and sat up to stroke its whiskers, not briskly as a mouse normally does but feebly and dreamily. She felt a rush of pity for it. But was it more than pity? Was this love? The feeling swelled past the mouse— past the fur on its chest made pink by the sun on the rug, the flimsy hands curved, even without a thumb, in the ballet position *arrondi*, as she knew from forced months at the *barre*—and on, to things a mouse must know, must live for, passageways, smells, and its own kind, and from there to things unknown to it because it had to be a mouse, a world of things going on somewhere, everywhere, with nothing to rule them.

No one would know of such a moment. It was hers. When the key turned in the door, the daze with the world in it was gone, and she managed to twist her mother's arm and be slapped for it until her ears rang.

Eventually her parents packed her up and sent her to stay with a great-aunt, from whom she could easily run away and who lost track of her altogether when she was fifteen. Few who did remember that girl's elopement a few years later with the middle-aged critic Lindenbaum would have opened her privately published little book, the first one, in all its hardness of heart.

Lindenbaum's friends were holding a dinner in New York for his seventy-eighth birthday. Sofya, who rarely left their building in Chicago where she wrote her poems and accusing letters at a high window overlooking the lake, hated being shut in an airplane, and theirs had landed in a snowstorm. She was calling down curses on the taxis absent from the front of their hotel, a small, choice building on which it was snowing so heavily the mansard roof was like a grave filling up between the brick walls of its taller neighbors. The sidewalk wore a deepening slush of ice and sand. "How I hate this terrible city!" Sofya shouted into his good ear.

Another poet would have seen curtains of snow waving in front of Christmas lights, a hotel's potted trees sheathed in sparkling ice. Lindenbaum was soothing her with a line from Shakespeare, "Travelers must be content," when the muggers struck.

"Oh no no no." Lindenbaum refused to produce his wallet.

"Do it!" Sofya hissed at him, never taking her eyes off the face of the one who had not said anything but had made the mistake of looking for a moment into her black foreign stare.

Lindenbaum's refusal was contrary to everything he had taught her about getting along among people far more desperate than herself when he had first known her in her youthful desperation. His memory was beginning to go, and with it his judgment. He was restless with schemes; he had just made over a portion of their stock to a dog-rescue organization. As she hooked his cummerbund, she had been lecturing him about his weakness for any and every solicitation that came in the mail. "Be a man, my darling fool! They all expect you to save them. Why must you? Stand up to them!"

So was this mad refusal to hand over his money her doing? Then to her horror she saw exactly what it was: not a refusal, but a wish to have a talk with the robbers.

"Listen to me," Lindenbaum said, attempting to grasp the hand of the one who had him by the lapel of his overcoat. The other hand was in a pocket with something pointed at him. An angry shove in the chest toppled him onto the sidewalk, whereupon in the cold, in the confusion of falling snow, the boy began to kick him.

"What are you doing, you demon?" shrieked Sofya.

Like a schoolboy, the other one actually answered her. "No, we—" Even knowing the pocket pointed at Lindenbaum held no gun but only a phone, he did not run away, as Sofya dropped to her knees and fastened herself to the leg the kicker was standing on. That one kicked as if the man on the sidewalk might be a lifelong enemy, until under Sofya's weight he too slipped in the snow and fell. At that moment the doorman, a huge man said in the next day's papers to have once been a tackle, slammed his bulk into the hesitating one, rolled onto the kicker and pinned him with his knee. He pointed with nothing but a whistle at the one who had missed his chance to escape, who instead of scrambling up lay with both hands in the air as if to pull the snow over himself.

"Kids," said the cop, when the EMT was getting Sofya back on her feet. She had begun a violent CPR, although her husband was breathing. "Right in the lobby almost. Morons."

In the emergency room they stabilized Lindenbaum and on the first night he did well. In the morning, when Sofya got out from under the shawl one of his friends had draped around her— for no friend of her own, if any remained to her in this city or anywhere, had appeared or called—the resident came to tell her the blows had bruised the kidney and lacerated the spleen, and that her husband's body had taken the rare response to such injuries of beginning to break down its own muscles. On the second hospital day he was worse; by the third he had sunk into a coma. That was Sofya's word; the doctors' calmer term was *lethargy*. "This is not coma," they said. "Lethargy!" she screamed to his friends in snowy scarves in the waiting room, as if it were a curse laid by the doctors.

That afternoon Lindenbaum woke up. As she bent to hear him, he opened his eyes a crack. "Sofi, Sofi, you should go home, let Kiki out." Kiki was their bird, set free in the afternoons to fly around the kitchen. So Lindenbaum seemed for the moment at least to have some sense of how long Sofya had been muttering and groaning and making her demands in the chair beside his bed with the shawl pulled up to her chin. Then his eyes flew open

all the way, his voice rose. "But the dogs? What about the dogs?
Who, who—"

"We're not at home, my fool, we're in New York for your
birthday! Bette has Kiki and the dogs." Bette was their maid,
older than Lindenbaum himself, rescued by him from the household of the cruel parents of Sofya.

Lindenbaum closed his eyes. In twenty-four hours he had
reached a stage the residents called obtundation. There was
groaning in the room, of the soul trying to stay in the body. A
day later, interrupting an open-eyed vigil coma, they called it,
that had seemed to Sofya to promise a wakening, the body, cruel
landlord, evicted the soul into the cold room of monitors, where
Sofya was screaming and trying to cram it back in.

From his room, where her shouts echoed down the elevator shafts and disturbed other floors, Sofya had to be escorted
to a cab, accompanied to her hotel, and helped through every
arrangement.

The names of these stages, each downward step of Lindenbaum's course in the hospital, appear in a cycle of love poems.
Because of these poems, the center of her fourth book *The Stages*,
Sofya won not only an important prize but a general acclaim. A
book of love poems had not come along in some time. As such
her book outsold the other poetry of its decade, and she acquired
more of a reputation than Lindenbaum had ever enjoyed. He
had been a minor figure at best; what kept his name circulating
as long as it did among those familiar with his essays, as well as
among the writers who had caught his benign and extenuating
notice, was Sofya's crusade. For Sofya spent years engaged in a
very nearly fanatical attempt to save the boy who had not kicked
Lindenbaum.

The one who had kicked him was seventeen, not eligible, at
the time, for an adult sentence. That one, after testifying to his
brutality, she left to his fate. But the other boy, the one who had
looked away, who had mumbled an answer when she screamed,
was twenty. As an of-age accomplice he was eligible for any
charge that could be applied to the acts of either one of them.

Though he had not touched Lindenbaum, he was convicted of murder.

For years, Sofya worked on his appeal. When the appeal failed, she attended his parole hearings as they came and went. Finally in prison he was one of those chosen to take part in one of the dog-training programs being introduced in the correctional system. When he was at last paroled, not as a result of Sofya's efforts but for distinguishing himself in the program, with her help he got into the state university where she had gone to teach Russian after Lindenbaum's death.

By this time she had retired from teaching. Though she was a celebrity in the world of poets, it was less as a poet than as a significant donor to the university that she was one of those invited to say a few words at his graduation. She was old, though not as old as she looked, being one of those who put up no resistance to age. She had to be helped to the lectern. Her hawk's face had softened into swags; her black eyes were quite gone, submerged in their lids. Before she was handed her sheaf of flowers and escorted back to her chair, she rambled on for some time about the work of her late husband, the critic Lindenbaum. Few attending the graduation of this giant university had ever heard of the famous poet Sofya, let alone of the critic Lindenbaum.

"We must wait and see," she said. She paused with a knobbed hand on her neck. When the audience did not break into applause, she sought to bring her speech to a close. "One of those who will graduate today is someone . . ." Here she paused again to fumble for the water they had poured for her. She turned around to glare at the speakers seated behind her, but no help came. "He is someone my dear husband and I knew in his youth."

There was no one to say that was not so. No one to say she was confused: no one else in the hall had any idea what or who she had been talking about from the beginning, or who he might be, a heavyset middle-aged man of mixed race walking up to receive his diploma, the oldest of the graduates.

He was heading for the stairs at the end of the stage where she was seated when she rose to her feet and tottered after him with her sprung hands dropping from the wrist. He turned, bent, and took her in his arms. This the audience applauded at length. Some even stood up. The robed speakers nearest to the two clapped loudest, as at some tender fact known to them. They didn't know this graduate any more than Sofya did, or than he knew her, or than anyone in the world had known her, except her readers and Lindenbaum.

Guatemala

∘ ∘ ∘

His son's girlfriend stuck one leg out of the car and followed it with an aluminum crutch. She sank the crutch into the sandy earth and took hold hand over hand as if she meant to vault on it, but she only hoisted herself and then lay back to reach a second crutch in the back seat. This was rapid, practiced.

She sat unwrapping a striped candy. "Get me the canvas one, honey. Here, you take that stuff."

Then she stood up. The legs were short for the body, and sprung backward, in a dizzying inverse of a knee. His son was hanging a bulging canvas sack from the hand-piece of the crutch, which was like a stick shift, black rubber grooved for fingers.

Well. This was Lupe, of whom Robert had been told and not told.

His son's mild face, flushed and broken out, had a broad smile. "My father," he said humbly to the girl. "Dad, this is Guadalupe! Lupe! Lupe McCann!"

Robert stepped forward with his hand out, saying to himself, Don't offer to help. "Hello, Loopy."

"Lu-*peh*, Dad!"

The girl got the candy between her side teeth and smiled a little gust of peppermint. One cheek was printed where she had been sleeping on it, and her bushy black hair stood straight up on that side. Below the tangles the face was pretty in a puppet way, with round eyes in matted eyelashes like bits of hairbrush. She propped herself and gripped Robert's hand so hard his thumb-joint popped. She sat down a second time and handed up two spiral notebooks with which he found himself pointing the way to the porch steps, as if she might not see them.

Halfway up the steps she stopped. "Wait! My machine!" Quickly Robert made way for the thought of a device, some pump or tank she must require.

"Got it." Billy was behind her lugging a box and a duffel bag, Robert's huge yellowed army duffel that the boys had each taken to camp long ago, ten years apart.

"Oh! Look!" Lupe was turning around and around on the hooked rug like a skier doing a swivel. Out the window lay the inky waters of the Strait of Georgia, with a white ferry passing in the distance and seagulls wheeling. "Oh, this I like! A real island, a real cabin! I'm so glad—I thought it might be one of those villas." So she knew there was Ann's money.

"Little lady," Billy said out of the side of his mouth, "I said cabin and I meant cabin." That was new, any sort of comeback from Billy. But was he Billy any more? Maybe by now, after six years in graduate school, he was Bill, or Will—though at twenty-eight he still bore the marks of junior high: nodding cowlick and fists in pockets. "What's with the others?"

"They missed the Nanaimo ferry last night and I guess they missed the one you folks took this morning. Sit down, sit down, coffee's on."

"My brother is never on time," Billy told Lupe. "He's the spoiled one."

Was there any truth to that? Robert could not have said. Of the past he had only a vague sense, once in a while, of a half-built house where a man on a ladder was hammering, and the man, though stronger and thinner than he was now, was himself, yet a sort of idiot, deaf and blind to all but a very few things. Down a hallway of doors standing open, in this vision, were a half-grown, silent boy and a smaller one who could not stand to be left alone. That was Billy, the toddler. No one else. Inexcusably, no mother. With no warning, no preparation of any kind, their mother had removed herself into death. A story so old Robert never went beyond the beginning.

"I see the bathroom," Lupe said, as if they were playing a game. "Under the ladder!"

"Oh, yeah, here . . ." Billy unzipped the duffel and rummaged. He handed her a flowered bag.

Well, the loft was out, for their room. How could she climb? Alan and Martine would have to sleep up there.

Lupe urinated long and hard while Robert talked over the sound. "Did you get a look at the wall, where the pylon came down? At the far end? I've got Smalley coming with some concrete. Sit down, sit down. I expect you had a wait for the midget, it's been full every day." Then he felt himself blush—why must he do this, in his sixties?—because of the girl's size. By midget he meant the little car ferry, not much more than a chugging raft, that took you back into the Strait from Vancouver Island, and out to the Gulf Islands. Billy, still wearing the dazed smile, didn't answer but sighed, cradled his mug and looked out at the water with eyes so bright he might have been getting ready to cry.

After a time Lupe came out, made her way to the glider and flopped down on it. It sent up a rusty creaking as she pumped it, poling with the crutches. She didn't stop until Robert brought coffee and then she leaned back, smoothing the faded seahorses with their afterimage of mildew. "Are we in heaven?" She had an odd, jokey voice, a bit . . . hard-boiled. Or maybe just playful. Was that what his wife would have said? He still patted along some dusty shelf for Ann's opinions. "That's a great ladder. I bet you built it." Of course Billy would have told her that.

"I confess I did. My wife and I." An off-kilter thing he wouldn't build today. But Ann had sat notching the rails by hand, with a hammer and a chisel.

"Put that over here, would you, Billy honey." A Mae West sort of voice, with another candy in the cheek. She delved in the canvas bag. "Every minute I'm here I have to sew. We're going straight from here to the wedding."

Robert said, "Wedding?"

Billy said, "Remember, Dad? We have Maria's wedding on Saturday? Lupe's sister?"

It was too late; now they were assessing his memory.

HE would cross his legs, turn a page, scratch the stubble on his neck. Some evenings he made no more noise than a moth in a lampshade.

He had opened up the cabin himself for the first time since his stroke. His sons lent it freely; blankets were hanging spread out to air on the loft railing, and the cake of soap in the shower stall was soap, not a piece of bone as it always had been in summer when they arrived as a family. His rod and reel were messily stowed; on the back porch there was fishy water in the bottom of the bucket that should have been turned over.

Could he keep his balance enough to fish off the rocks.

In the medicine cabinet where he put his pills he found a box of condoms. Wildflowers sat on the counter in a mason jar, holding down a note in a precise hand: "we both thank you alan for a week of sweet serenity."

His sons had had a phone put in, and both had been calling. How many sea lions had passed? Was the woodstove working? It had always worked. They meant was he counting, was he cooking. What would he be like when they got there.

"I'll show them," he had told Loretta, his office temp. She had him flexing the affected arm.

"They don't know!" she said. "You *tell* them! You say you're fine!"

When his secretary Rose Fitch retired, personnel had sent a temp, with the promise of a real assistant—they weren't called secretaries anymore—once the job was posted. But after the stroke, Robert had put in for a full-time position for Loretta. Usually the agency sent girls, but Loretta was a woman in her fifties, with pictures of children on her screen saver. They were her foster children, she said proudly. She was divorced, with no children of her own. She had gone in and screamed—of the truth of this Robert soon had no doubt—until the agency let her keep several of these children with her on past the age of eighteen. They were grown now; the pictures were old.

Loretta came from a temp agency but she brought a folder of references and letters of commendation with her. Soon she had things organized more efficiently in the office than his old secretary Rose had in twenty years. Often he heard her outside his door, getting up to walk to and fro in the high heels she wore despite her weight, as she pored over files she was going to enter into the computer, stopping now and then as if she couldn't believe what she was reading. After a few hours, if he opened his door, she liked to take off her glasses and say, "Whoa, Honey!" The glasses had dug deep marks on either side of her nose. They were reading glasses and after wearing them all day she couldn't see a thing. At the end of her first week at work she took the glasses off, dropped the pearl chain that held them onto her bosom, and whether she could see Robert or not, told him the story of her life.

It was largely the story of the foster children and the courts. Jobs, long-ago marriage barely figured. Loretta spoke of her life with a combination of perplexity and satisfaction that pushed the pink skin of her forehead into thick even ridges like crayons, which in later weeks he would be half-tempted to lean over and press with a finger. He knew not to do that, not to touch an employee, male or female, or let his bad arm graze one, or say anything suggestive. Suggestive of . . . what? Of the body. A subject Robert would not suggest to anyone. He was not like some of the others his age in the firm, bumping into girls at the copiers. He knew what would offend; he kept up.

He was surprised at himself for listening patiently to Loretta while the office doors opened and closed for the day and the elevators rose and sank. Normally he would have made some summarizing remark to cut such a session short. He always put a firm stop to any employee's attempts to bring personal business into the office.

Loretta had arms that could heave the stuck drawer out of the filing cabinet. She had a big head of hair, the blondness of which

varied every month or so from yellow to the color of manila file
folders to off-white. He knew she feared she would be done out
of the job while he was on leave. Every few days he had been calling in from the cabin to tell her to sit tight. "Call me if anybody
even looks sideways at you."

"I guess I will!"

"I mean your job."

"And you do like I told you. Don't fool with any *blueprint*.
You made a promise. The only thing you do is you squeeze that
little ball."

"I'm crushing it."

AROUND the glider, sheets of a dress pattern settled on the
floor. Billy was bowing along scooping them up like dropped
underthings. Robert drank his coffee with a mild exasperation.
Ann had sewed. The filmy hissing paper might once have sent
him into that dry, unspecific, widower's craving, itself a memory
now.

"Yeah, put it there. In front of the window." Through the pins
pressed between her lips the girl employed a sort of singsong, as
if she had to go through a calming litany for everyone present,
like a coach, or an animal tamer.

"Her sewing machine. Lupe's the maid of honor in the wedding," Billy said proudly.

"Matron of honor! Don't forget I'm divorced. Or maybe I'm
back to being a maid."

"You're welcome to put the sewing machine on the desk,"
Robert interrupted. But he would have to move the piles of
books. How in fact would she carry anything? A frying pan, a
child? How would she live?

It was obvious. She would get hold of someone to help her.
Someone with a conscience, someone weak, a man who could
be manipulated. A boy. Billy.

"Here." Robert got up to move the books.

Billy got there ahead of him. He held up *The Golden Treasury
of Natural History*. "Back to school?"

"Thought I'd learn a little something."

"It's never too late, right, Loop? Dad spent all his life as a structural engineer."

"Not quite all. Some of it may remain."

Slime molds are like plants in some ways and like animals in others. He had found a box of the boys' old schoolbooks in the closet. Paging through them he felt a settling-in, a release of independence, a sinking. While he read he could squeeze the ball. He still had powers of concentration that he could summon, but he didn't want to read fiction or anything from his own field.

"What you do, you get right up in their face!" Loretta said when he went in for his temporary disability. He had gone straight back to the office but he was having to brace himself when Loretta brought in anything new for him to do. "Blueprints," she would say with a grimace, putting them in his basket. He delayed signing off on anything. With bridges there was no leeway. He no longer had his eye for detail. No one had to tell him he had received an insult. That was what the doctor called the stroke: *insult.* Perhaps that was why he was so full of suspicion. The word was out that his good nature could not be relied on. He would wait until the elevator was empty; he would slump against his office door once he had it shut on all the well-wishing and offers and compliments.

Some agreement had been reached above his head that he was not quite ready, he was going to have to build up to it. A longer leave had to be put through; he went through the formalities but his application snagged on a young man in personnel, whose memo Loretta snatched. "Too simple for the minds down there! I'm going. I'll explain so they get it." That was the last he heard of the snag; the leave came through the next day.

"Well, hello there!" said Lupe. Two seagulls on the mossy windowsill were peering in as she positioned the machine on the desk. She ducked, disappearing below the sill, and both gulls skewed their heads to see her.

"Would you look at that," Billy said. "They like you."

"Sure. Sure they do. I was a seagull in my former life."

"You were," Billy said, coming up behind her and beginning to massage her shoulders. "A scavenger, right?"

Lupe laughed; she crossed her arms at the elbow and flapped her hands. Her build was slight, but under the bulky sweatshirt Robert had noticed volume, a slinging back and forth of globes. She had let her head fall back to laugh and Billy bent over it, presumably to press his lips to the red upside-down mouth. Robert could not see exactly what was going on because their backs were to him, but they stayed that way for several seconds.

He couldn't do what he usually did after breakfast, sit down and leaf through the old books all morning until he fell asleep in the chair. The question was whether he was resting up, in this state in which a furious impatience blinked on between long dazes that were like standing at an abandoned bus stop.

"Jeez." Billy was back to *The Golden Treasury*. "'The lace-wing fly has to lay its eggs in a special way to keep the first lace-wing flies that hatch from eating up the eggs that have not yet hatched.'" Now Lupe was down on the floor by the window, with her legs out in front of her, mounds of shiny orange material between them. There was no way it could be comfortable to sit like that. She already had the pattern pinned to the material and she was cutting. Orange. Orange bridesmaids. A color to make even a normal person look like a clown. She cut fast, paying no attention to what was coming out behind the shears as they snaked around the pins making a dancing gasp.

"So Dad. A hatchet-footed animal with no head. 'They use their feet as burrowing tools. Sometimes they pull themselves along with them.' Who am I?"

"A cripple!" Lupe sang out from the floor, and laughed with what Robert was beginning to see as an absurd merriment.

"Cut it out, Lupe," Billy said.

"I already did!"

"You know what I mean," Billy said in a crooning tone that set Robert's teeth on edge. "Listen to this. 'The softly colored rosebud jelly is pretty at night as well as in the daytime. It shines in the dark.'" Lupe grinned at him from across the room. "'This small animal catches its prey with its long tentacles. The tentacles are sticky.' OK. 'A starfish, let us suppose, comes upon an oyster. It fastens one or more of its arms to each half of the oyster's shell. The suction disk holds its arm tightly to the shell. Then it tries to pull the shell open. At *first* the oyster can hold its own—'"

"Whoo hoo." Lupe yawned broadly. "I'm done with this part. I'm tired. Why don't we take a nap."

"So Dad . . ." Billy was apologetic. "What if we did rest up for a while before they get here? Would you mind?"

"Not I," Robert said, picking up the mugs. "I've been known to take a nap myself."

"Other room, Loop, that one's Dad's." Billy followed him into the kitchen. "You know, Dad. I just wanted to tell you something. I don't know if you . . . I just want to say . . . Lupe is the smartest person I've ever met."

"Well now, that's a compliment all right."

"And I want you to get to know her."

"I hope to."

"Dad? I just want . . ."

"I hope to."

It was too cold to go outside and stay there. Robert fed the woodstove and put the radio and the fan on for noise and then he went into his room and lay down. He took the sea life book in with him. This was a book that drew his eye; he left it on top of the pile on the desk, where he could glance at the picture on the jacket, of a little open-mouthed fish with eyes on stalks. The fish was hiding in seagrass, in its black eyes a look that stopped Robert no matter how many times he noticed it, of wondering sadness.

He was in bed a good deal anyway, at the wrong times. He wouldn't get under the covers until the night was half over, and then it seemed he never moved off his back until the sun hit him. After that he'd lie half in and half out of sweaty sleep for an hour, two hours, before he got to the window in his pajamas, jaws pried apart by the first of countless yawns. Then he would quickly get the stove going, and catnap until midafternoon in his chair. Then he would really wake up.

No one would put up with him if he went back to work in this condition, worse than when he left. Soon somebody in the elevator would be saying, "Robert Mallow has come to a complete standstill."

HE thought at first that Alan had hurt himself, but he had merely cut his hair so short the dents in his skull showed, and dyed the stubble an iodine color. After the hug and the kisses on both cheeks, which Alan always imposed with an aggrieved smile, like unwelcome treats, he held Robert at arm's length and said, "So how *are* you?"

"I'm in great shape!" Robert said heartily.

Then came Martine, Alan's second wife, absently chewing her dark lips. She too kissed Robert twice, but she was French-Canadian, from her it was natural, merely a cool touch, faintly scented with resin because she was a painter.

By three o'clock they had carted in half a dozen bags of groceries and finished handing their bags up to the loft. Alan pressed his ear to the door of the bunk room. "They really are asleep in there, aren't they. One of them snores. So what's all this on the floor?"

"The books? The books were packed up, but I got them out. I've been getting a kick out of them. The rest of it—Lupe's stuff. You've met Lupe?"

"Haven't met her yet. Hey, I remember these books! So where were they?"

"In a box in the loft. I went up. I did. I was careful coming down." He had nearly taken a dive off the ladder with the box.

"*The Book of Knowledge*. So"—Robert was getting tired of this airy "so" of his sons'—"are you acquiring knowledge?"

"Too late for that." Robert forced a chuckle.

"If we look at our old schoolbooks, for a minute we are seven years again," Martine said dreamily. "In my grammar was a little blonde girl with a white dog. I thought I would grow to be like her. I thought it was possible, *voila!* I could be a different little girl, so simple, just turn things a little, a little . . ." She tilted a frame with her hands.

Alan was slipping off his shoes as Robert groped for a pleasant remark about dark hair. "So, what about the art stuff I sent? Bet you haven't unpacked that. Drawing would organize you, you know. Prime you. Free the inner engineer." Sometimes the tone Alan took with him caught Robert off guard, unaccountably bringing around a gloomy image of himself shedding tears in a darkened school auditorium when a prize for art was not won by Alan. Ann was beside him letting him grip her hand, and Alan, a little boy of eight or nine, was at the end of a special row in the front, of those who might or might not win a prize. He was waiting. They could see it in the back of his head, tilted slightly, pink in its transparent crew cut.

Alan had found work at last, not on some dinner stage this time but as a drama therapist. He was working in a nursing home. At least he had paychecks, new shoes he might have bought with his own money. From his mother he had enough to be comfortable. That was part of the trouble, for both boys. Of course it might attract women. Did attract them.

Alan tilted his chair onto one leg and spun the loose handle on the oven door with his feet. The points he was going to make, he said, were not his own ideas but those of a colleague, a master art therapist. First, no matter how badly off you were, drawing—the following eye, the copying hand—retaught the brain.

Robert wondered briefly how long Alan would hold on to this job if he didn't know when he was making a nervous, bitter face, if he didn't know a certain kind of attention paid to the person you were trying to encourage had the same effect as doubt. Robert knew this from his own physical therapy. He knew the ones who helped the situation and the ones who made you clumsier and raised your blood pressure.

"You smile," Alan sulked. "I see this every day."

"I don't smile, believe me," Robert said, putting up his hands. Martine wandered around the room just as Lupe had done, albeit with a lithe, soundless step, inspecting Alan's old framed pencil drawings of crabs and urchins and starfish. "This little boy I see, with his pencil," she wailed suddenly, "where is he?" Alan didn't answer her. "Robert, what are you doing?" Martine gave his name the French pronunciation. "No, are you sewing?"

"That's Lupe's dress. She's a bridesmaid. Matron." Robert lowered his voice. "She looks all of twelve, but apparently she's been married."

ALAN snapped the catch of the mess kit in which he had soaked beans all night in their hotel room in Vancouver. He was as pleased with the beans as if he had smuggled them in. At thirty-seven, with plenty of money, Alan still traveled as if he were hitchhiking across Europe. "Sourdough!" He held up a plastic container. Martine was spilling onions, tomatoes, celery, and carrots out onto the kitchen counter.

"I do hike out once in a while for provisions," Robert said, and she gave him a preoccupied smile as she popped the cloves out of a fat head of garlic. Spices, mustard, brown sugar, vinegar. A ham hock. "It's for the whole weekend," Alan said sharply as Robert eyed the bottles of red wine, a row going halfway down the counter. "*Et voila!*" Alan drew two gleaming knives out of black sheaths. "I came prepared. Look at this, Martine! Remember these?" He rattled the drawer of battered utensils.

"I did take your advice, as a matter of fact," Robert said. "Yesterday afternoon. I got out the stuff you sent and I tried a sketch. I put it in the trash."

Martine threw down her knife, found the wastebasket and dumped it out. She smoothed his crumpled drawing of the rocky point, and looked at it as she might have looked at a burned dinner. "Mmm. We will draw! Robert? Why not? Alan will cook and we will draw! Where is your paper?"

At her insistence, they sat on the floor. Alan set brimming jelly glasses of wine beside them. "Cheers!"

"Somebody's going to have a very big headache," Robert said.

"For the drawing, energy comes from below," Martine said firmly, putting a piece of charcoal in his hand and guiding it to the paper with her chapped fingers. "From the earth. The line, you will pull up from the earth. Now color, if you are painting, will come in from all sides, everywhere."

Does everyone have a screw loose now? Robert asked himself, as he always did soon after the arrival of his sons and whomever they had in tow. And if he said a word, they thought he was nuts. Worse, now he had an official status: post insult.

"This I can't do," he said.

"Robert, you can do it." Martine had the straight black hair swinging against the neck that he associated with artists and with Frenchwomen, loose shorts, though it was cold early April, one arched foot out in front of her in a canvas sandal. The foot was very smooth, as if she had put hand cream on it instead of on the chapped hands, and had slim, fierce toes ending in dark red toenails. "I think that Alan's beautiful drawing comes from you. Yes! I sense this."

Robert paused to turn over this evidence that Alan had never said anything about his abilities. "I can't relearn at this stage," he said petulantly. "I'm a draughtsman. I'm almost seventy."

"So?" said Alan, not even arguing—when Robert was still a few years away from seventy.

Martine scooted closer to Robert. "I am thirty-nine." She pressed the darkly tanned skin in the V-neck of her shirt. "And I have this year learned to weld. You will like my pieces, I think. They are new, they are very, very big, almost industrial. For the engineers! For you! I am waiting only for you to see them. I want you to see also what I am doing in oils." She made a fist. "Very big. Not like those little acrylics you have liked before." He liked the way she said *ac-reelics*, as if they were something floating and beautiful. He saw someone fishing, casting over smooth water. He could not remember Martine's paintings at all.

Going along with her, he produced a drawing of the wood-stove. "Matisse!" said Martine, watching him while the onions sizzled. "But no, no, *absolument,* no shading."

"Engineers!" cried Alan from the kitchen. "They can't leave anything out." Robert was getting tired of the word *engineer*, too, in the mouths of his sons, suggesting as it did an old crackpot bound to some disagreeable, repetitive act.

The latch rattled and Billy and Lupe stood in the doorway rubbing their eyes. Lupe's hair was even more askew.

"Billy!" cried Martine, jumping up. "And here, here is Lupe!" First she kissed Lupe on each red cheek, and then Billy. Alan did the same. "I have seen this dress you are making, Lupe!" Martine said. "This color! Very beautiful! The color of the lobster."

Lupe gave a shout of laughter. "Three lobsters! I'm doing the bridesmaids too. It's the old two-way taffeta from the fifties. Come and see—they're long, floor length. In my case, not all that long. See the sleeves? See the sort of bustle, all those gathers? Mine's the only one that has that. Chic, *non*?"

"Ah, *oui!*"

"And what's this?" She stood in front of Robert's drawing. Martine had taped it to the wall with the ones from Alan's childhood. "Is this yours, Martine, so fierce?"

"It's mine," Robert said.

"You all draw, in this family."

Did Billy draw?

To the thumps Lupe made situating herself, the sewing machine responded at length with a gentle, syncopated purr Robert could feel in his feet. He was suddenly weary. Wood smoke had made his eyes heavy, wine in the afternoon had brought on the yawning, unstoppable once it got going. He waved Alan, coming with the bottle, away from his glass, and leaned over to take a book from the floor. But when he had it in his lap his hands went slack, his head hummed, right in front of them he could feel sleep overtaking him.

He was giving a presentation. He and Loretta were at a banquet. He had the slide carrel but the slides were not there. "Oh, no," he whispered, as if his heart would break. He heard Loretta clump heavily down the stairs to find them and he waited in front of the audience for a long time, until finally everybody got up to leave and the banquet tables were being cleared — he was very hungry and had not been served even one of the rolls he could smell in the covered baskets — when he woke with a jerk, covered with sweat. "I had a dream!" he said plaintively, in the empty room. It took a while for his pulse to slow down.

He couldn't tell how much time had elapsed, but the four of them were in the kitchen. An echo of whispering hung in the stuffy cabin. He smelled the bread from his dream and his mouth watered shamelessly. A lid had been lifted, a cloud of fragrant steam billowed out of the kitchen. Billy came in and banged on the frame of the steamed-up front window until he had it open, and to Robert's relief stark, rain-cold air rushed in.

"I've had it with sewing and I hate cooking!" Lupe announced to Robert. "What did you dream?"

"Nothing."

"Was it a nightmare?"

He didn't answer her. Had he made noises? "How long did I sleep?" he called into the kitchen.

"A while," Lupe said gaily. "What a place for sleeping! There's that smoky smell in the pillows. I snuggled down, I could have slept a hundred years, except Billy made me get up. Don't worry, you were cool. You don't gag and gasp like Billy."

"No fair!" Billy shouted from the kitchen.

Alan came in, glass in hand. "It's seven. You fell asleep at four." He looked at his watch. "Pretty soon we'll have bread."

"But look," said Martine. She held up her spoon and in a second the beans began to move. Very gently their skins rippled in the cold air from the open window and split open. "If I draw this, as I would have before I gave up the drawing," she said with a scowl, "it will be called a domestic picture. A women's picture."

"And you will be called a sentimentalist. But me too, if I could paint I'd paint these little pods!" Lupe placed a hand on her heart and began slathering the air with an imaginary brush. "Pods, are you going to burst open and impregnate us?" She investigated her soup bowl. Robert wondered if anything mental went with the physical defect. "You didn't see *Aliens*," Lupe said, catching his look. "And now, we ask permission to consume your bodies," she continued, speaking to her spoon. "Oh, Alan. *Mes compliments!*"

Robert cleared his throat, and asked sternly, "What are you majoring in, Lupe?" She was an undergraduate, Billy had written him.

"I am not exactly majoring. I am thinking, though, of being a writer. See those notebooks on the bench? Those are my life story. Billy says it's a mem-mwah."

"Lupe has had quite a life. Several lives, actually," Billy said, and Lupe flashed a grin.

Robert said, "That would be after you were a seagull?"

"How did you know? I'd have to say yeah, it all started with my birth as a mammal. This bread, Alan—" she said with her mouth full.

"Lupe's done just about everything," Billy persisted.

"How did you and Billy meet?" Martine said warmly.

"It's funny how everybody wants to know that. Well, it was like, once upon a time a frog came up on land and next thing, she met an emu. OK, it was in the cafeteria at school. You know the ladies who sit on the stool with their press-on nails on the keypad and say, 'Plain burger?'" She preened her own bitten nails. "That was my latest job. In this country, I receive a special letter in my file, for being able to do these things."

"In Mexico Lupe broke horses, because she could speak to them," Billy said gravely.

"Is that so? I believe there was a best-seller on that subject," Robert said.

"A tonal language, I would think," said Alan. "Wine, anybody?"

"It has more to do with the breath," Lupe said.

"In L.A. she was a gang infiltrator for the police department. Girl gangs. Spanish-speaking. She also worked in a couture house in Paris."

"Now I'm between jobs." Lupe tore off bread and ate fast, the way she had cut out the dress, and looked up to find them all observing her. "I'll have to watch out when I get to this point in my memoir, this lull."

"After dinner you will read to us from your book? I think we would like that," Martine said, to Robert's dismay. "In the place where you grew up, your parents were . . . ?"

"Parents—no. Place—no, not really a place. I grew up on the road."

"They were orphans," Billy said. "They had to keep coming down from the highlands, even crossing the border, into and out of the country."

"The highlands," said Robert.

"I do not even know what is your country," Martine said humbly, leaning forward.

Lupe let go of the spoon with it still in her mouth and twanged it with her thumb. "Guatemala," she said, removing the spoon with a delicate motion. "My country long ago."

"She should read it to you!" Again Robert had the feeling Billy might burst into tears. "In the highlands, villages were erased. Farmers had stakes driven into their chests. You won't believe it. Lupe's parents—she saw them shot. She was four years old. They had her hidden in a bag of coffee."

"Green coffee," Lupe said.

I don't believe it, Robert thought. He almost said, "How did you see out of the bag?" Villages, stakes, the highlands. Something told him the girl was a child of middle-class professionals, like everyone else in the room. The disturbed, possibly cast-out child. That California voice. The incongruous surname McCann. The way she said "sentimentalist." The way she had said, "I'm back to being a maid." He was beginning to pity his son, and fear for him.

"Where exactly were you, on the road, growing up?"

"Sometimes, walking along," she said patiently, looking not at him but at Billy. "Sometimes"—the black eyes narrowed as she daintily scraped a last spoonful of soup—"I was in the trunk."

"The trunk of the car," Billy said.

"If there wasn't enough room," Lupe confirmed. "Because there were a lot of us. Assunta, the woman who had us, had to make a getaway from time to time, with shoes and food and so on. And crutches, of course."

Robert said, "How do you happen to know French?"

"Know French! Ha-ha! *Merci, monsieur*. It's an act, really it's high school French. In high school I was here already. I was in San Diego."

"And then of course you were in Paris."

"Yeah, right, in the sweatshop."

"Lupe is one of those people who . . . who . . . who *picks up* languages," Billy said, stuttering with pride. "There was no way she could go to college, of course, no money, because of course they had to come . . . come down out of the highlands with nothing." So much for her being an undergraduate. "I mean, they had nowhere even to spend the night, and once she got here Lupe had to . . . she had to have operations, and sleep in a car, in her casts, and be raped. Don't worry, she is open about it. They were picking fruit, for God's sake." Billy voice climbed and cracked. "And then she got married!"

"Married," Robert said. "Is Spanish your native tongue?" The girl had no accent.

"Dad's an engineer," Alan said.

"Actually, I spoke another language, that I doubt you have heard of. An Indian language. The name McCann—that was the guy I married."

"Darren McCann," Billy said, almost as proudly as he had spoken of Lupe. "She was sixteen, he was twenty-eight. What a loser."

"You met him?" Robert said.

"You can't meet him, he's in jail," Lupe said. "And Billy, I don't want you to say that. I told you. His family is very good to me." I'll bet they are, Robert thought.

"I'm sorry," Billy said.

Robert said, "And the sister who's getting married on Saturday? Was she in the trunk too?"

Lupe looked at him with a little squint. "She was there, yes," she said.

∘ ∘ ∘

MARTINE came down the ladder facing the wrong way, forward, so that she had to turn her long feet sideways like an Egyptian on a frieze. " Robert?" she said, though of course it was he, sitting at the desk holding the canvas sewing bag. One side of the lining formed an inner pocket, with a nametag sewn to it. "Lee Ann McCann." *Lee Ann*.

"Do you use this ladder, Robert?"

"Hardly ever."

"It is not very safe." Martine came and sat in the low, slatted chair beside him, the children's rocking chair. Pinecones dropped on the tin roof and made it ring. "Solitary figure," she said. Out the window Alan was a small white blur. He had thrown out his arms and was stretching and dipping in slow motion. "His t'ai chi." Martine seemed to want to include Robert, not leave him puzzling.

"I thought you did that in the morning."

"If you are very drunk you can do it whenever you want."

"Billy and friend are out there too," he said. "Down the bank. You would think he'd have the sense not to let her roam around on the rocks in the dark. In the rain, in the middle of the night." He heard his querulous tone; it was almost one o'clock.

"The moon, the moon!" they could hear Alan chanting drunkenly as he climbed down.

"*Vraiment*," said Martine. "Thank you, we are all awake."

Alan rushed in and whirled around on the rag rug, scattering a faint spray and smiling with his teeth bared. The skin of his face was twisted when he stopped, as if it had not kept up with him. He flopped down on the rug and began working his fingers nervously into the weave, as he had as a child.

Robert didn't like the look of him. In the semidark his white face was puffy under the orange fuzz of hair, the chin line loose. Why, he's middle-aged, Robert thought. A middle-aged drinker. All this — pretending to be a boy. He's as tired as I am.

Martine sat rocking back and forth in the little chair and shaking her head, holding her knees up against her chest with her thin, tanned arms.

Alan jumped up, sloshed wine into a mug, chugged it at the counter and poured again.

"Why not go back to bed?" Robert said.

"I don't think so."

"Where *are* you going?" Martine said.

"Back out. Might have a midnight swim." Alan leaned around the screen door to wave at them.

"But he does not swim, of course," Martine said to Robert when the screen slammed.

"I know that and I expect he does too." Robert had been a swimmer in college; he had a lot of stamina in the lap pool even now. Everybody in physical therapy commented on it. To his lasting chagrin neither of the boys had even learned to swim: both of them clingers to the side, refusers to jump. In high school Alan had come out of the silence that had descended on him with his mother's death; that was when he seized hold of his eccentricities, and turned funny and scornful. "If God meant us to get into the water he would not have given us clothes."

"You know Alan wants to divorce me," Martine said. How would Robert have known this? Though he had noticed her eyes seeking his all evening with some grievance. "So that he can live with his friend for a while, his friend, *vous savez*."

"His friend," Robert said, bringing up a deep sigh.

"He has brought him here, that boy. That is his choice, *n'est-ce pas*? But I do not want to divorce him for this reason. I don't see why I must do this, I don't see why why why." She banged her dark knees together with her palms, and then wrapped her legs in her arms. "Where is the family he promised to me?" Her lower lip stuck out and trembled.

Ah. And these were people, four of them, whom Robert hardly knew. Not his sons any more—though Ann might have known them, somehow made them familiar. Two strange couples who had driven for days and ridden ferries, not to console him for what had happened to him, not to cook soup for him, but to perform thus at midnight, with stances and gestures. I don't want to hear, he thought. I've come away.

"I will not do it. I will not let a little shit come into our house because Alan is the actor, the artist that this boy will never be, and eat the food we cook, and spoil life." A strange thought. Could Alan really be an actor? "I don't care about this *in love*, I don't care! I am his wife! I don't want to hear about *in love*! Where is his work now he is *in love*? That is what I want to know! Where is it if he can be so *imbecile*?"

"I would think if you sit tight it would all blow over."

Martine gave an angry, impatient moan and glared out the window.

Billy and Lupe had rounded the point and were working their way along the second tier of rocks. They waved, but not at the house. They must be able to see Alan. They had stopped to fumble, both of them, with the crutches. "What are they up to?"

"I can't see exactly."

Robert opened the screen door and went out. The rain had let up and the moon had gone behind thin sailing clouds. When it reappeared Robert could see Billy and Lupe struggling with each other. "What on earth are they doing? Where's Alan?" Wind blew his voice away.

"*Attendez!*" Martine, close behind him, whispered so fiercely it raised the hair on his neck. She jumped off the porch and started to run, scrambling and sliding on the rocks. Robert started after her. "No, no, *mon dieu!* Billy!" Billy crouched alone, waving a crutch over the water. "No! She is down there! How did she get in? Alan! Alan is in there! Billy! Don't let him! He can't swim!"

"Billy can't either!" Robert yelled, teetering to pull off his shoes. He sank a foot into the icy water and lost his balance. He went in half toppling, half skidding on the kelp and the barnacles underneath it, which felt like saws. Cold fire stabbed to the center of each bone, where it seemed his fainting self had been living undetected. Martine was in the water, slugs of black hair down over her face, and she caught him, tried in the quakes of shivering between them to pull him forward. "Save him!" she cried.

A little way out a head was bobbing rhythmically, like a dog bringing in a stick. Two heads. Alan had gone in after Lupe.

Billy had dropped onto his stomach in the sloshing water on the rock and lay groaning, dipping the crutch in the reflections like an oar. Alan reached for it. But no, it was Lupe—*she* was reaching. She was towing Alan.

Martine too groaned. "*Mon dieu, mon dieu.* Look at her. I knew it, Alan, I knew you have gone crazy."

"Come on!" Billy shouted. "Get out, get out, get outta the way, they're coming up! Lupe!"

Martine went on wading out but Robert obeyed. He had no feeling in his fingers and he used his wrists to haul himself back onto the rocks, the chattering of his teeth making his head nod with a kind of wild approval.

Lupe had Alan under the chin, as if she were bringing in just his head. She was barely above the water, barely swimming, just the one arm turning like a wheel with one spoke. How could she swim at all? Her left arm came slowly out of the water and up and around, out and up and around, and finally her hand grasped the hand-piece of the crutch. She rolled onto her back and passed the head to Billy. Martine got under the shoulders and Billy strained backward, whereupon Alan's long body came sliding and bumping up out of the water onto the kelp, as if they had rehearsed, as a team, just this ponderous transmission—Martine and Billy shoving and pulling cruelly, as though they didn't care if parts tore off—of something like a rolled-up rug. Alan's only role was to breathe rasping, speechless chords. Blood was leaking along his forehead.

Then Lupe came up out of the water like a seal, on her elbows, and Billy took her under the arms as he would have a child and hoisted her onto the rock. He wrapped her in his arms as if he could soak her into himself.

"Alan jumped in!" he croaked finally, letting go of her. "Alan, you idiot! He jumped in! We saw him! We saw him do it!" Staggering on his knees back to Alan he lifted him by the shoulders and shook him so hard his head made the kelp splash. "God damn it. God damn it, if you're gonna kill yourself do a better fucking job of it. You risked Lupe's life." Alan said something unintelligible, blinking watery blood and letting his head roll with abandon, as if he were acting the part of a victim.

"Yes, go ahead. Kill him," Martine said through her hair. "That is what you should do. I think so. Put him out of his misery. Smash his head. Kill him."

THEY were dressed for bed, each wrapped in a blanket, but they didn't go to bed. Martine had lit candles and spread the towels on the clothes rack. They steamed by the woodstove. Lupe had actually gathered more of the orange material onto her lap and was pinning on pattern in the half-dark. Alan lay on the glider under Ann's old cross-stitched quilt, with a pillow-case tied around his head. "I'm sorry," he said every now and then. He accepted the mug of coffee Martine held out at arm's length.

"We will have wine, but not you, Alan, you are *drunk*," she said, and Robert experienced a small relief because she used a voice of unshocked exasperation, the voice a schoolteacher might use to deny a troublemaker his moment, his having achieved any disruption worth noticing.

"Lupe? Billy? I'm sorry."

"No shit," said Billy.

"He *is* sorry," Lupe said.

"I don't know why you did that, Lupe, or how," Alan said, bowing with folded hands.

Lupe said brightly, "I went to camp. I was the lifeguard."

"Martine?" Alan said, turning his big eyes, now full of tears, on his wife. He *was* an actor. But Martine stood over him with the malignant look of a child who is going to kick another child.

"You could be dead," she began. "We could be pulling the sea-weed out of your pretty teeth. Here" — she stamped her foot — "we would have a puddle. A smelling puddle."

"Stinking," said Alan. Something boyish crept into his face, something abashed and foolish and at the same time sly.

"Don't dare to look at me like that!" Martine stamped her foot again.

Gazing up at her, Alan allowed a smile to appear. He touched the turban. "I must be the sheik," he said.

The turban was coming untied, exposing a red seam in his skin, running into the hairline, with white edges curled back like a snail's foot.

For a minute Martine stood over him as they watched. When she moved, it was to swish the skirt of her dark red robe with a knee. "I wonder why we did not go to look for a doctor who will sew his brain back into his head. Perhaps we do not care about him very much." She folded her arms. "Why should we? Just because he is charming, and a sheik? When we know all about them, these sheiks. How they are. Why should we save him at all?" She sat down and put her face in her hands.

"But why not?" Lupe got up and swung forward, breasts swimming under the yoke of her flannel nightgown, to lean over and half embrace Martine, who sat up suddenly and hissed at Alan, "And did you thank this child?"

"Hey, I'm twenty-nine," Lupe said.

Alan said, "Lupe, I thank you a thousand times. I am yours. I mean it. I have become yours. I am now your responsibility. I'm absolutely serious. Don't you think she should have to take care of me, Martine? Of both of us, in fact?"

"I will take care of him for you," Martine said to Lupe, snatching up a wine bottle by the neck.

Lupe said, "Spare him! If you kill him we will have to bury him. How will I get these dresses done in time for the wedding?"

"Well, now," Robert said. "The wedding. What do you say we go back and start all over again? What if I said . . . oh, what if I said I've been giving some thought to getting married myself?"

"My God," said Alan. "That is to say, who?"

"Who?" cried Martine and Lupe together.

"I'm kidding you."

"I do not think so," said Martine.

What made him go on? "But there is a woman in the office right at the moment."

"Who?"

"Well, my secretary."

"Your secretary!"

Loretta! As if Loretta would marry him!

Loretta talked on the telephone every day. She talked to a man; he could tell that. Her voice sank and her chair creaked as she ran it idly back and forth on the acrylic runner. "Oh no you will not! Nossir! Not at my place! You know I have grandkids! Stop that right now!" If Robert came in she rolled her eyes and turned her thumb down on the man on the phone, but she did not hang up.

Loretta might kiss Robert, as she had when he came out of the hospital. She might tie balloons to his chair, and bring in a cake she had made herself, but that didn't mean she would marry him.

Nevertheless he was flooded with relief at the thought of Loretta and of his office. He would be back in less than three weeks. "It went all right," he would say. "I got the seawall rebuilt. Of course, I had to do it without a blueprint."

"What's her name?" Lupe had pulled herself close to his chair. He told her. "So, and it doesn't matter to me one way or the other," he added in a whisper, "but who is Lee Ann?" He was safe, momentarily, in a vacuum of calm at the thought that it was so, it didn't matter to him; whatever his earlier suspicions, he had lost interest in them. But if that was so why ask the question at all? Why? And it was too late. Lupe had veiled the lower part of her face with the blanket from her shoulders, and above it the eyes studying him were black, unreadable without the rest of the face. It might be they were sharp with curiosity and mischief, but agreeable, as they had been. They might as easily be sad, as sad as the eyes of the gaping fish on the book cover, for they had set off a sadness in him that spread, warm and bitter. "Lee Ann. That's Darren's sister. My sister-in-law," Lupe said behind the blanket.

He couldn't understand what she said next. It might have been a language of Guatemala. An Indian language. It might have been the language of horses.

"I am sorry, Robert . . . your fiancée . . . I want to know . . . but now I am so tired." Martine was pulling the red robe around her, closing her eyes. "Move the towels so they will not burn, will you, somebody? *Merci*, and wax is melting, I think. I smell it. And keep us warm."

Billy moved the towels back from the stove, blew out the guttering candles, opened the grate and began stirring up the coals with the poker. Alan limped over and hunched beside his brother. In the firelight they made hoods of their blankets and waved the heat at themselves. With their backs to him Robert couldn't hear what they were saying, but it seemed they were conferring rather soberly and officially. They seemed to have something in common that he had not suspected. They seemed to be men, men who had appeared while he slept a hundred years. He supposed they were doing their best to form an idea of a woman who might marry him. A woman pleasant and elderly, settled in her habits but having her reasons. Thinking, no doubt, all of them, of his secretary Rose Fitch.

All but Lupe, who sighed, "Loretta! And look! The moon is back! It's yellow! Who wants to go out before we go to bed? Come on!" She clambered to her feet with the energy in which Robert recognized an old, put-away, restless woe. In a few minutes she had them all outside, standing on the bluff wrapped in blankets, like figures who had made their way down out of the highlands and reached the sea.

The Stabbed Boy

○   ○   ○

THE summer of the stabbing, he attended Vacation Bible School. Who took him there, along with his sister, who did not survive? His teacher, Mrs. Rao, from the Methodist church where the Bible school was held. How did she know them? Had anyone in his family ever been to a service there? That was for his biographers to answer.

His sister was in a class down the hall, with the kids who were already in school and reading. She was seven years old; he was five.

Because there was polio then, on the first day the teacher handed out a note for them to take home and after that each kid came with a thermos or a jar of his or her own juice. For him, Mrs. Rao brought a clean glass and poured out juice from her own thermos. She did it for his sister too, because he and his sister were her helpers and the three of them got there early. Sometimes she used the time to play the piano, always telling the two of them that it was out of tune. He came to think he could hear what she meant.

One day Mrs. Rao took him upstairs into the ladies restroom, past the open doors of the still room of wooden rows for which he did not have the word *sanctuary*, and she combed his hair with a little water. Another day she washed his hands. In their workbooks they were doing Put On the Full Armor of God, which he would find later to be words of the Apostle Paul, about whom he would write a poem when he was in his fifties. They were pasting silver and gold breastplates and helmets on an outline of a man with bulges in his arms and legs. "A giant," he said. Then and afterward, he spoke in bursts of one or two words. "No face." "It's a silhouette," said Mrs. Rao. *Silhouette.* It sounded like a bird, not a giant. He had been careful not to get paste on his hands, but she washed them anyway, leaving him with a clear memory of gray water with bubbles in it going down the drain of the church sink.

Now that he is famous he sometimes brings up Mrs. Rao in interviews. His story is not known; it is not in his poems. He's in L.A. now, and in his adult life and travels, he has never even met anyone familiar with the small once-industrial city in the Midwest where he was born. So it is not unusual for him to be asked about his youth, urged to recall something that might have set him on his path as a poet. One of these interviews in which he gave credit to Mrs. Rao's attention, her eyes, piano, black hair in a sort of coil—for this hairdo he had yet to find a word—resulted in the phone call that led to his third marriage.

"Oh my goodness, it is you! It's Lisa! I was Lisa Rao. Lisa! The Raos's daughter! I'm visiting my daughter here in town and I just had to call you up. You're right there in the phone book!" He had a little speech for deflecting this kind of admirer. But what a coincidence! She was sitting at the breakfast table and just happened to open the entertainment section of her daughter's paper and there was the interview, and there, her mother's name! "I was in Vacation Bible School with you! I can see you now, that little plaid shirt you had on every day!" Tactless reminder, and what could have possessed him, that he invited her to meet him for a drink? He must have seen her as coming at him straight out of a church basement in Michigan, from a table of paste and scissors, a woman who would say grace before drinking her juice and never come upon the life-altering taste of alcohol.

He wouldn't have recognized Lisa Rao, or seen in her any of the Indian reds and golds and graces he had added to her mother over the years, but in the bar she walked right up to him. He had chosen the place to send her on her way, a dark bar with hunched permanent occupants and a smell of beer in the floorboards. Quickly she drank two rum and cokes. Like him, she had had two marriages. She said Frank, her favorite, had died three years ago and while they had had their rough years, there were things she missed a great deal. She suggested he come to the motel where she was staying. Her daughter had too many children to allow for a guestroom. He went with her and nothing came of it because although her way of lowering her eyes in the grip of her own imaginings had not escaped him in the dark bar, she was much too old for him, his own age. But they met again the next day, and over time and her persistent phone calls and visits to L.A. they became friends, and finally he married her. It was his one good marriage. She cleaned up his house and banned his drinking friends in favor of a private rite for occasions ending in the bedroom.

His sober friends were relieved that it wasn't one of his students this time, but they compared her to Nora Joyce: she was uneducated, crudely outspoken, and bossy, while he, the poet, as a result of what they called "the damage," was a ruin. Under the charter of long friendship they listed his traits: could someone like her have any idea what it meant to join forces with this most embittered, tense, infantile, drunken, paranoid, alienated, critical, silent, secretive, and easily hurt of men?

Of course Lisa knew that first night that there would be scars on him, all over the chest and ribs, where his mother had stabbed with his father's Buck knife, in search of the heart. "What an awful thing to do to a little boy," Lisa said in a practical voice. Her finger rubbing with no awe on the fat seams of scar on his naked torso made them seem a simple thing, almost something that might be discovered under the clothes of any man, just one more in a tangle of things in the past, some of them ugly, that a decent person could only shake her head at. "Ah. And your poor sister who didn't have your luck." His luck!

That night in bed, as if he were any old friend, she reminisced.

"We lived not all that far away, but I couldn't come over to the trailer park, not even for trick-or-treat. None of us kids could. We were the Asian kids, so proper. I always wanted to. You-all had that little house thing, at the gate. We called it the witch's house, even before that happened. My mom went, she went right in there because she knew you kids were in there. She wanted you out of there. She talked to your mom. She said your mom should be in a hospital."

His father had been the manager of the trailer park until he ran off. Thereafter, by virtue of living in the gatehouse instead of the trailers, his mother was the manager, but she never did any of the things his father had done or went outside or answered the phone. People stuck notes in a hole in the screen, left broken fans and sink pipes by their step, and torn-out stove burners and bags of garbage. Their own stove was black with the overflow of things his sister tried to cook.

He was not in kindergarten, because you had to have the shots. His sister was in second grade and had the shots; his father had seen to that, Mrs. Rao told him, giving him a choice: a father running off, ducking into the woods behind the propane tanks, or a father taking his sister for her shots. Some things allowed this choice of what to remember.

When he went back to Michigan with Lisa the first thing she did was take him to see her mother in the nursing home.

At the sight of Mrs. Rao he stopped in the door. He would not have known her, any more than he had recognized a five-year-old girl in Lisa. "It's Robbie, Mama, Robbie Forney," Lisa said. Mrs. Rao lay on her side and did not speak, though she was awake and breathing quietly, her eyes open and looking at him. The first lines of a poem came to him. There was no way to hug someone lying in bed and he was not a man who would try that, although now he sometimes found himself wrapped in the heavy arms of Lisa without knowing how he got there. He was a famous man, but once he was her husband he meant the same to her whether he was a known poet or nobody.

He stared at a cup of water with a bendable straw on Mrs.

Rao's nightstand. Feeling shaky doing without his drink, he picked up a plastic fork in cellophane and scratched at his wrist. "Robbie's a professor now," Lisa said. She didn't say "poet." To him she said, "You can call her Mama, or Gloria. Call her Gloria. I guess Mama could be anybody, but Gloria is her. Take that chair."

He sat down. "Mrs. Rao," he said, very low.

Mrs. Rao might be ninety-seven and lying there with white hair, but she had the same big eyes in smooth heavy lids. She looked back at him. The irises had gone a lighter brown. Far down in them was a table with scissors and paste, and his sister sitting on Mrs. Rao's lap, having her fingernails cut with a pair of round-tipped scissors. His sister had laid out the scissors herself, each on top of the armor man from the teacher's workbook, while he chose the locations for the big jars of paste and the flat sticks they used to get it out. He would have no children, so for the rest of his life he would not recover the smell of the paste.

Mrs. Rao lifted his sister's thin long hair from her neck and drew it up in a ponytail. "Like mine," said Mrs. Rao, whose hair gleamed with comb-lines and bars of light that traveled up and down the black, offering the eye a quiet for which there was not a word. His sister got down and went off to her own classroom. This was not the last day of her life, a day hidden even from his poems because there were no words for it, the day of who and why. This was a hot summer day in the first week of Vacation Bible School. He remained at the table, carefully tearing from their perforations in the teacher's workbook a set of pages containing breastplates and helmets and metal shields for the front of the legs: a page per child, enough for each one's silhouette to have on the full armor of God.

The Blue Grotto

o　　o　　o

IT was after midnight. Capri was counting out three minutes, with Elizabeth folded in her lap. At the age of five Elizabeth still wouldn't open her mouth for the thermometer, and Capri had to hold her arm down to keep it pressed in the armpit. She had unbuttoned the pink pajama top and carefully taken the arm, not much heavier than a table knife, out of its sleeve. The child seemed asleep. "Are you with me here?" Capri whispered.

They were sitting in the window seat in the baby's room, where Capri had almost fallen asleep after his last bottle, looking out at the water. The security floodlights fastened to the big houses across the lake made white stakes in the water. You felt like spinning out into the clear night and weaving back and forth among them. A vague feeling but it had a torment in it. The houses over there are bigger than this one, she said to herself idly. Those on the suburb side were right on the lakefront; this one on the city side was a block up the long bank from the water. Back ten blocks to the west was her own street, everything getting quickly smaller between here and there as if you were looking in the wrong end of binoculars.

She knew families in every block between here and her own house, from babysitting. She was the sought-after babysitter, though Tia was making inroads, without even taking the baby-sitting course, on the strength of being her little sister. If they couldn't get Capri they'd ask for Tia, despite her punk clothes and her maroon hair. "Our kids are going to send you girls to college!" more than one of the fathers had said, to both of them. Mr. Yates had said it again to Capri last week when they were gone eight hours. When she was twelve, Tia started right in at what Capri was making. She didn't have to come up laboriously past all the evenings of surprised, disappointed smiles as Capri explained that everybody was charging more now. "Well, now," an outspoken father might say, "we might have to get a wage freeze in place here."

"It's not the big money, over there," her mother would say. "The Yateses aren't the ones *on* the lake. Here's somebody in the paper making eighty-five million for running a company. How do you like that? Bet that guy's a winner." If her mother flipped through the paper, she was in a good, if irritated, mood. If she just stared at the page, it was a sign that she had been made to think of the things that stood in the way of her plans. Capri didn't answer her mother when the subject was money, guarding against the next subject, which could be her father. He was tied to money, in her mother's mind. She swore he never sent any. Capri did not believe this. She knew he would send something, even if it wasn't the sum her mother was waiting for so that she could cut back to one job and begin saving to travel.

Her mother had made only one trip in her life, on her honeymoon. One trip down to Oregon, camping in a van, and then, defiantly, laughingly, down to nothing but gas money, back home: that was it. She was still waiting to travel. There were places in the world she saw as absolutely waiting for her. Provence. Italy. Capri and Tia looked at each other. When their mother talked about these places it was as if they, her daughters, were the skeptical parents.

Capri took the thermometer out. One hundred four. She realized that she had not shaken it down, but before trying again she put Elizabeth on the window-seat cushion and went to find the Tylenol.

When Capri came back Elizabeth was sitting perfectly still, and put her lips delicately to the spoon. When she swallowed the red liquid, she shuddered, giving off heat and the silent whine that hummed from her body. That was normal with Elizabeth, the feeling of a whine. This time she was getting over the flu.

"It never fails, when I have a busy week, she's home," Mrs. Yates told Capri. The girl was sunk among the sofa cushions, breathing with the little hitches of one who has stopped crying. "And I couldn't call you, because of course you had school." Capri did not feel like telling Mrs. Yates that her mother let her take off from school to babysit. Mrs. Yates had a job with what she called "the Commission." Capri did not know what it was but she knew Mrs. Yates was a lawyer. Usually she wore suits but tonight she was wearing a silver dress with uneven pieces floating off the skirt like seaweed. Capri wondered why Mr. Yates didn't do the job that must be a husband's and tell her that her right cheek was redder than her left one, but she looked much better than usual, with all the makeup and earrings dangling to her jaw and giving her face a surprised, hopeful look.

Mr. Yates crossed the room with the baby on one arm, his black shoes flashing under the lamps, and lifted his daughter's chin. "Cheer up," he said firmly. "Capri here is going to feel lousy if she has to look at that face. Let me see a smile. That won't pass. Overruled. Hey, there we go." Elizabeth's smile was the worst Capri had seen on her, as her father gave her a kiss on the hair.

"How many times have we left her with Capri?" Mrs. Yates said to him as he handed the baby over to Capri. "Should I do something? Do you think she's going to give Capri trouble?"

"She's all right. She's been sick," he said, and to Capri, "Don't let her breathe on the baby."

CAPRI put the thermometer back in her armpit. "Hold your arm in tight, like this. Grab on to that sucker," she said in a TV voice. She knew how to talk to kids.

You had to add a degree to armpit temperature. This she knew from the babysitting course in middle school, where Mrs. Inigo had taught them about charging appropriately for such a vital job. "A vital, vital job." Mrs. Inigo was young; the boys who took Spanish from her called her Mrs. Ego because under her eye makeup and tender gestures she was a feminist. It was well known in school. She had four earrings going up the rim of one ear, like rings for a tiny curtain, and she was not Spanish; her name was Dawn. Although her husband was from somewhere among the countries Capri thought of as dangling from America, it was not he who had taught her Spanish, she made clear, but travel and long study. Travel in particular.

The girls were always telling Mrs. Inigo they intended to hitchhike all the way to South America as she had done, coming back with a husband. Capri was not one of these. In her house their mother's wish to go places was a kind of quicksand they all had to step around. But it was a good thing she had taken Mrs. Inigo's course: the fathers were right, if she got to college it would not be with her mother's money from Supercuts or her phone-survey job, but with these folded checks held out for Capri to come forward and accept, or pressed into her hand along with the extravagant thanks. "Thanks so much, Capri. You saved us again." "You don't know what you did for me today by taking them." Sometimes the mothers seemed ready to cry when they were looking at what their kids had drawn with her and thanking her. The fathers were not as emotional. As often as not they would be trying to get her to understand something about the ordeal of whatever evening out they had had.

All the children in these big houses were young, though the parents were not particularly young. They were all quite a bit older than her own mother, even though several of them had new babies. Mrs. Yates kept saying Capri's mother looked like a high school girl. Over the years Capri answered steadily. "She's thirty-two." "She's thirty-three."

The baby lay wheezing softly in his crib, but Elizabeth was out of bed again, standing in the doorway of his room, where Capri sat in the dark. "I don't feel good."

Unwinding her arms—she had been holding herself as she watched the lake—and stretching them out, Capri said, "Come here, honey."

"I don't feel good," the girl said again, without moving.

Capri got up, went to her and scooped her up.

"Ow." A whisper.

Capri felt the heat of her skin when the pajama top came up. "Sit here, OK? I'm going to check you again."

The child sat tilted back. As Capri passed his crib the baby gave a gasp and flailed for a moment, blindly lifting his head off the mattress and bowing it around like a caterpillar. She put her hand between the shoulder blades and he settled back.

Robert. Robert and Elizabeth. The names were reserved like parking places for later. Capri liked to call the baby Bobby and Baby, so he could hear the syllables bump each other. Babies liked words with double sounds, blowing and popping sounds. The girl she called Lizzie. She still had to make friends with her every time. At the same time she sometimes had the wish to tease and corner a child so flinching and wary, so sliding-away, so dissatisfied by everyone except the father. But lots of children were this way, she knew, rich or poor. They didn't want you; they wanted just one person, the mother or the father. Usually not both. This one was a father's girl.

Capri was fairly sure she had been one herself. Her most specific recollection of that time was of sitting in the front seat, no seat belt. ("You will all be driving someday," Mrs. Inigo said. "Car seats and seat belts if you ever *ever* put a child in a car! And the child is in the back!") She must have been five or so, Elizabeth's age, because her father was still there, in the family, and she was with him in the car.

How did she get all the way from there to here? How did she come to be in the Yateses' house watching Elizabeth and her father, and with a shamed attention, as if it satisfied her?

Why did you keep thinking you could get back to a certain point? How did it happen that there was one life, and then a different one succeeding it, and maybe another and another, like trips farther and farther away when you had not gone home from the first one yet?

Her father had reddish blonde hair — the hair Tia had under

the maroon—and thick, light eyebrows. He kept banging the heels of his hands on the steering wheel in time to the loud music on the radio, and she discovered in herself a determination not to think, as her mother would, that it was not necessary to do that.

"On a level street, don't have to use the gas much," her father was telling her above the radio. "This is a machine that just rolls along if you let it. Don't even have to steer all that much." She liked the idea of the car rolling along on its own with the two of them inside. She had cut her tongue on the glass-like grooves of the hard candy he kept in the car since he had quit smoking. "Let's have a looksee," he said. He stopped banging the wheel and looked over at her when she put out her tongue.

Everything about her father's face was strongly pleasant to her. This was a memory blunted with use. He said, "You know, I think you need another one for that." It must have been summer: the sweat on his T-shirt, the sticky wrapper. "You're my girl," he said.

That day or another day, her mother was wearing cutoff jeans. She had her hair in a braid and they all four sat at the supper table. Her mother was talking fast and then crying, and then she threw a glass of milk that hit the refrigerator and broke into skidding bits on the floor. Tia spilled her own milk. Everybody scrambled around the table like musical chairs. On Tia's heel was a scar from a knife of glass. It could be seen today, even touched from time to time when they were painting their toenails.

Capri held her breath and sopped at the milk with the dish-towel, and when she opened her eyes her father was down there with her, sweeping glass into a dustpan. When she got the milk cleaned up he said something to her, as Tia screamed, and their mother, with incomprehensible low groans, squeezed and picked at the dripping red heel. He said, "Thanks, Cappy."

Mrs. Yates called Elizabeth "E." When Capri heard this "E" she thought it was not really a nickname. She did not care for the initial, the removal of a name, nor for the occasional references made by Mrs. Yates to the name Capri, which reflected on her mother. "Has she ever *been* to Capri?" Mrs. Yates once asked, but at the time Capri had been thirteen and unsure what Mrs. Yates meant when she said "*Copp*-ry"; it sounded like a local town, or worse, some class you took, like pottery.

"I don't know." She had looked away, though she did know, if she had understood the question, that her mother had never been to Capri, having left home at seventeen to get married in Discovery Park, in a circle of tambourines. Her new husband was nineteen. In Capri's room there was a picture of them standing on the bluff above the Sound, her father's hair short because he was thinking of joining the army, her mother windblown and smiling, a little bouquet with flying ribbons in her hands.

They had driven to California in the van, they had come back, they had had two children. So of course her mother had not been to Capri.

But it was one of the places she talked about going. Islands were her favorite. She was going to Hawaii, she was going to Bermuda. But first Capri, where there was a cave that filled with blue light when the sun shone: the Blue Grotto. "I will get there. One of these days I'll be sitting there in the blue light," their mother said. She showed them a brochure. Capri carried around a distinct set of facts about this little island of mountains. So did Tia. They didn't like the word *grotto*, a word for a body part or something under the street. But it had a sound of importance, of something guarded or hidden, even religious, so that it seemed their mother was not just longing for beaches or fun.

They began to joke about it: "Where did you *get* those earrings? They look like they came from the *Blue Grotto*." "We took off today. Lin and me." "Where?" "We went to the *Blue Grotto*." Lin was Tia's boyfriend. He was from Taiwan and had been Tia's boyfriend from the time she was eleven; now she was thirteen and couldn't babysit the kind of hours Capri did—twelve, sixteen, even twenty hours a week—because she was glued to Lin so much of the time. Half the time they didn't go to school. Lin lived with his uncle and came and went as he pleased. So did Tia, for that matter.

"My mother thinks things will get better when Tia's done with middle school," Capri told the guidance counselor. This was not her mother's opinion but her own. She based it on the fact that for herself, at the end of middle school something had changed. She began to babysit almost every day, and she experienced not so much a lessening of her feeling that things could not be made right, and that she would never really be alive, as a suspicion that this did not matter as much as it had seemed to. It was probably how at least some other people, adults, felt as well. Still, Tia's behavior did not seem to have its root in either of those feelings. Tia had no doubt she was alive and no memory much before Lin; she did not even remember the loud little girl she had been or the screaming when the glass stabbed her heel, or the apartments, or their father. With Capri's help she searched her memory. "He wasn't tall," Capri prompted. Tia screwed up her face. "Nope, nothin'," she said.

Elizabeth was shivering. Capri knew that bundling up a chilling child was not good. You had to cover just enough to stop the shivering but not enough to heat the body more. It was an art, Mrs. Inigo said, that they would be glad to know when they had their own children, if not before that in their babysitting careers, knock on wood. They laughed at the thought. They were twelve. Having children. *Having* them.

"There have been some terrible babysitters," Mrs. Inigo had told them the first day. "Ignorant. Kids who put rubber bands around little boys' penises"—there was only one boy in the class but the whole class stirred—"to keep them from wetting. Kids who opened up a can of beer and let toddlers wander into the street. But those things are not peculiar to babysitters. *Parents* have done those things. So, for the stereotype, we substitute— *you.*" Mrs. Inigo pushed up the woven bracelet she wore for some cause, and raised her hands over them. "You are the new kind of babysitter. You are responsible in a new way. When you've finished this course there will be things you'll know more about than the parents do. I guarantee it."

Capri took the thermometer out. One hundred four point two. That meant one hundred five point two. She didn't remember hearing a fever that high mentioned in the course.

"Come here," she said, picking up Elizabeth, who weighed hardly any more than the baby. "Come back to bed."

The girl was shivering strongly now and at the same time holding herself stiff in Capri's arms so that it was like carrying a small chair. "Ow," she said again in a tinny voice. "My neck hurts."

She sank the hot points of her fingers into Capri's arms as Capri tried to lower her onto the bed, and whispered, "I can't, my neck hurts."

Here goes, Capri thought, but no tears came. "Sit up, sweetie. Here's your pillow. Just sit here and I'm going to call your mommy and she'll be right here. Your daddy, I mean." The girl bared her undersized teeth and began a shallow, toneless sobbing through them, holding still with hands on either side of her on the edge of the mattress, like somebody sitting on a windowsill who might tip down into the street. Capri turned back and pressed her lips to the hot forehead. "That's a girl."

Capri called the number on the pad by the guestroom phone. No one answered. On the bed was the bag with her T-shirt and toothbrush in it. She was spending the night because they would not be home until morning. They were at a fund-raiser that was going to end in a champagne breakfast. The clock on the table said 1:15. She called the number again.

Downstairs she looked for the Babysitter's Friend, the card she taught all her families to make and keep near the phone. Eventually she found it stuck in the yellow pages. There was the pediatrician, Dr. Abrams, who, she knew, would not be at his office number at this hour. He was not, nor did he have an answering service or an emergency number as pediatricians were supposed to. His home number was not in the phone book. Down the list were the two names marked "neighbor." She took a breath and called the first one. After eight rings she tried the other one. They were not people she sat for, either name. She tried to think who her mother would take her or Tia to if they were sick. They were never sick enough to go to the doctor; their mother was always saying, "Thank God that blew over."

She carried the phone into the living room and looked out at the dark water, thinking. The moon had moved, the row of lights lay on the water unwavering, now there were stars.

She called her mother's cell and then she called home. Lin answered. "Lin, is Mom there?"

"No," said his polite, sleepy voice. "She's not here—quit it, quit it, it's Capri—she went over to David's." Tia came on the line. "I'm hitting him. He wasn't supposed to answer. What's the matter?"

"A kid is sick and I can't get hold of anybody. I just wanted Mom to come and get us and take us to the ER."

"Well, she's not here. She and David went over to his place. Why doesn't she answer her phone? Hey, don't tell her Lin stayed. God, Lin's so dumb. It could have been her on the phone. Are you going to call nine-one-one?"

"I guess I'll just call a cab."

"Yeah, that's good. Well, sorry. Sorry, Capri. Whoa, that's going to be fun."

After she called the cab she went up the stairs two at a time and ran water onto a washcloth. Elizabeth's face was a dull red. She looked asleep but she opened her eyes and gave Capri a tense, unusual glare, eye to eye. "I can't move my head," she said angrily. Capri peeled away the other pajama sleeve and smoothed the wet cloth over her forehead and cheeks and then her shoulders and her thin chest with bone just under the skin like a plate under a dishtowel. "Shhh," she said as the ticking sobs began again. "Shh, honey, it's OK. We're going to the doctor. Put your top on. Here, I'll put it on. It doesn't matter if it's a little bit wet. Let's see, do you have slippers?" No answer. She found them in the closet, and a pink bathrobe. "He-ere's one arm, he-ere's the other arm, all done. You come and sit at the top of the stairs while I get Bobby." The girl didn't move. Capri picked her up and carried her down the wide hall to the top step.

"Hey, little buddy, come on up here." Capri gathered up the baby as smoothly as she could, blanket and all. He began smacking his lips and fussing as she looked for his bag. Where was the bag? It must be downstairs. Bottles. She would have to take formula. He was waking up now, rooting in her neck.

"Come on, honey," she said, pulling Elizabeth gently by the hand.

"No." The narrow eyes menaced Capri.

Capri got them both into her arms. Downstairs she had to put them on the couch to fill the bottles and write a note. The baby went back to sleep. She saw the restfulness of his curved eyelashes when she picked him up. It would be easy to love this baby. He slept, he received his bottle with joy, he sank against you, he had no questions, no wish that things be different, no longing yet for any specific person. There was a shy ease about him. Not every baby had it, only certain calm, lovable babies. It was simple: if you were lovable, people loved you, guarded you.

In the cab she said, "I can't find the seat belts."

"Must be down in behind the seat," the man said. "Can't get 'em if they're down there."

In the cab the chilling started again, almost as if the child were making lunges to get out of the circle of her arm. She was no cooler but she had stopped crying and despite the jerking of her body she seemed to be asleep.

When they stopped, Capri said, "I only have three dollars."

"It figures," he said. "You go on in there, go to the desk, see if they got a cab fund. Tell 'em."

She got out with the baby and reached in with the other arm to heave Elizabeth up against her side. "Ow," Elizabeth said, but did not cry, all the way through the automatic doors and up to the desk. The crying seemed to be over.

"This girl has a high fever, one hundred and five," Capri said. "I need somebody to look at her. Do you have a cab fund?"

"No, we do not." The woman at the desk came right around from behind the glass and lifted Elizabeth from her. She was a tall woman with glasses on a chain and she looked like a teacher. "That's quite a load," she said. "Here, we'll just let her stretch out."

Elizabeth didn't say she couldn't stretch out but she gave out a high-pitched sound that was both a scream and a whisper.

"Her neck hurts," Capri said. "She can't lie down." The woman set her down carefully on the gray couch. Everything in the room was gray or blue-green, including the pictures of gulls and herons on the walls. There were a few people, not many, scattered around the room. One other baby, in an infant seat on the floor. The mother looked fixedly at Capri and shook her head. An aquarium was bubbling beside her.

"I came in a cab—" Capri began. Now that she was sitting down she found she was breathing too hard to speak.

"You got anybody else with you?"

"I'm the babysitter—"

"Just catch your breath, baby."

"I can't get hold of her mom and dad. Not yet."

"All right, now, all right. We're going to have trouble treating this little baby girl without the parents. Mm-hm. Mm-hm. Well, we'll see what we can do. Plus don't you worry, I think your cab just pulled out."

THE woman at the desk and the nurse were looking for Mr. and Mrs. Yates, along with somebody they had called, a man in a tie. They were going through all the big hotels looking for parties, and waking up lawyers in Mr. Yates's firm. So far, nobody knew where the Yateses were.

Elizabeth was having a lumbar puncture. "They're tapping her spine," the nurse explained to Capri, though Capri knew what it was, as anyone would know who watched TV. "Is she in the operating room?" Capri said. Her arms were almost numb from the baby's weight. "No, she's right here, down the hall," the nurse said. "You can go see her in a minute. Here, let me hold him for a minute. Here's your chance to go to the bathroom, right down there."

"Thanks. There's his bag if he . . . but I'll be right back." She wanted to make a phone call but she didn't want them to listen. Down the hall she found a pay phone; they still had one, and one with a directory. She found the name. "This is Capri Miller," she said. "I don't know if you remember me or not but I was in your babysitting class three years ago. I was the one with . . ." She couldn't think how to describe herself.

Mrs. Inigo's voice woke right up and sounded as it had in class, challenging. Capri imagined Mr. Inigo lying there, letting his wife answer the phone in the middle of the night because she was a feminist. "I do remember you, Capri," Mrs. Inigo said.

"I'm sorry to call so late, or early, I don't know which. I'm at the hospital with the kids I'm babysitting."

"Tell me what's happening," said Mrs. Inigo.

She told her. "Listen," Mrs. Inigo said at last. "You've done well. The trouble they gave you was because of liability."

"I just . . . I just . . ."

"I think right now you should go and sit down, Capri. It's in their hands now. If you can find a machine, get yourself a cup of coffee. I really think you should do that. Even if you don't drink coffee. The thing I'd like to do is come and be with you, but I can't, because of the baby." Tia had not told Capri about any baby. Tia had never said Mrs. Inigo was pregnant.

Capri pretended this was not so. "Oh, I've had coffee since I was little. Thank you," she said. "I'm sorry to have woken you up. How *is* the baby?"

"She's fine. I see your sister in school, Capri," said Mrs. Inigo. "I hope life is going well for the two of you. I hope you're not taking any shit."

When Capri hung up she thought about this. She remembered Mrs. Inigo herself saying in class that Spanish-speaking men did not think well of women who used bad language. She wondered if Mrs. Inigo tried to please her husband in any way. She wondered if Mrs. Inigo knew she could drive him away and be alone.

THE doctor who sits down beside her has those pop eyes that blink and get wider and wider until the next blink. It is as if she has to keep shutting her lids to settle her eyes down or they will go wild. Capri doesn't think this is a good feature in a doctor. But she has a calm voice. "Elizabeth is very sick," she says slowly, more or less as if this will have to sink in. "We think she may have encephalitis. That's an infection in her brain that sometimes comes along after the flu. Very rarely. We don't know why."

"She's going to stay here," Capri says.

"Oh yes, she is. She is a sick little cookie."

"Could I go back and explain to her about her dad? I know she's worried." Capri keeps talking to the rhythm of the blinking eyes. "It's the middle of the night, he's not here, it's confusing. I think she ought to see me."

"Well, she's on her way to the ICU right now. About to be. She's not worried because she's not conscious and I wish we could get our hands on the parents."

Capri shifts the baby and inhales the soft fumes coming from him. Even wet he smells like bread. "You mean she could die."

The doctor casts her wide eyes up at the long-necked herons in the painting, standing in water. "We certainly hope not," she says, after a bit. "We're just going to have to get her turned around, that's the first thing." The baby gives a low, rasping growl. "This one's sure a sleeper," the doctor says. "Doesn't know a thing. Doesn't have the foggiest idea, does he?"

"I was going to change him, but I don't want to wake him up."

"Don't wake a sleeping baby."

"Oh, this one wouldn't mind, he's happy no matter what."

"That's the way to be," says the doctor wearily, closing down her big eyelids. "Want me to take him?" and when Capri shakes her head, "Do you drink coffee? Charlene, is there coffee left?" Charlene brings coffee out of the back in a cup that says OVER 40 AND FEELING FOXY. "I'll tell Lee to wait a minute on taking baby girl upstairs," she tells the doctor. Capri likes the way she calls Elizabeth a baby. "This young lady can go see her, and then she can come on back and take it easy. Meanwhile I get my turn with this little guy." She holds out her arms.

Elizabeth is lying on her side on the gurney with her head on a big snowy pillow so crisp it looks like paper. It is paper. Her legs are drawn up and her arms bent close to her body. Her eyes are open but she pays no attention to Capri. Her pink pajamas are on the counter, and the line of a hanging IV pouch is plugged into the back of her hand, which is taped to a little board. Another tube comes out from under the hospital gown. Coming close Capri says, "It's OK, Lizzie." The usual pinched expression has been wiped off the girl's face by her open mouth and the flush that puffs out her skin. The complaining feeling that always hangs in the air around her is not there. Again Capri whispers her name.

She slides her fingers into the damp hair and lifts it back from the forehead, laces it carefully behind the red rim of the ear, and looks for a long time. The ear, ribbed and glowing, reminds her of the inner leaves in a head of cabbage. How strange, these leaves on the side of the head. How strange the head is, in fact. Objects on it like little vegetables, if you look at them.

And people think faces are beautiful, and think of them, certain faces, all the time, she thinks bitterly. The child's face comes back together as a face, but there is something unpleasant in it, even so. It looks stretched downward and fierce, as children look straining to go to the bathroom.

"Lizzie," she says. "They're going to make you feel better now." With that, a certainty rushes over her that the things that could make Elizabeth feel better will not happen.

You can't make anything happen, Capri tells her silently. You can't make your mom and dad come right now. You think they don't like you and maybe they don't for some reason. But now you're sick. It will be different, when they come. If you died, they'd be different people. Capri can see them. No longer dressed up, full of instructions. No more shining shoes, heels, earrings. No. Tear-streaked, tired, swatted down. She could almost cry for what Mr. Yates will feel if he remembers his good-bye to his daughter last night, so long ago. He will have to regret it forever. She is visited by a brief joy as fierce as Elizabeth's clamped face.

She stops. I don't mean die. I don't mean that. They can't help it.

The young man comes into the room to wheel the gurney away. "Now wait a minute, this one ain't yours, I know that," he says.

She steps away from his wide smile. Something exercises in her chest, like air in a sticking balloon, a sensation she hopes is not the beginning of tears. He throws his hip against the table and wheels it in a circle, a tray with Elizabeth on it. Capri sees the soles of Elizabeth's feet, and the jiggling bag of liquid. She sees that Elizabeth has athlete's foot: peeling toes and cracks in the red skin at their base, and wonders if anyone but herself and the orderly have noticed this about her. It seems her duty for the moment to notice everything, in the absence of anyone else. She is struck by the separateness of each member of the Yates family, including the baby asleep out there, now in Charlene's arms, giving off his odors like a secret he easily shares. When you breathe on his head it breathes back at you the scent of a sweet roll. No idea who is holding him. No idea, ever, if someone should steal him now, of where he came from. The lack of any use to each other, any protection, that they are, his family. All out in the night at once, scattered. Any one of them could be steered down a hall to an elevator with the wrong person responsible.

She imagines her own father stretched on such a table. He would be lying straight and not in such disorder as Elizabeth. She grabs for the scene as it recedes. At the same time she drops a short way down, into a knowledge that he *is* somewhere. Not suspended just out of reach of her mind, but existing—sick or well, putting on his clothes, eating, driving with the radio on. If he's in the same time zone he's asleep right now. Asleep as if nothing were happening. Groggily her thoughts swerve away.

She has to get back to the baby. She wishes they had let her bring him in with her, with his sweet smell and his luck of being the second-born, the one at ease. Was there some way to transmit the luck of one life into another?

The gurney, like one of those jamming grocery carts that do not seem built to go on their swiveling wheels, takes its awkward path to the elevator, carrying Elizabeth. The elevator doors close. Charlene puts the baby back in her arms and she sits in a chair uncomfortable for sitting with a baby because of the metal arms. Pushing the chair out of the way with her foot she lowers herself onto the blue-green carpet and leans back against the wall, letting the baby sink onto her legs. She looks up at the bulb in the lamp and closes her eyes. Her ears are ringing.

She can feel him against her legs and in her wrists and hands as she steadies him, but gradually she feels herself broadening out, her limbs going slack. She puts her head back, under the lamp. Behind her lids everything is dark, with the lightbulb still there in gold, moving slowly out of sight like a ship, and then fan-shapes, outlined in a bright blue-green, begin to rise and fall all over the background color. Now and then she can hear the movement of people around her and even the bubbling of the aquarium at the far end of the room. She watches the scene behind her eyelids. Now there are gold tracks all over the dark color. Everything is far off. She is not waiting. I'm here, she thinks. I'm in the Blue Grotto.

Later or Never

○   ○   ○

ON the days Lawrence could walk, Cam sat with him in the old grade school. His house had a ramp but there were days when he could do stairs, and they would negotiate the seams and curbs of two blocks of sidewalk and the school's railed steps in order to drink coffee at a table in the entrance hall.

In place of the children who had worn the edge off the marble steps in two troughs, the high-ceilinged classrooms now held shops and restaurants. Sometimes those old children could be seen standing up close to photographs hung in the corridors, pointing themselves out, prim or devilish at their desks. "See those holes? Those are inkwells," they would be saying with a hopeless pride, to kids who must be their grandchildren. Great-grandchildren. Cam thought the kids in the pictures looked like orphans. Dressed up, dark around the eyes, staring with grins and scowls into a time in which the classroom, the teacher, and they themselves in their bunched-up plaid shirts and bloused dresses did not exist. Yet there they were behind glass, jittering in rows like kids anywhere, waiting to be let out the doors and onto the buses lined up in one of the pictures on their bicycle-sized tires.

"Did they all wear white?" Cam wanted to know. "The girls?"

"Little brides," said Lawrence, tipping back his head. "Brides of knowledge." He raised one of his eyebrows at her.

"So how did you keep clean if you went to school in a white dress?"

"Clean wasn't so big, then."

Cam didn't say, "How do you know?" After all, she asked these questions. And Lawrence had an interest in many subjects far afield of his own, which was French literature of some time period.

He was squinting out the open doors at the hedge that bounded the parking lot. He spoke a line in French. "A poem," he explained.

"Yeah," she said. She could have said, "I mean, look at your face. French poem."

"The blue sky. The blue sky is God, the only difference being that it exists. The hedge, the sun over there? All in a poem." This seemed to please and agitate him at the same time. She hoped he would not recite the poem.

The hedge was seething with tiny birds. His eyes were giving out on him but he always noticed the same things she did; like her, he was always on the lookout for something. Something sudden but expected.

For Lawrence, she could see later, the thing watched for would have been more specific than it was for her: some change in the course of what was happening to him. He had the kind of MS in which the body rapidly divorced the brain. She knew about it from a semester on disabilities; it was the worst form but there was a chance of reversal. She told him that. She should have known that instead of arguing he would bring in his poet. His poet was Mallarmé, the subject of his book, the one he had published as opposed to the two rubber-banded stacks of paper in liquor store boxes in the closet.

"Chance, yes," he said. "Not *a* chance. A throw of the dice never will abolish chance. 'Le hasard.' *Le* hasard." She knew *hasard*; she had a string of French words now. She knew when he was quoting; she knew when it was his poet because of the way he held up both weakened hands like a conductor, two fingertips of the right just meeting the thumb.

His book had received one review, and she knew the name of the person who had written it. Lindenbaum. "He did say it wasn't a biography, but by *Jesús*"—he always pronounced it the Spanish way and then apologized because Cam was Catholic—"the man knew his Mallarmé."

"If it wasn't a biography what was it?" At one time she had expected he would give her a copy of it but he never did. She knew where the copies were, in another box in the closet.

"*Une vie.*"

They had both seen the birds swoop in, dozens of them, and make themselves invisible in the hedge, so it seemed to be shifting of its own accord. "God of the weak," Lawrence whispered. "God of the little birds, protect them now." To Cam's mother, the way he looked saying this would have been proof he was crazy. But Cam knew these prayers of his. He liked to put his palms together and roll up his eyes. It was something he did when they were watching the news. "Oh God, we ask that you turn the general, as he testifieth before the Congress, to stone. Also the attaché with the briefcase."

"Fob," he was explaining. "The prayer for the birds. Fob, who wrote about animal life."

"Fob," she said obediently.

"F-A-B-R-E. He's saying a prayer that the owl won't snatch the bird." With his better hand he made a snatching motion. "Snatch the mouse. Fabre doesn't hold it against the owl, even as he describes how it's done. Every chew. Except of course an owl does not chew. He swallows. Vomits out the little bones et cetera."

"Whatever it is, somebody's gonna know all about it," Cam said. "And then tell you."

"You're right." He said it warmly, turning to face her. He liked exasperation. He was a child that way, always goading somebody, a teacher or a mother. She knew that.

"There's that face," he said, something his mother also said to Cam on occasion. "That baby look," he said. "Know how a baby, certain kind of baby, won't smile at you? That baby will …

she'll drink your blood before she'll smile at you. You could turn inside out and she would just look. And you know she thinks you're already inside out, you're so ugly and frightening and you smell."

"I don't think that."

"To a baby we smell like zoo animals. To a baby." His face emptied, the way it often did when he remembered something not connected to a book, and he turned away, so she was able to do a mental drawing of his profile. His skin was sweaty and drained of blood, almost the gray of a pearl. A freshwater pearl, like her grandmother's present. When she was in her cap and gown, her grandmother had fastened the strand for her. It barely met around her neck. It burst the same night, when she went off to drink beer with Ray Malala. Ray had been her friend since St. Benedict's, the new fat boy in third grade, because both their fathers had died. By high school Ray was a DJ everybody wanted at parties, and a football player. By then being Samoan was a plus. He got her the place as the team water-girl. The guys liked her but they didn't get around to going out with her. Ray, on the other hand, had acquired a fair amount of experience over the years. "All right, listen, Cami," he told her when he took her home after graduation, "don't you be doing no more stuff like that right now. Hear me? I'll tell your brother. Here's your beads."

A freshwater pearl had dents, though, and Lawrence's face, familiar to her eye and her mind's eye, was uncommonly smooth, except for one crease between the eyebrows. No one would read his age in the features, which, despite the cheeks rounded by prednisone, reminded her of the smooth, heavy-lidded face of Rose of Lima. He had the same look of secret pride and refusal. The picture of Rose in her First Communion book, *Our Saints and How They Lived*, was of a statue. The tapered plaster fingers didn't even have knuckles; this was Rose before she dipped her hands in lime so as to scar them. Cam's Communion class drawing of the face of Rose, sleepy and secretive under a crown of roses, had stayed on the refrigerator until it curled around the magnets. For weeks after her father's funeral she would check it for a miracle. Rose of Lima's miracles were not listed in *Our Saints*, though she had performed them or caused them to happen or she wouldn't be a saint, and as not only Dominicans but Jesuits too had sworn, more angel than human. Even then, Cam knew herself to be half-pretending to expect, and finally faking the expectation, that Rose's lowered eyes might open. If they had, it would have meant her father had arrived in heaven, if there was a heaven.

In time, like her brothers, she had a list of reasons not to go to Mass. Then she heard her mother start the car and drive off alone because of having a husband who was dead and kids who wouldn't go with her to Mass, and that ruined the hour anyway. Years of Sundays. By the middle of high school she was doing better with her mother but she discovered she had let God dry out like a plant.

o   o   o

ONLY a certain kind of person, the kind you could be pretty sure would not pass by, would pause to figure out Lawrence's looks. "There's something the matter with that guy. He could be fifteen and look forty or he could be forty and look fifteen. And that girl with him. Fat." Though Cam knew she was not fat, so why put the word in the mind of an observer? She was tall and solid but with large bones and a body mass index within the OK range, she knew that from her nutrition course. Not so big, in the eyes of some people. Pacific Islanders. That, she knew from Ray Malala. Columnar, Lawrence's mother said. He often told her what his mother said, which was a way of taking her side against his mother. And in fact Lawrence was thirty-nine, so the observer's second impression would have been the right one.

His mother's name was Daisy. Cam knew it was a name his mother had given herself, the way she had given him the name Orion and left it up to him if he wanted to change it in high school. He named himself after T. E. Lawrence. Cam must have seen the movie? Peter O'Toole? Cam defended herself. Where would she have seen that?

"Of course I changed my mind, about Lawrence. But it was too late."

Daisy was a small, pretty woman who must, since she had had Lawrence in her teens, be at least in her fifties. Cam listened for any mention of the parents who must have been around and had some feeling about what was going on, when their daughter was pregnant with Lawrence. She could imagine her own mother's reaction. She could see her face. And her father's, if he had been there—no way would he have let a boy who got his daughter pregnant dodge his responsibilities.

A designer, Daisy called herself. Her garden pieces in glass and cement and her elaborate stone figures mortared into walls cost a fortune and were featured in magazines. Cam admired them when Lawrence showed her photographs. The bulky figures were not exactly people. They were Daisy's idea of myth, Lawrence said.

Daisy wore eye makeup, and leather pants with high heels, and did not look like someone with the muscles to work in stone or cement. Drawings. That's what she said the figures were. They gave the effect of being trapped in the walls looking for a way out, but in a lazy, drugged way, like bears in a zoo. At the same time, their stone faces or muzzles or whatever they were, raised from the background and pointed skyward, wore half smiles, "to make rich people feel at ease," Lawrence said.

"They're sculptures," Cam said with the confidence he expected of her where art was concerned.

"Reliefs," Lawrence said. His mother wouldn't use the word *sculpture*, because that would land her in the hell, she said, of galleries. People with MFAs writing up wall-cards.

"Did she want to be a sculptor?"

"Of course," he said.

Daisy was a drinker, Lawrence said—as if that excused her from all the responsibilities she left to others—but she worked in her studio all day first. The idea had wandered into Cam's head that Daisy might lead her into the presence of a white-haired couple on a yacht, holding martini glasses, who would say, "You must have a scholarship to"—what was a famous art school?—"right away."

Often Daisy took men along on her travels, but she had no fear of going off on her own in pursuit of ideas for her designs, into deserts and ruins and villages where the women mixed bowls of paint and dipped their fingers and printed symbols onto the mud of their houses. She made friends with these faraway artists; she preferred them to people near at hand—like her son, Cam thought—and wrote them letters, without the least proof, Lawrence said, that they could read English.

Daisy had a lot of travel coming up in the fall and before she embarked on it she fired the other two shift nurses, both RNs, who took care of Lawrence, and hired Cam, who had no real degree, to live in. There was every reason to do this, Daisy said. Each nurse had had her own way of tormenting him. The older one, Iris, had her own physical complaints—her back prevented her from using the lunge belt to get him onto his feet on a bad day—and talked all day on her cell phone. The other one, Sharon, teased him, sampled his wines and used his computer. Sharon wore tight jeans and tanks and used a tanning bed; Cam saw the bend from the waist for something dropped, and the backward arch when sitting, for something out of reach. According to Daisy, Sharon had not bothered to remove her browsing history from his computer, showing that she had looked him up and done a search for his ex-wife with the different last name, and even his child. He had a son.

There were no pictures of the son. Daisy never said the word *grandson*.

When Cam revealed to Daisy that her mother feared gossip because Cam was moving into a house with a man, Daisy grinned and said, "The poor dear." At least I have a family, Cam thought. My mother doesn't make me live with some slave so she can leave the country. I go see my grandmother. My parents were married.

"Your *mom* called me," Daisy said early on, when Lawrence

still had Iris and Sharon and they were seeing how Cam worked out on an eight-hour shift. That's all that was legal, eight hours. But Daisy didn't care what was legal. "Your mom called just to make sure everything was OK. She calls you Cami! Cami with an *i*?"

It was Daisy who had written the ad: "Mature, cultured companion for invalid. Medical credentials."

HE bores her until she has to yawn and stretch, until she almost says, "I'm not one of your students," but something in him so unsuspicious, so ignorant in proportion to his knowledge that it's almost a kind of sweetness, stops her and lets her stand it. Not that he would notice whether she could stand it or not. Though at times his eyes will pass quickly over her like a flashlight. When she wore a plaid shirt of her brother's, he said, "Don't wear that."

He has dropped his head back so he seems to be scanning the heavy school light fixtures strung on cables. She knows he is trying to fill his chest with air.

Just before he got sick—so even Daisy can't claim that was her reason—his wife divorced him to marry someone else. Moved three thousand miles away, taking their son. Cam pictured a little boy having Lawrence's wide greenish cloudy eyes, with a permanent crease between the brows, staring hopelessly and knowingly over his shoulder as a woman dragged him away. A blonde in glasses. Cam knew that much. She knew because the wife wasn't the forbidden subject; from the beginning he had talked about her, a woman who couldn't see a foot in front of her, and ran in marathons, and made him go to parties he hated. A woman with long blonde hair her students mentioned in their critiques because she played with it while she lectured. But a woman who lectured, a woman with a Ph.D. When Lawrence spoke of her it was the same as when he spoke of his mother. Women. Women who existed to torment or exhaust you until you simply . . . simply . . . simply—here he conducted with his hands—put them out of your mind. Cam listened in the

understanding that this was a race to which she did not belong
and for which she did not have to answer.

But how old was he—five? ten?—the son looking back as he
was dragged away?

HER drawing, when he looked at it, did not surprise Lawrence.
She saw that. He had expected it.

Later her mother expressed the opinion that the drawing
should have been entered in a contest before she ever let it out
of her hands. "A contest. For one drawing," Cam said. "Right.
I didn't want it anyways."

Lawrence would have let her know about it with an eyebrow
if she said "anyways." Or "somewheres" or "lost for words" or
"on accident."

Now he had seen three of her drawings. "Don't show these
to my mother," he said. "She'll make suggestions." Cam didn't
tell him Daisy had one of them, the one of him. It was the one
he had let her do while he was in the chair by the window, why
not, it was what he did all day, though by *Jesús* there ought to be
a skull on the windowsill. He could sit forever looking out the
window. Not only now, he said irritably. Not just this particular
summer quarter when he was not teaching—as if he would teach
again in the fall. Looking out the window was an occupation for
all seasons. "*Sickly spring, lucid winter*, et cetera."

She didn't tell him she had met twice with Daisy, once for coffee while she was still working the morning shift, and once right
before she moved in. The second time was in an old hotel, by the
fireplace, for wine and what Daisy called snacks—perfect little
dollhouse dinners on plates thinner than the heavy napkins. They
had finished two bottles and ordered a third. Daisy did most of
the drinking but Cam kept up her end. She was underage but
nobody asked her. She didn't look it, with her size and the kind
of face she had, "not so much scowling as . . . solemn," Daisy said,
as if she had come to respect Cam's choice of face.

In the early hours of this occasion Cam had laughed a good

deal more than she usually did because Daisy knew how to be funny about herself and her art and her son, exactly the same way he made fun of her, showing no pity. "Where were we? Lord no, no more pinot. Take it away! I admit he didn't have the best example, growing up. But—he appealed to women. That is something that cannot be helped." She filled her glass and Cam's. "*She* ran off with a bore from the business school. Of course there were plenty left to comfort him. Coming around. For a while."

The telephone rang all day. He answered it or he didn't, depending on his mood. Cam could have told Daisy that. No one, man or woman, came.

At some point in the evening Cam was drunk for the second time in her life and knew it and gave in to the impulse to flop over her canvas bag and pull out the drawing she had made of Lawrence. Daisy looked at it in silence and then she tried to stand up. She had some trouble getting out of the deep chair because she had already met somebody else for a drink before this. "You hold this, I don't want it on the wet table." Then she was gone a long time, fifteen minutes. Finally Cam followed her to the ladies room. You could suffer a clot or a hemorrhage at any age; Daisy could be sprawled under the door of the booth.

There was Daisy, at the big softly lit mirror with her eyes shut. She had a mascara wand out, lying open among crumpled tissues. "I can't find the top," she said in a hopeless voice, losing her balance. Cam picked it up off the floor. "Where did you put that?" Daisy rasped, when Cam was in the booth.

"I just gave it to you."

"I mean that picture."

"In my bag."

"Don't show me things like that, oh, no, no, no," she said when she joined Cam at the table some time later. "Sign it." She never asked if the drawing was for her; she just took it. After Cam had signed it Daisy sat with her eyes shut. Cam decided to order two more plates of the miniature crab cakes with caramelized onion, even though it was Daisy's treat. She beckoned the waiter over. She felt Daisy had put things in her hands.

They would talk on the phone, they would make lists in his kitchen, but this was the only evening she and Daisy ever spent together, socially.

THE bookstore in the old schoolhouse was gone. Taped boxes filled the space where bookshelves and display tables had stood the week before.

This upset him but he pulled himself together. "Good thing I brought my own," he said. He had sent her back into the house to get it, the scuffed little *Les Symbolistes,* from the pile on his bed that she knew to leave when she pulled the covers up.

It was early afternoon, shadow just leaking from under the cars in the parking lot. A group of girls came up the school steps, laughing and talking on their phones, slapping the marble with their flip-flops. She recognized them; they were from her high school. At the top they wheeled and set off down the hall, one of them showing a roll of skin above her cutoffs. That one had been in her art class. Cam had liked her; she liked people her own size and bigger, liked to think of them standing in front of a mirror seeing if they could pinch the number of inches of belly that meant fat.

She leaned, as if a current from them had swept her. She couldn't tell if they had seen her. She was two years ahead of them, or at least of the one she knew from art class. Out in the world. Despite the C's on her transcript, she had finished her CNA at the community college in a year. Once she was certified it was easy to find a job with a home health agency. Probably just speaking English, Daisy said later, got her that job. For two months she had cut thick toenails and helped old men take showers. Not many agreed to it, half of those who did would not let her into the bathroom, and every so often one of them who did, sitting on the shower chair with water streaming off him and calling her "a big gal" or "a doll," would ask her for something she had to pretend not to understand. She changed their loose gray jockeys or pajama bottoms or long johns or reported on the fact that there was nothing to change them into, and sometimes, though as a home health aide she was not supposed to do what either a nurse or a housekeeping aide would do, opened the bathroom door on messes that would throw her schedule off for hours.

Then she saw the ad for Lawrence. She quit the agency the day after Daisy interviewed her. The salary was more than either her mother or her brother in the service made. To everything she said, Daisy's reply was, "Mmm, yes, so, mmhmm . . ." The next day Daisy called her on her cell while she was trying to talk her way into a huge old guy's apartment while he blocked the door with his belly—never mind finding soap in the cat-smelling dark behind him and getting somebody his size into a shower stall. Daisy said, "I think we can work this." As if it were a scheme between the two of them.

Nothing about mature or cultured. Cam hadn't even met the invalid. Why was his mother hiring her when he was a grown man, a college professor? Because his mother had the money. And he didn't want to interview anybody, so why should he? That was how Daisy saw it, and apparently Lawrence too.

"He's just like me," Daisy said. "He was."

IF he is in the bathroom Cam doesn't go into the hall because she doesn't want him to think she is listening. If there is cleaning up to do, she does it later. Sharon told her she would need to get in there, and showed her the 409 under the sink, stored in small jars because the jug is too heavy for him to lift. The time is not far off when she will have to rinse him off, bathe him. Touch the knobs of spine she can see under his shirt.

This was part of the routine for the other nurses. Sharon made sure Cam was informed about his "endowment," as she called it. But with Cam, for some reason, he is back to shutting the door. He even locks it. It's an old door, with a sticking lock. He doesn't realize that with his hands the way they are he could get shut in there. Things like that happen. People get trapped. In her week of training at the agency they learned how to take a door off the hinges. She has already made sure the hinges aren't painted over.

Daisy put in a big open shower with bars, but he has to seat himself on the chair, and Cam can hear him stumble and knock it against the tile or knock it all the way over and have to take his time scraping it into position.

In the garage, draped in a tablecloth, sits a wheelchair more expensive than a car, that Daisy will have to sell on eBay unused. In a crowded hall rented for the memorial—who are all these men and women Cam has never seen, saying they have lost him?— Daisy will say, "There's that face," and having never touched Cam before, close in on her with a hug that knocks the breath out of her. And there, the blonde wife, with a husband trailing after her, and there a tall sullen boy of about eight, with no crease between his eyebrows but unmistakably thin and careful and watchful, there at last the son.

ALL at once the tiny birds burst out of the hedge like spray out of a nozzle. His eyes widen, meet hers. Clearly he saw it, whatever he says about his vision. No one but the two of them saw it, she feels sure. "Ah," he says. She waits; always he has to put words to what goes on. He begins. "Once, anything could fly." Is he more cautious than usual? "Of old, that is, anything could be depicted with wings. Even snakes. The Egyptians, the Phoenicians, the Judeans . . ." He pauses, looks into his cold coffee.

The girls from her high school come by, going the other way. This time they all give a wrist-wave—so they did see her before, and identified her and talked about her.

The one she knows says, "How's it going?"

"Good. What's up at school?" Then she remembers they must have just graduated.

"Good," they sing out, and give the wave again.

Lawrence sits up straighter while this goes on, because girls are near, but he doesn't really notice them. He has no idea Cam knows anyone, anywhere, except him. He is concentrating. "One and all, they esteemed a winged cobra," he goes on. "And the winged snake, remember, in . . . in . . ."

Cam says, "Yeah, that guy."

"In Herodotus." He smiles. Then she can tell by the way he chews on his lip and says, "He saw the wing-bones," that he is tired and they will have to get going. Waiting for him to let her take part of his weight so he can stand up will take a while. Half the time in public he leaves the walker collapsed. Sometimes even walking he'll carry it for as long as he can and then have her carry it.

Wait. He is not quite ready to stand. "Last night I was at a party having one of those conversations where you're buried up to your neck and people are going to step on your head." She knows he means a dream; he wasn't at a party; he was in his study looking out the black window and she was in the living room watching TV.

He recites in French. She stretches, gives up on holding her face in what her grandmother says a woman should never part with, a pleasant expression. A willing expression, as if French matters. "*Biting the warm earth where the lilacs grow*," he says, just barely lifting all ten fingers.

"That would be you-know-who," she answers. Then she's sorry because the tone of exasperation that normally pleases him has caught him off guard.

After a while he says, "I'll show you something." He has made a decision. "Let's see the book. The book, the book."

"Sorry." She gets it out of her bag and gives it to him. The way he takes it, carefully in one hand, makes her think of her mother handing the missal across her to her father at Mass. Her father parted the halves of his coat, felt his chest as he always did, and sank onto the kneeler. Was he taking the right medications? A weight of shame for all of them in her family settles on her. When he sat in his chair at home, did she, Cam, bring him anything? She bows her head. She says to Lawrence, "I don't think my father had any books."

"Never mind." The flashlight look. "As Molière tells us, reading goes ill with the married state."

"The married state." He likes it when she simply repeats his words.

"See this?"

She shrugs; it's in French.

"'With his times,'" he reads to her, bending close to the page and following his finger, "'the poet should not involve himself.' Da da da . . . here it is: 'he should work mysteriously with regard to later or never.'" He holds up his hands and spreads them triumphantly. "Ah! With regard to later or never."

She shrugs again, to hide the yawn.

"That's not what I want you to see." He is feeling among the pages with his stalled fingers. Finally he comes to an illustration, covered with a sheet of onionskin. "Here we have," he says, beginning to smooth the cover sheet like somebody stroking a kitten. Finally he lifts it by a corner. "Here we have. Ah."

She studies the painting of a man. It must be a painting, though it is in black and white.

"There. Manet. Manet painted him. Everyone painted him. Sadness incarnate. You see?"

She nods.

"Having a salon of *Symbolistes* did not protect him. He was a bourgeois like everybody else. He lost his little son Anatole. This picture," he adds, "was painted before that happened."

To him, that was logical. She could understand that. She understood everything he said. The order in which things happened might be nothing, when you thought about it. Your life was there, like your fingerprint, inescapable. Why not? Each year filling with what belonged to it and to you, and flushing away what was going to turn out not to be yours. A disease could seem to come out of nowhere. A job, a person. Not out of nowhere. Yours. It was all lined up like the school buses. Rose of Lima had foreseen the day of her own death.

He closed the book and leaned over to put it in her bag, resting his forehead on the table as he did it and for a second or two after. That was a first.

He prepared to stand up. They looked at each other in their shared life. Everything was familiar. It was all coming to pass as if they were reliving it, what they would do now or later or never.

Two years later she would be a wife, her husband not someone she met after Lawrence had died but a man she had known since grade school. A friend of her brother's, a friend of Ray Malala's. She would go on drawing but nothing would come of it. She would never, with all her children, be as married as this.

Street of Dreams

○　○　○

THE children knew how to be quiet. They knew how to make
sure the blinds were closed and the shades down, or to play in
hallways where there were no windows; they knew to flush the
toilet once a day, while the recycling truck was grinding or someone ran a lawnmower next door. They knew how to cram sleeping bags into the three computer boxes and tape them and shove
them into a closet while their father went to the door. He picked
up a clipboard and put a pen behind his ear before the real estate
agent got the lockbox open.

He was a real estate agent himself and knew how to put the
other agent at ease, how to call the children in, introduce them,
send them to play in another room — "They have stuff with them.
I like to bring them along when I'm doing this" — indicating his
clipboard, while in the other room they would be grabbing a sock
or a Kleenex and stuffing it into their pockets. He would explain
the balloons tied to the FOR SALE sign: "Yesterday we thought we
had a buyer." Balloons would allow for some coming and going,
some glimpses of children. Sometimes an agent saw the balloons
and just passed by, like a soldier of Herod.

If an agent came alone, their father would say, "We'll get out of
your way. No, really, I can come back any time and finish up." If
a client came too he'd say, "Isn't this great?" The houses were not
the best by any means. Usually they were on the edge of town,

in an area where yards lost their fences and flowerbeds, sidewalks disappeared, and cars parked in ruts. "Great little place!" he would say, and this would be a clue to the other agent, if she was on the ball, to say, "Well, it's our lucky day! It's still on the market."

They would drive around, eat at Taco Bell, go back in a couple of hours for the boxes. From there they would go straight to a different house.

Sometimes, in houses with electric ranges and power, they cooked. Gas was usually off. They never used the oven, because a hot oven door was a giveaway. They didn't fry because of the smell. They boiled. You could boil potatoes, along with eggs for your next meal, and mash up the eggshell and bury it under pine needles. Every once in a while, they boiled chicken thighs, but the smell was strong and they were left with bones. Carrots you could eat without peeling them, and bananas and apples, putting peels and cores into a ziplock bag. You had to be sure it wasn't full enough to pop, inside the computer box.

Their father always remembered to take the bag to their school and drop it in the Dumpster. He was very neat, careful, and patient. He was the opposite of their mother.

While they were in school he did the laundry at the apartment of their mother's friend Melissa, who was at work. He had the key Melissa had given their mother, long ago when their mother was well, with friends and a job. At the beginning of this period, while their father was going to the hospital every day, before he knew their mother would not be getting out, they had let themselves into Melissa's apartment while she was on vacation and stayed for two weeks.

They knew not to tell their mother anything about that, or the yard sale. Everything left from it was in a U-Store, an aluminum room they could have lived in except that it had no windows or bathroom. Mandy knew you had to pay rent or someone would pile the furniture outside in the rain. But if that happened their father had a plan. He could put everything under a tarp on the cement slab beside his friend Gary's trailer. They could even prop the tarp and live under it. "You're as crazy as she is," Gary said. The slab was a foundation for a house, but it was old now and had a big crack where Mandy and Cody stuck their hands, pretending it led down into the center of the earth.

Their father needed to sell a house and he had not sold one in a long time. He had the hours they were in school and that was all, because he wouldn't leave them alone even though Mandy was eight and had skipped a grade. She was in fourth grade. Cody was six, in first grade.

Child Protective Services caught up with them but it took the agency six months. It had them on the books already because of things neighbors had said about their mother.

The last house they stayed in, out in the country at the edge of a pine forest being cleared, was on the Street of Dreams. There was no street yet, but five houses were already furnished for the coming tours, each with its own grounds landscaped to match it. There was a castle with a moat and a black and white timbered house with a hedge cut into animal shapes. At night Cody was afraid of the dark because the streetlights weren't installed, but their father moved the three sleeping bags close together and gave him a flashlight of his own.

They were not in the beds but in the laundry room of the biggest house Mandy had ever seen. The front door had a huge brass knocker that would echo out over the pine stumps the day Child Protective Services arrived, and gold-edged ribbons sealing the six toilet seats. The table was set with platters instead of plates, and glasses as big as pitchers, and thick, tasseled napkins. The couches and chairs were huge and heavy on the deep carpet, and nothing creaked or rattled or made any sound at all, as if, before their father with his smile of promise turned the key, giants had lived as secretly as they were living in the house.

Who Is He
That Will Harm You?

∘ ∘ ∘

"I HEARD what you said to your girlfriend."

"Why do you say that, 'girlfriend'?" She looked up, stretched out on the couch with the Sunday paper, into his frown. "I mean, I don't say *girl*friends. A friend's a friend, right?"

"I heard what you said. You said what you'd put in an ad."

"What?"

"What you'd *advertise.* You were on the phone."

"I'm not following. So now—*what?*"

"You said, 'Slim with big breasts and fat toes.'"

"Oh my God. We were talking about our bodies. Jeez."

"I heard."

She put the newspaper over her face. "It was Teresa from school. Saying what she would put in one of those ads in *The Stranger.*"

"What about you? Did you put an ad in?"

"Yeah, right. I totally did. I'm looking for a guy with a—"

Something happened. When she opened her eyes she was lying on her back with things on her. Papers. She was under a low roof. Half under. Table. Couch. Glass thing dangling. Lamp. She funneled through time, and found her name. She was Mary

Ann. Her head hurt. Down the room a blurred man stood with his legs apart.

Earthquake? She lay there in the prickling of details that weren't really thought. Her mind was joined to her body in a combination of exhaustion and alertness. She couldn't tell if there was silence or she was deaf. At length she heard her own voice produce the sound, if not the words, of a question. No answer. Her mind tried to sleep, but she kept her eyes open, thinking with a slowness like moving in a bath.

Dennis. She knew him. Dennis.

Her tongue was sore. Seizure. But pain . . . her head . . . huge . . . a word for it . . .

She was in medical school. There.

Dennis. Not helping her. She let her breath out. "You."

"I what?"

"Hurt," she said, drawing up her knees. She could move. She could produce words, she was seeing double but she had her speech centers. "You." She raised a finger off the floorboard. Where was the other hand? On an arm twisted back along her head. "You. Get. Out."

At that he took one broad step, grabbed the lamp and hurled it. The cord whipped after it and somewhere glass shattered. She rolled her eyes up, seeing the underside of his jaw and thinking— and at the same time noticing that she was thinking—strategically. She had her second realization, and with it a knowledge of what the word *realization* meant. He was panting. It might not be over.

There on a level with her were his feet. In socks, if he kicked. "Oh God," she said. Her voice surprised her, a normal groan as if she were telling him how much reading she had to do.

"Oh God," he responded, but he had backed away, he had sat down. That was good. Not on the couch, on the rocking chair, and he was rocking it, of all things, so hard it ground on the wood. If she shut one eye she could get two flushed, small, handsome faces condensed into one.

How long was she out? She was starting to give a history. She had speech, she was speaking reasonably, and the person listening in the ER would be somebody she knew. A nurse would be best.

The phone rang, with a muted sound. "There's your call, there's Mom," Dennis said in a mincing voice, or was that her imagination? Did she have her imagination?

Her finger kept softly touching the leg of the coffee table. I hit a table. Marble, from Goodwill. Iceberg. We call it the iceberg. So she had her mind. The brain works to repair itself, just like blood, which wants to clot. It doesn't want out into hair.

"Is there more to this?" the nurse would say, or maybe just, "OK, cut the crap. What happened?"

He did it.

She started over. Maybe he hit me with a lamp. I don't know. I don't remember. I don't remember getting up this morning. What day is it? What time is it?

What a comfort it would be, if a nurse were to say, "Three o'clock." The day would be half over. They would have figured everything out.

Why was there no question of tears?

She turned her head and vomited, an act requiring no effort on her part. The phone was ringing again. So, Sunday. Her mother called on Sunday.

How was she going to get to the ER?

Now she saw in his face something she had not learned about in her years of learning everything rapidly and well. But she detached herself from the sight and went limp as he shoved the iceberg, toppling her books, and dropped to the floor half beside and half on top of her, tearing newspaper out from between them. I wonder if I'll beg, she thought. No, this was something else. He had started to cry. He sobbed, banging the floor with his fist. Would someone come? "Don't you know you can't talk like that? Big tits and fat toes? Don't you know that?" She could barely hear him. He weighed her down, her head pounded. I think maybe he killed me, she told the nurse.

AFTER a couple of years she never referred to it. People did not encourage that, as anyone back from an illness or a travel ordeal, her father said, or even from travel without an ordeal, will tell you. He was explaining not to Mary Ann but to her mother, to soothe her mother and give her some rest from talking.

People who had known Mary Ann when she was in medical school knew of the episode; that's what they called it, as she did herself. What else to call it? She had not been murdered.

WHEN they moved her out of the ICU she had her own window. Across the street stood a big tree where there was a bird the size of a goose or an owl, even bigger, too heavy for the limb it sat on. No, no, not a bird, merely leaves, the giant leaves of the tulip poplar: her mother brought one up to her room to prove it. There was no bird as big as the shape she was seeing. But a bulky green bird with a half-open beak sat there day after day, neck craned to peer into her room. The nurse she liked fixed her pillows and said to her mother, "Must've escaped from the zoo."

"I'm sorry!" her mother said, almost in tears with the leaf in her hand.

"I don't care," Mary Ann said. "Let it sit there."

"Oh, it's worrying you," her mother said. "It's making you uneasy."

"No."

HER friends put all his things in two boxes to be picked up. They glanced through a scrapbook Teresa found wrapped in a lab coat at the back of a drawer. Drawings, dozens of clippings about random subjects, photos of Mary Ann cut up and pasted into collages. His name, Dennis Vose, written hundreds of times. Somebody came to collect the boxes. Her parents were in touch with his lawyer—he had a lawyer!—and through the lawyer he had turned over the key to her apartment. He could have given somebody else a copy, her mother said. "One of his henchmen?" her father said from the big hospital chair. They were both professors but her mother had taken an indefinite leave of absence from the English Department. Her pacing, her bringing up things from books, her fury of analysis, always broken at its height by tears, did not bother Mary Ann as much as it bothered her father, who sat with his hand over his eyes beside Mary Ann's bed with its rails and gears.

FROM the bathroom of the new apartment she could hear Teresa on the kitchen phone. "Yeah. Yeah. Yeah. But . . . Yeah, but how do we convey to her . . ."

Teresa was staying with her until her mother could get there. She had passed her Activities of Daily Living—they wouldn't discharge you until you had mastered those—but she was going to have to have somebody for a while anyway. That was fine, but she was not going to leave Seattle and go to Portland to be with her parents. Nothing and nobody was going to make her leave her physical therapist, Nolan. On her last day in inpatient rehab, the PTs clapped while she was having the tantrum about Nolan. People with some aphasia, they told her—"some" was what everybody said she had, and it would resolve, most or all of it—would almost always find they could curse.

Nolan had to call her mother to explain that some patients developed a dependency on a particular therapist. He said that as an outpatient Mary Ann would ordinarily have somebody new but he would go on working with her himself as long as she wanted.

"You're a lucky girl," the nurses had told her when she was first sitting up and listening to what was said to her. "Medical students get the royal treatment." "Pretty ones. No kidding, they have a special saw they use on them." "Don't listen to her. Seriously, you should have seen these guys taking care of you."

Every resident who came in went over the whole thing with her. The nurses' account was shorter and had blood and mess in it. From when she arrived in the ER still pretty much herself and talking, downhill fast. Intracranial pressure. When that went high enough a team came in and sawed into the skull and lifted a section of it off, to be frozen and put back on later. In a case like hers, where the piece of bone turned out not to be sterile, they used plastic. A piece of plastic, said one resident, as expensive as a car. A used car, Nolan said when she got to him. He made her half dozen procedures sound like a science project she herself had undertaken, well done but not all that complicated.

Bone or plastic, the piece was held in place with snowflakes.

Snowflakes. The snowflake, the surgeons explained in their careful, tiring way, was a little half-inch plate that fixed the piece back into the skull with screws. The plates got their name from the spokes sticking out from them, into which tiny screws were sunk. "Think of a dance floor in your skull," Nolan said, "outlined with spangles."

Teresa said Mary Ann would be playing tennis again soon, and they would be running their morning miles, but Nolan made no mention of that. Nolan never spoke of a possible improvement until it got close. *Milestone* was a not word he used. But Mary Ann was getting around, growing her hair, starting to read. Doorknobs and shoelaces gave her trouble, and forks, and stepping out of reach of the hug Teresa wanted to give her first thing in the morning when she wandered into the kitchen in her bathrobe.

"You know, your sweet little fat guy Nolan says we can go ahead and talk about anything that comes up," Teresa said, pouring her coffee and Mary Ann's milk. Mary Ann no longer liked the taste of coffee.

"Why are you looking at me?"

"I'm just looking at you. You're looking at me too, babe."

"Am I different?"

"Well, you've had a little work done. A little makeover."

Mary Ann didn't laugh because a laugh had to be assembled from scratch. Once she had laughed at everything. They all said so. You could tell where Mary Ann was sitting in a lecture hall. "I don't mean looks," she said to Teresa.

"Neither do I," Teresa said.

"MARY ANN, he yanked you by the arm, hard. I saw him. And then the time you were dancing at the sink. He spun you around. You snapped your fingers. You thought he was doing some flamenco thing. You thought he was going to dance with you."

"I did," said Mary Ann, not making it a question.

"He pushed you. He was furious. I know this. *You told me.* He said, 'People can see in.'"

"They could, too," Mary Ann said. The big windows of the apartment where she had lived eight months before came back to her clearly, with plants on the sills. Were these plants she had now the same ones?

"You talked about getting a cat." Teresa seemed to have a drill, a list she worked from, of things that were normal and things that were not normal. Mary Ann saw that the list was scrambled but could not be sure where Teresa came down on some of the items. "He kept going to see his family in Canada. You liked the same music. Music was a big thing to him. You knew him three months. He said he was studying for the GREs. You didn't say you had lived with guys before. He is, I admit, an incredibly good-looking guy. You told your mom, 'He's the best-looking man I ever saw.' You told your mom everything."

"I did."

In his backpack he had kept a pill container, and when she clicked open the compartments for the days, they were all empty. She didn't know which of Teresa's lists this would go on. Sometimes a thing that seemed in his favor, such as the fact that he had cried and played "Come As You Are" all day the day they heard Kurt Cobain was dead, was on the wrong list.

Teresa picked her up from PT so often she was getting to know Nolan. "That Nolan," Teresa said. "He used to be a wild child, know that?"

"What do you mean?"

"He went here as an undergrad and then he trained here. Said he used to live down at the Blue Moon."

Mary Ann didn't ask what the Blue Moon was.

"He was a drummer of all things! He drummed with some band."

How did Teresa know that?

"What a little sweetie," Teresa said.

SMELLS. Detergent, for instance. That smell contained the time she said, "Jesus you waste a lot of electricity." Dennis worked out every day in the fitness room in their building, and after he showered he put in a wash. He didn't mix his laundry with hers but went down to the basement machines by himself and came back with a small, folded pile. When she said that, he stood there with his back to her, holding the laundry against his chest. She put her arms around him from the back and she could feel the heartbeat shaking his body. Gradually it slowed down.

"How come you don't criticize me? How come you don't get mad?" she said. "Like when I swear. I know it bothers you."

"You know it but you do it," he said without turning around. "Is that the idea?"

AFTER a year her mother was the only one who talked about it. Only her mother craved an exact tally of what had been altered or erased, and searched for it in photograph albums, in Mary Ann's old transcripts and letters of acceptance.

He had pleaded guilty. Something was wrong with him so he was in a private institution. Where? It didn't matter where. Wherever it was, he could not get out. Her mother assured her of this until her father said, "Gail, that's not something Mary's worried about."

She didn't worry. Even later, when her mother was in bed dying, Mary Ann was not worrying. Her worry centers were gone, Nolan said. He wished his were.

"You need snowflakes," she told him.

FOR a while her friends would remind her of things, explain things, question and prompt her. Reason with her. They liked to tell her stories of herself, how she had drunk beer half the night and aced the anatomy exam, how when they got their grades she had climbed onto the iceberg and danced.

After a while she saw less of them because more than a year had gone by and they were in their clinical rotations. "It breaks my heart," her mother said. "Where are they? Where's Teresa?"

"She's at her apartment," Mary Ann replied. She was the logical one now.

"The only person you see anything of is Nolan."

"I see the doctor. The OT. I see those people downstairs. I see you and Dad."

"I wonder if Nolan knows who you really are," her mother said in her new voice of thin argument.

Mary Ann didn't argue any more, with her mother or anyone else, the energy for it having left her. It was to Nolan, now, that she told everything.

"She means who *she* thinks you are," Nolan said. "She can't help it." Nolan understood everybody. He had to. Once the doctors were finished, he took over. In serious rehab, with the Hoyer lifts and the parallel bars, you saw it all. "We get the guy who makes the winning touchdown at three o'clock, and at six he gets hit by a bus. Whoever thinks they're somebody, they're right. Some body." Nolan didn't interfere with their pride, but he didn't throw compliments around either, just eased gradually into his system: moving the limb in question or getting squared away with the non-limb. Not looking back. Not forward either, any distance into what might or might not be achieved. Just right in front of you.

They were not allowed to skip a session but they could feel free to yell at the top of their lungs; they could curse, weep, soil themselves for spite. Nolan said it was a pity the doctors didn't get to see what some of these patients had in them, the pain they volunteered for, the feats they were capable of.

Mary Ann saw the doctors step inside the gym in their hard shoes to make suggestions. When Nolan was the one who knew. There was mind and there was body, and on the washed-out road between them, he waited for her every day. At their wedding he said, "I know two things: what bad luck is, and what good luck is."

SHE held her baby, touched his ear. Tory. Sometimes her love for him sent a shudder through her so strong it woke him up if she was holding him. All things fell to one side or the other of a line like a tennis net: safe or unsafe.

"Your mother was just the same, when you were a little one," her father said. For her mother had died.

Now whenever she read about a man who had run over his girlfriend or gone after his wife and kids with a shotgun, she checked the name, she read to the end, she turned on the news. This was a few years before you could track people down on a computer. It couldn't be him, though; he was in a hospital, probably in Canada. He was Canadian.

"He put that accent on," her father said on one of his visits, with a deep sigh. "He wasn't Canadian." She saw that her father, and if her father, then others as well, had information she did not have. "Dennis Vose . . ." her father began.

"It's snowing!" she said from the window.

"It's not going to stick." For a minute she was in two lives, so clearly did she hear her mother say that. The wet snow trickled down the pane and she had the unwelcome thought of her mother as she had been long ago, when she was still an English professor and had ideas about everything, including the weather, art, poems, the health of children, what to wear, what made people believe in a God, and how her friends wished they had a child like Mary Ann, whom she had decided on first looking into her eyes, burning with infant wisdom, would be named after George Eliot.

"Not for the looks," her father would always add.

The baby woke up crying. He gave her a wild look, and when she picked him up he shivered as if she had found him lying out in the snow instead of in his crib. Already, after so few months of life, it seemed a baby could be visited by dreams. "I'll always, always come," she told him.

WHEN he was old enough, they told him she had hurt her head and there was a plate in it for protection. With fingers infinitely gentle, he liked to tap and rub her scalp, exploring for the snow-flakes. Of course he didn't know what had happened to require them. She didn't want her son to think of such a thing, her warm-hearted, dreamy little boy with his spontaneous songs. Nothing prepared you for motherhood, for the tide that knocked what was left of any other life right off the shelf, while you waded around it and sloshed it out of your way, with your child held close, held above it, above all things.

"I was a drummer," Nolan said. "That meant you had to drink like crazy but not lose the beat. For me it was one or the other, so I went back to school." He was talking to her father, who had perked up as he always did when Nolan was around. They had driven down from Seattle to give him some exercises for his arthritis. He liked talking to Nolan, sitting at the breakfast table with Tory on his lap. "I had a physiology professor tell me why not forget the whole thing, join the navy," Nolan said.

"What? What?" her father said in an old man's loud voice that made Tory turn to look up at his face. "You could have taught *him* something."

"Hope I won't have to," Nolan said.

She had a different handwriting. Strong smells gave her a headache. She no longer had any blue clothes. She prayed. Not to God. But when she was waiting for her son at the door of the preschool she prayed steadily. Not because she was anxious. "Don't worry," the aides were always saying. She was not worried, she was praying him back to her. While the other mothers talked by their cars, when the high syllables of the last song rang out behind the shut door, the prayer intensified until it was answered.

She and Tory, whose shots were behind him, were watching the clinic fish steer in and out of a pearly castle when suddenly the woman who had come out of one of the doors behind the receptionist turned into Teresa. She was heavy, with blonde hair instead of brown, and a stethoscope around her neck. She looked up. "Oh my God," she said, steadying herself with a hand on the receptionist's shoulder. "Mary Ann!" She ran out into the waiting room and hugged Mary Ann as if she had been searching everywhere for her.

"And this, this beautiful child is yours? Your little boy?" said

Teresa, squatting down in front of Tory with her hands out in a way that said to Mary Ann that she might clutch him.

"He's shy," Mary Ann said.

"I'm not shy," he said.

"Oh my God. Mary Ann! Come into the back, come into my office so we can talk. I don't have a patient right now. Are you waiting—who are you waiting to see?"

"Dr. Cooley. We saw her. We're just waiting for a prescription."

"I'll tell her I've stolen you. Oh, this is unbelievable. I'm just here on a locum, I don't even work here. Oh my God. How many years is it? And how old are you, little buddy? I bet you're . . . five."

"I'm five," he said.

Mary Ann couldn't pin down when Teresa must have graduated and gone away, so she said, "I haven't seen you in a long time."

"Nine years? Ten? Is he your only one?"

As if there could be another. As if this love could be repeated. Mary Ann nodded.

"I have three," said Teresa as if to apologize. "I married Alex."

"Alex . . ."

"You remember Alex."

"Oh, yeah. Yeah, I do, I think."

"We went to Chicago for our residencies and then he did a fellowship year," said Teresa, leading the way into an examining room, "and then we lived in Chicago again so I sort of don't know what happened to anybody. Sit right up on that stool, sweetie." Tory had already climbed up and sat swinging his legs. "Mary Ann, Mary Ann. So. How are you?"

"I'm fine."

"So-o . . . tell me."

"Tell you?"

"All about you."

"Oh, OK. Well, remember Nolan?"

"Of course I remember *Nolan*."

"We got married."

"You got married." Teresa did the thing with her hands again that made Mary Ann think she might be going to grab her. "And had this beautiful child."

"I didn't get pregnant for a long time, but then I did."

"Yes, you did. I can't believe this. I can't believe I'm seeing you. And your son!"

"We live here," Mary Ann explained, to settle her down. "Nolan's at the same place. The hospital."

"Where's my Spiderman?" Tory whispered to her.

"Everybody just scattered!" Teresa went on. "We just came back and I've hardly seen anybody from the old days. Well anyhow, I'm a pediatrician. Can you believe it? Who would have thought? Did you think I'd be an old married lady in Peds? Remember when I was going to put an ad in *The Stranger*?"

"Here he is," said Mary Ann, handing Tory Spiderman from her purse.

"That's all I thought about in those days. I know I went out a lot but I didn't have the boyfriends, like you did." Teresa smacked herself on the forehead. "Did I really say that?"

"What, about boyfriends? I guess so, I guess I did. My mom kept pictures of me with some of them."

"Your mom! How is she?"

"She died."

"Oh, I'm so sorry. I'm sorry to hear that. Was she ill?"

"She just . . . got worse and worse." A vague shame came over Mary Ann. She didn't know what her mother had actually died of. Her heart bent in on itself: her mother had never seen Tory.

"What a shame," said Teresa. "Things were hard for her. Did she live to know about Dennis?"

"About Dennis?"

"That he died?"

"Dennis? He died?"

"Oh dear. He did. He died quite a while ago."

"Did he get out? What happened to him?" She saw Dennis walking out the door of the institution and being hit by a bus.

"Oh dear," Teresa said again.

"It's all right," Mary Ann assured her.

"Well, I'll be in trouble with somebody for this. He jumped off a roof." Teresa said this in a whisper. She made a steeple of her hands and turned to Tory. "But, this wonderful boy! And—Nolan! Why don't you run in here after your appointment so we can really catch up."

"We already had our appointment. Why did he?"

"Good lord." Teresa sat down. "What do you know about Dennis?"

"I don't know, I guess nothing."

"He was in and out of those places for years. I have a little patient like that right now that I'm referring to the Vose Center." Teresa took some glasses out of her lab coat pocket and put them on to look at Mary Ann. "You know about the center? For when the whole thing starts in childhood. No? I've had to be in touch with them a couple of times. The Vose family." For the name she put on a little accent. "A big deal. Oh, Mary Ann." Teresa got up and threw her arms around Mary Ann and hugged her as if she would never see her again. "Oh, I hope I haven't made things harder."

"Things aren't hard," Mary Ann said when she got loose.

All this she explained to Nolan on the phone, after she took Tory to school. She was trying to get used to the all-day kindergarten. She told Nolan what had happened to Dennis Vose. There was a silence and then Nolan said, "I have to say that I knew that."

"You didn't tell me."

"I didn't. I'm sorry," he said. "Do you think that was the same thing as a lie?"

"No," she said. He tried to tell the truth but he couldn't always do it. You couldn't if somebody asked you at work, for instance, if their scars made them ugly.

A SHORT fat woman in an orange smock answered the door, eating a candy bar out of the wrapper.

"Carolyn," a voice called from deep inside. "Will you see if

that's our visitor? Use the viewer." But the woman had already
said "Come in."

Mary Ann stood still. There, past the French doors opening
onto a long room with urns of flowers on stands, was the marble
table. The iceberg. With the rest of what was in the room in pink
and white and gold, it became a piece of whatever that kind of
furniture was called.

Not from Goodwill. From this house.

"Am I speaking to Mary Ann Kemp? This is Mrs. Vose." This
voice, a flat voice with pauses and little slurps as if the person were
eating, was asking her to visit the Voses in their home. Where did
they live? In The Dales. North of the city on the Sound.

They wanted her to come that same day. "I can't get out there
unless there's a bus," Mary Ann said to the voice. "I just drive
around here. Just in the area."

"We'll send a car," said Mrs. Vose.

She called Nolan again and he said she should go if she wanted
to. He had heard of The Dales. He didn't think she needed to
have him with her. He would pick Tory up from kindergarten
and take him back to work with him, where he could have a good
time on the rings in the gym.

"But I always pick him up," Mary Ann said. "I'm always
there."

"Just today," Nolan said. "Let these people say they're sorry."

"Sorry?"

"Sorry they didn't tell you. Sorry they didn't give you a heads-
up back then that their son was from someplace else all right but
it sure wasn't Canada."

So she called back. The car Mrs. Vose sent was a pickup truck,
driven by an old man. He said he was coming off his shift at
the gatehouse. After he said he did some driving for the Voses
because they didn't get out in a car much since the stroke, he
was content to drive without having a conversation with her. By
way of the freeway, The Dales wasn't that far after all. The man
smoked with the window open, and at the end of one cigarette

he slowed at a gatehouse and saluted the face in it, and then after some hills and circling around they turned into a driveway.

"Thank you very much," Mary Ann said, but she couldn't remember his name.

He didn't get out of the truck. "I live down the road," he said, gesturing at some woods in the distance. "Four o'clock, I'll be back." She wondered if she should have had money to give him.

"This is Carolyn, our daughter-in-law. Dennis's wife. Come with us, Carolyn," Mrs. Vose said. She was old and walked with an aluminum cane. She lifted it and for a minute Mary Ann thought she was going to give Carolyn's legs a tap with it to get her going. Carolyn had finished her candy bar and Mrs. Vose took the wrapper from her and put it in the pocket of her dress.

Mary Ann got the smell of a cat. Not strong, but there. She liked cats and looked around for one. She and Carolyn sat on the couch, the Voses in wing chairs covered in pale green stripes and roses. Mr. Vose was a heavy man who wheezed when he moved, sucking in the flushed rounds of his cheeks. Another old woman came very slowly and sideways into the room. She set down a big tray of tea things on the iceberg, and they didn't introduce her so Mary Ann saw that she was the maid.

The mother, who had a small, childish, lined face, a perfectly shaped face Mary Ann had seen before, poured unsteadily from the big teapot, and right away she said, while she was stirring, "We're told Dennis was happy when he was with you."

For just a minute her heart had gone out to Mrs. Vose because she had trouble with her speech and had to keep wiping her mouth with a handkerchief. When she said this about happiness the father glanced at Carolyn.

Mary Ann said, "I don't know." You didn't have happiness or unhappiness as a memory. You had specific things like your face in the steam and suddenly behind you in the mirror another face. A certain kind of music being on all the time. "I don't know," she said again. She had something she was going to say, though. "In your twenties"—here she was quoting her mother—"you're having fun, you aren't ready, you aren't ready for . . ." For what?

"Dennis was not in his twenties. He was thirty-five years old at the time," his mother said.

"Thirty-five," Mary Ann said. A year older than she was now, the boy crying in front of the TV because Kurt Cobain was dead.

"This is a picture of his wedding," Mrs. Vose said, taking a photograph out of her pocket along with the candy wrapper, which she shook off her fingers onto the rug. "He married Carolyn while they were there." Carolyn did not seem to have to be included in the talk. In the picture a fattish couple stood in front of a cake, smiling—Mary Ann would have said idiotically, but she knew, now, never to use such a word.

"He always wanted marriage and a family," his mother said. "From an early age. That was all he wanted in life."

"Well, Dorothy, we knew that was unlikely," said the father.

In Mrs. Vose's way of speaking, halting but irritable, Mary Ann began to feel some threat, as if some crude or ugly word might come up the middle of what she was saying. Carolyn seemed to be dozing rather than listening, except occasionally her head would snap up and she would look at the father with a dog's mild anxiety.

Coming up the freeway beside the man in the truck, Mary Ann had decided to tell the Voses that she had loved their son. Now she saw that the word *love* could not be trusted on all occasions. And in reality, she loved only her own son. Oh, she loved Nolan, or liked him more than anyone else. But her son . . . her little boy: for him, for him, something had been turned on and even after it filled her it never stopped, there was always room for more of it. So she was not after all going to use the word about anybody else.

"Actually, the center has been around since the twenties," Mr. Vose said. His bleary, helpless gaze seemed not to match his words. He seemed to want her to know something. Was it that they were sorry? "Later we came in with some backing in Dennis's memory and they renamed it."

"That was where Dennis lived?"

"From time to time, in the early years, yes, he did stay there."

"He developed schizophrenia," said the mother, training her eyes, wide in the rings of old skin, on Mary Ann.

The father wheezed even attempting something as simple as taking off his glasses and rubbing his eyes. "Usually that type of thing won't show up until the teens. But in his case it was a little earlier."

"He would never have hurt anybody. Something would have to provoke him," said Mrs. Vose, taking her cane and stamping it twice into the rug, which sent up dust. "Something."

"Dorothy," her husband said.

"You're alive," Mrs. Vose continued, to Mary Ann.

"Dorothy."

Another woman, not as old as Mrs. Vose and the maid, came to the door, took a look at Mrs. Vose and another at Carolyn, and went away.

"Somebody just told me," Mary Ann said. "About Dennis. I didn't know about that."

"About what?" said his mother.

"That he ended his life." Those were the words suggested by Nolan. "Teresa told me. My friend from medical school."

"Of course I know who told you," said Mrs. Vose, fussily swatting the air. "She called us to let us know, last week I believe it was."

"This morning," said Mr. Vose.

"I haven't seen her in a long time," said Mary Ann. "I'm not sure how long but I did see her today when I took my son to the doctor."

"You have a son."

"I do. I have a little boy, Tory. He's five."

Mrs. Vose was wiping her mouth. "Five," she said through the handkerchief.

SHE had learned to type with both hands, but she was typing with one finger, to keep an arm around Tory. Sometimes he hit the key for her. "V," she told him. "O." He loved the alphabet; he had known the letters since he was three. Not just to say them: he could read. He could use the computer.

There were pages on Dennis Vose, Sr., benefactor of the Vose Center, with his wife Dorothy Suttler Vose.

The Vose Center. The web page had a picture of a campus, and another of a smiling, attractive child. The child stood still among trees; the nurse behind him had on a white uniform. Nurses didn't wear white uniforms any more, they wore ugly print tops and white pants, or scrub suits. Mary Ann knew hospitals. In the cafeteria of the one where she had lived, she still met Nolan for lunch. She still ran into people in the halls who had known her at different times. When they spoke of those times they did so in certain ways, depending on which time it was they were recalling. She recognized the ways; they didn't mention the episode but they all knew more about a period in her own life than she did. They cared more. She had her snowflakes.

At any rate she knew people didn't wear what the nurse in the picture had on. They didn't wear what Dorothy Vose had had on that afternoon either, a navy blue dress from some dim time, with big, chipped buttons and a pocket where you put a picture of your son's wedding.

If they had invited her in order to say they were sorry, they had forgotten to do it. By the end of the hour Mrs. Vose had lost track of things, and seemed to think Mary Ann had come to bring them something. Several times she inquired as to how Mary Ann was going to get home. When the deep chimes of the doorbell sounded they all sat up straight in relief, except Carolyn, slumped against the cushions. "Her medication," Mr. Vose said softly to Mary Ann. He wheezed on the way to the door, where Mrs. Vose said, "Where is your coat?" and Mary Ann said, "I don't have one, it's summer," and Mrs. Vose said, "Oh, at this time of day my mind wanders so."

Mary Ann got into the truck. The man had the windows down to let the cigarette smoke out so she leaned her head out to call a good-bye. Mrs. Vose was ducking and twisting her shoulders, trying to keep her husband from guiding her back into the house. Because her mind wandered. If you lost your son you would search, you would have promised to, your mind would not rest.

IT was late and they sat in the kitchen listening to music while she told Nolan about the cane and the wedding picture and Carolyn. She told him about the iceberg. "But I doubt if they sit there," she said. "In that room. I bet they go someplace else in the house. Where the cat is."

They had the CD player turned low so as not to wake Tory. At the end of a hard day Nolan still put on Nirvana. At work he liked music on and when you were his patient he would play whatever you wanted, as loud or soft as you wanted. When she was in rehab, Mary Ann had not been able to choose. So Nolan said a select few of his people liked to do their PT to Nirvana, which did them good and did him good. Because of the groan. Any song by Nirvana had the groan, he said. The howl. "Things are far gone, but yet a song is being sung about them," he said. "And not only that, a little bird told me Nirvana is your favorite."

That made her jump. She saw the tree with the green bird. Things like that would happen to her then, even though she quickly knew he meant a person had told him and it was Teresa.

That was early in rehab, when she first knew him. Even then, he didn't say "*was* your favorite." He put on certain songs and waited to see whether she liked them. Not whether she remembered them. Whether she liked them. "Sort of," she said. "Sort of not."

"You know something about you? You don't pretend," he told her, his first praise.

She finished telling him everything and then they just sat there listening. After a while he said she wouldn't want to know how much beer he and his friends in PT school had put away to the tune of "Come As You Are." But you didn't have to like a song for it to take you back. Music she had once loved, he said, might make her want to go back to a time before he and she knew each other, let alone were married. She said no, it didn't do that.

Tory was on the stairs. "*Come S.U.R.*," he sang in his high voice.

"OK, man, come on down," Nolan said, and he came into the

kitchen in his Nemo pajamas and stood near Nolan's chair. He put a hand on the leg Nolan was keeping time with. Finally he said, "Why did the man jump off the roof?"

"Well, my guess," Nolan said, "would be it must have been Spiderman." He looked at Mary Ann to see if she thought that was a lie.

Search Party

○　○　○

THE sun comes up, low beds of cloud pull apart, the shapes on the ground turn into cows. Very quickly the sun is round and hot. One cow after another picks up a foot and puts it down, pushing up gold bubbles in the mud they have all been making where the dirt is bare of clover. Their red sides steam, they chew, they stand in a half-circle looking at Susannah.

AT the age of three, Susannah Floyd wandered out of her yard in a northern county of Virginia and tumbled down the embankment of the railroad track that passed a hundred yards from the house. She found she could not climb back up through the blackberry vines, and began to walk. Scratched and whimpering, she walked a mile and a half in the rail bed, and when the banks fell away and the track ran into the open she veered off across a cattle guard, under a gate and into a field of Herefords.

Hours later a search began, but no one came upon her in the bowl of three hills on the Bayliss place where she stopped. She sat down where the tractor had repeatedly dropped its back tire off a shelf of fieldstone into a groundhog hole, making a dirt hollow screened by clumps of burdock. There she remained to rock and cry and suck her scratched arms until she slept.

The next day was a Sunday, and the largest search party ever assembled in that part of the state fanned out to look for her: the rescue squad, the Eagle Scouts, all the members of the VFW who could hike, the Lions, state troopers, police from four towns, and neighbors on foot and horseback. Several churches sent their youth groups; a hermit widow who kept dogs and shot at hunters showed up with a bloodhound. This proof that the widow listened to the radio caused opinion to shift in her favor afterward, even though the bloodhound did not find Susannah. Emotion in the search party was at such a pitch—hands being wordlessly shaken and held and eyes locked across all boundaries of age and rank, among dogs wandering with slowly wagging tails—that from a distance it could have resembled the springing up of the Peaceable Kingdom, except for the people holding up cardboard signs saying NORTH & CASE'S WOODS and EAST TO DUMP.

It was midsummer, when the days were long. Most of the searchers headed in the wrong direction, down the long gravel drive from the house out to the road, or straight across the two big unmowed clover fields to the woods. A few took the railroad track but went toward town or did not go far enough the other way. All day in the heat, they were assembling in the Floyds' yard to compare routes while they drank jugs of tea the neighbors kept filled, and setting out and straggling back and going again.

The sun went down around nine, leaving fiery pink trails that painted the glasses and tear-streaks of people taking leave of those intending to search through until morning, and after that, the moths came out and a dozen flashlight beams went bowing across the Floyds' clover field into the woods. The night grew unusually cool.

In the early part of the day, when they started up again, there was fog and the clover heads were loaded with wet. They sopped the pant legs, people recalled, or if you had on shorts your bare legs were washed as if you had gone into a sluice. You could write on the pale, wet film on a leaf of burdock and leave a dark green word. By ten the fog had lifted, the fields steamed. Black shade under the locust trees in the fencerows pulled the cows in and closed over them, leaving the grass blank and bright.

That morning, Susannah's mother, who had been taken to

the hospital the night before, seven weeks early, gave birth to a miniature, flaccid girl, who was passed from hand to hand into the incubator, and given the name Mary Jo, to tie her, however briefly, to the life everyone was worried the mother too might try to leave behind.

The mother of two children dying or dead might do anything, especially a woman whose nerves might be excitable. It was not clear. The stories said yes and they said no: if she seemed a little off-center, she had not grown up there and no one could say what behavior in the present crisis would be in keeping with her nature, or just what her nature had been at all up to that time. Nobody had been taken into her confidence. If you went over with a pie, this woman gave you back the pie plate at church. She did not seem to bake. But Tom Floyd's attachment, by all reports, did not require pies and cakes. Everybody knew Tom, and this spoke something in her favor, that he had married late and married her. On the other hand he had met her in a lodge in the Smoky Mountains, at a dairymen's convention. She might have been a secretary for the association; she might have been working in the lodge, even as a maid. No family was heard of; she was alone. There might have been past difficulties of some kind. It was not clear.

As the sun climbed outside her hospital window and no news came, however, she did not throw herself out of bed to wrench the window open and jump the three floors. Women who were not searching were clustered around her bed holding her to life with murmurs and touches. They did not have to be on close terms with her to fall into talk of husbands and visitors and vegetable gardens. No one spoke of children.

Some of the time they were lingering before the wide glass on the same floor to look at the unfinished newborn, motionless except for the tiny rib cage flaring and closing like a bird's mouth. They studied the eyes of the masked nurse and the doctor coming and going all morning shaking his head. They were in agreement about the baby's hands, minute and dusky, with a poise everybody was accustomed to in animals on the verge of death.

Outside in the heat the pastures and roads of a five-mile-wide strip of the upper county were swarming with people, dogs, horses and inching cars, looking for Susannah.

It was July, so dry and hot the tomatoes were banded like pumpkins. The troopers agreed that it looked bad: two nights, one of them freakishly cool, the third hot day coming, the soil conservation map showing ponds curled in every basin and little creeks, though the heat had narrowed and slowed them, still running heartlessly everywhere. The railroad tracks themselves, with culverts, cinder rail beds strewn with glass, and bridges. Copperheads sunning. Yellow jackets in the fences. Old wells. Bulls, certain dairy bulls in particular. The rescue squad brought out ropes and a grappling hook.

Later that day, the Monday after her disappearance on Saturday, Susannah was found.

In later years the sisters often heard the story of how each of them escaped alive, to everyone's surprise, from the fate that had seemed to await her. For Jo the story's interest was soon worn out; she did not care for stories of birth, or fate, or what family one fell into. About herself she cared only for what came later, after the meager fingers the women were pitying in the incubator had flexed and taken hold.

Jo's friends in art school spoke in grim or offhand ways about their own families. Susannah heard them on her visit to Chicago, girls and women going on about themselves as nobody, man or woman, ever would at home. These women were not even really Jo's friends—Jo steered clear of women—but only her classmates, talking on the steps.

This was Susannah's first trip away from home, and she was examining the art students, their uncut hair, and their outfits not unlike her father's milking clothes. It was 1969, in the spring. Most of them were older than Jo, older than Susannah. Jo was drawing them; her newsprint pads were full of their bodies, looking somehow frail and old-fashioned in the nude, Susannah thought, regardless of how big and firm they were there on the steps of the art gallery, or how confident. She sat with her baby son; she had left her two-year-old with her husband Larry's mother. She had just buttoned her blouse from nursing for the first time in public. She wondered if her milk would be affected by the marijuana smoked in Jo's apartment and the unpleasant stories everybody who came in, everybody Jo knew, was always telling.

One of the classmates on the steps had an older brother who had tried to murder his high school girlfriend. This heavy woman, steadily smiling, was relating the details to Jo, who turned her back to the wind and tied up her portfolio. A dark girl with braids, and that stamp of the un-included Susannah recognized from grade school, kept saying, "Oh my God. Oh God. Oh my God."

"He was sick, and they just didn't realize," the woman said. "He's been on a supervised farm for six years."

"Farm life," said Jo gruffly as she turned away. "Come on," she said to Susannah.

"We were not close. I feel badly about that. If I'm smoking good stuff I'll tune into him, I'll have dreams where I go and get him," the heavy woman persisted, looking off toward the lake. "I'll just go and take hold of his arm and pull on him to come, like I did when we were kids."

"Does he come with you?" Susannah said, hanging back.

"It's like he's in mud or something. No. No, he doesn't." The woman had a meek, peaceful smile. It was a hippie expression that was appearing on young women all over the country, which Susannah had not seen before this time, but remembered later. Jo didn't have it, then or ever.

"That's probably a birth dream," said the one with braids, the one they all ignored. "Or it is if you try to pull someone out of water." She made a face, and added in a schoolyard singsong that went with her braids, "It's not my idea."

No one answered her, and to break the silence Susannah said, "Well, I used to have a dream, for years I had it, about pulling the bull out of the creek. Jo? Remember?" Jo snorted. "Our father had to winch the bull out of the creek when he broke his leg. He was a big Holstein bull," Susannah went on. She saw that none of them knew what "big" meant in this case. They had turned to look at her politely. She gave a little laugh. "Well, so I wonder what that would mean."

"You'd have had to dream about it before it happened," Jo said scathingly, "for it to mean anything. And I'd hate to think what it would mean. Anyway, we have to go."

Susannah gathered her things off the steps with one hand, trying not to jostle the baby, who was not a good sleeper. The heavy woman was still smiling. "I'm interested in babies," she said doubtfully, as the baby's eyebrows reddened in preparation for a howl. "I think I might like to draw them."

"Babies!" said Jo from the sidewalk. "They don't even have faces."

The baby cried shrilly as they began to walk, interspersing choked hiccups with his cries. "God, is he going to explode?" Jo said.

A man who had stopped directly in front of them on the sidewalk spread out his arms, blocking their way. "Hey, don't I know you from AA?" He had a red face that was too alive and interested, and too large. Shaking his big head like a calf, he fixed bloodshot eyes on Jo.

"Alan, this is my sister. She knows you don't know me from AA."

"Come on, Jo," the man said in a strangled voice. "Just listen."

"Alan, just leave me alone. I've told you. Go home," Jo said, and she pushed past him. Susannah followed her. When she looked back the man had sat down in the middle of the sidewalk.

"Babies!" Jo resumed. "How would she draw them? If she could draw in the first place. I mean they have expressions but no face. What exactly is a baby anyway? What is it?"

"I don't know, Jo," Susannah said to pacify her. She held her son against her chest, looking surreptitiously at his flushed face, which was just smoothing out and losing its distress. The baby eyes met hers. This was not like looking at anybody else in the world. There was a force in this face that grasped you like a fist, a force from which it seemed some people, like Jo, might have to be protected.

"No offense, Susie," Jo said, contrite. "Your kids are beautiful, both of them. Are you worried about that guy? That's just Alan. *He's* in AA. I don't even drink. I can't, just like Dad. It makes me sick."

"He was awfully unhappy. He's still sitting back there, Jo."

"He's going to have to straighten it out for himself. I can't do it for him."

Jo's early photographs were of farm machinery. Later she expanded to livestock trailers and veal feeder-cages and slaughterhouses. She photographed them empty, washed down. She photographed quarries and dams, and strip-mining dredges in West Virginia. In time, galleries showed these photographs and art museums bought them. This surprised Susannah. Machines and parts of machines were what it all added up to. Probably no one who did not work with such things would be able to identify the bars, prongs, saw-edges. Strong light with no feel of sunshine to it, metal dripping water, corners of bleached landscape out windows or behind tires: these were not the light and shade or the tools or products of any identifiable enterprise.

But this opinion—Susannah was not as backward when it came to art as Jo seemed to think—did not keep her from seeing the property in the photographs that was Jo's, and that made people want to look at them. Her angle. Jo's pictures showed this thing of hers the way you might hold up a root that had got into the plumbing and been skewered out. Or this part of it had been skewered out, and anybody looking would know worse remained. At the same time Jo did not exactly disapprove of it, whatever it was. She was guarding it, possibly, as a dog will guard something inedible it has found.

When Jo visited, she would wave the children's questions aside angrily. "These aren't magazine pictures!" she would snap, to their bewilderment. Susannah's boys were afraid of their aunt, of her harsh teasing when they made any claim on their mother's attention, but the girl, Stephanie, intended to be an artist herself. It was she who hung over the back of the couch when Jo sorted proof sheets, and who was a slave for years to Jo's stories of ugly episodes in the lives of artists and poets and people considered the agents of beauty.

All this was exasperating to Susannah, though less so than the stories of their own past, as they were still circulated at home, were to Jo.

For Susannah, the stories had a music that was sweet no matter how many times she heard them, and she heard them with some frequency, from teachers, from nurses while she waited for her births, from people in church and women in stores. Jo asleep in her incubator, feeble and veined but actually unsubdued by the smallness of her welcome, signaling with her thin, unchanging rhythms if not a bid to live, at least not a readiness to fade from life, "just lying there, so we all thought, we'd say . . . she doesn't know she's been born." And she, Susannah, living those days as secreted away, as potentially nonexistent, as if she too were not born. But she was sought: all the fields of the county were alive with searchers.

The stir being made, over two children who barely existed! The searchers were lifting the moldy sides of the collapsed chicken house, parting rows of corn with their arms, calling from hilltops, leaning into pole barns. They were trolling the big creek with branches, by tree roots where the current had dug out pools, and getting down on their hands and knees to see under balers. Twenty grade-school children, led by the minister's wife, could be heard singing the loud songs of Vacation Bible School, where Susannah would have been in the nursery on that Monday morning if she were not lost. Susannah heard all of this, when the story was told. She heard the panting and slobbering bloodhound, dragging the hermit widow on a path of her own that no one else took.

There were whistles blown in the woods and homemade gongs banged by some of the older women. They had been on the phone the first night conjuring up past toddlers, children who would have sat up at the language of spoon and pie tin, and replied to it, before they would answer to the sound of their names. But there is an age of not answering, they said.

All the activity got the cattle bawling in the fields. In later life Susannah told her children that she could distinguish claims and threats and simple explanations in the voices of cattle. This was a disputed talent of hers. She had it only partly because of growing up on a dairy farm, where her father's Holsteins, though he had given each one a name, remained strangers. She thought of them as indoor cows, forever being driven into their stanchions like huge children into their cribs. Most of them would not hesitate to throw a haunch into you, or pick you up on a bony head and pitch you into Fauquier County. So her father said. He controlled them with shoves and a flat voice, but the lead cow's ball eyes took in the approach of anyone who lacked his authority. She would roll out her gray tongue and jolt her full udder with her hock. "She's not sure about you," he would tell Susannah, setting her on a ledge. "You're near about the size of a dog." They had no farm dog, and could not expect to have one; their mother feared dogs. "And here"—he would put Jo up—"here comes the puppy."

Susannah believed that her knowledge—her hunches, as they came to be called—came instead from the time she had spent in Bayliss's cow-calf herd, from whatever it was that had kept her there two whole days. There was debate, that would still come up, as to what it could have been. It had been the Herefords, she knew. In her dreams, they swung their enormous heads back, like heavy bells, against the flies on their shoulders. Jo was the artist but Susannah took pride in being the one who dreamed every night and recalled it all in the morning.

Asleep, in the middle of falls from heights or insoluble multiple-choice tests or driving with no steering wheel, she had come to expect the appearance of cows, a circle of white-faced cows. She would lean forward, right out of whatever disaster it was, and look between the blunt red knees. She would be able, staring with unspeakable pleasure, to see calves through the legs, as they watched with outstretched necks but kept their distance, and the dark pink heads of Big English Red clover plunging under the weight of bees. Some of the clover would have already gone a brownish violet in the heat that the dream somehow conducted.

The heads swung back. There was a foaming in the air, of flies starting up all at once. But someone was coming. She was so hot she would throw off the blanket and wake up. No matter that she had been dreaming of the ordinary landscape where she still lived—though she lived in town now—she would experience the stunned, triumphant feeling of having gone through the earth to China.

Sometimes she woke up with sound in her ears, the hum a cow draws up from the bags of her neck to address her calf, and the infantile m-m-m the calf makes in reply. Her husband Larry knew about this. "Cattle say much?" he sometimes said at breakfast.

THEIR mother never made peace with normal life. She lost her place in it and then she forgot it. She forgot about shoe sizes and the Methodist Church and friends for her daughters, and her own friends, if she had had any before, and eventually about combing her hair or the girls' unless she was reminded, or giving baths, or going into town, or going forth at all from her place at the window where the slipcover was tanned by the sun and her cushion was squashed thin. Once in a while she reconstructed accomplishments she had had, or thought she had had, but she burned red stripes onto her hands with the skillet, or ran the sewing machine needle into her finger, and these things made her cry quietly, almost tearlessly, not at all as Susannah cried at first when she saw what her mother had done to herself.

Sometimes, too, she groaned, about nothing they could see, in a protest that did not really disturb them until they got older. Before that it was just a noise coming from the living room, one of the sounds of the daytime, like a kitchen chair being pushed back or the tractor belching, way out on the back of the farm.

In time—in high school, when they began to put thought into

her—they thought she was hardly any different from the crazy woman with the dogs, except that she would not have shot at people or gone out to rescue them.

What could be said about her? That sometimes she spoke and made perfect sense, but speech could not be touched off in her by anything that was said to her. That every night, while she was still eating with them, she stood up from the dinner table and went to bed as soon as it was suggested to her, although if they woke in the night they would hear her moving around downstairs. Or they would hear, through the floor, her voice suddenly speaking, sharp and afraid. And then the creak of the stairs and their father's voice, and water running in the kitchen as he filled the hot water bottle for her, and the stairs again as he came back up with her, in the days when she still slept upstairs.

There were no pictures of her to study later, of things she might have done in the time when she did things; certainly there were none of her on the couch with her hot water bottle, slumped in the sun flooding off the windowpane, with the radio on. Even after they got a TV she liked the radio. She didn't really listen. If they asked her a question about a program, she would give them a slow, appalled look, and sometimes she would close her eyes.

That was all later. At first she just needed help.

She needed help when the hospital finished with the baby Mary Jo and let her come home, after many weeks. Their father hired a woman to live with them, a girl, really. Stevia, the daughter of the tenants who had worked the farm down the road for twenty years and had so many children nobody knew where they had all got to. As the oldest of the six that remained at home, Stevia knew how to take care of children. She took over Susannah and the baby and most of the housework.

Stevia was a laugher, a chaser, freckled all over in a sandy pink, the possessor of movie magazines and Little Lulu comic books and a red vanity case full of cosmetics, with a mirror in the lid. She was devoted to home permanents for Susannah and three-heart barrettes for the baby's fine hair, and a succession of styles for herself derived from pin-curl diagrams in her magazines, which she called books: "Hand me my book!" "Where's that book with Janet Leigh on it?" Susannah and Jo paged through those magazines kissing the ink lips of movie stars, ran up the back stairs and down the front and through the living room past their mother with Stevia in pursuit. They sat in kitchen chairs on newspapers having their Toni's, with shudders as the lotion crept down their necks and Stevia hissed "Stay still! Stay still!" and the smell bloomed up around their faces with its tender promise of change.

These things took years. Almost six years. For Susannah those years had an aura of put-off effort that was like being on a school bus that is still a long way from your stop.

Stevia did not read to them, though she took them to the library when their father said to, and brought back books picked out by the librarian, who was Mrs. Bayliss of the Bayliss Polled Hereford place, where Susannah had been found.

Mrs. Charlotte Bayliss had been among the legendary group seen from a mile away rising over the hill in the late afternoon bearing Susannah aloft, calling something that could not be heard. She was one of the women who took an interest in their family. She treated Stevia in a funny way, as if she were the same age as Susannah and Jo. Sometimes she walked them all down the library steps and out to the car, and peered in to see the groceries. "Tell your momma hello, now," she always said. Stevia always gave Susannah a secret cross-eyed look as Mrs. Bayliss went back up the stairs.

From Stevia's trouble with what was printed under the pictures in her magazines Susannah knew, eventually, that she would not pass easily on to a library book. But Stevia knew how to draw people and showed Susannah, and Jo in time, how to do hair and noses, and lips, a top and a bottom, and she drew hundreds of girls, pressing so hard her dimpled fingers bent backward at the knuckle, always erasing until everything was perfect, and sweeping the eraser dust off onto the floor, where they rolled it under their bare toes.

Stevia was fat but she had a lot of slow-burning energy for coming up out of a chair and grabbing them, toppling them onto her wide, freckled knees and tickling them.

Sometimes after dinner a car horn honked for her and she went out the door and was not there to put them to bed. On those nights they left their father sleeping under the lampshade with his *Farm Journal* and tiptoed down the back hall to her room, and pulled open her dresser drawers, stopping each other when they creaked.

They lifted out the nylon underpants inflated with Stevia's shape, and untangled the huge yellowed bras from the Avon jars and the pink canister of talcum powder, with the holes in its lid never quite closed, so that everything in the drawer was roughened with powder, and held them up against each other in voluptuous disbelief.

"Shh! Someone's coming!" They froze at the sight of their mother in the doorway. Before she drew back into the hall she said something distinctly, she said, "Your mother wouldn't like that."

Jo said, "Stevia made us give her all our meat. She took it home on Sunday." Susannah did not remember that. She could not really see how it could have been so, because of getting meat off their plates and into the refrigerator and keeping it there until Sunday, Stevia's day off. And their father had been there somewhere watching over things. He was certainly in the house in winter, when there was less to do outside.

Susannah tried to hear his voice from that time, laying out rules or giving directions to Stevia, but she could summon him only in his commanding passage among the cows and in the smell he still had: the little wake that followed him of grease and gasoline in the knees and seat of his pants where he wiped his hands, mixed with soap from washing udders and the smell of the truck bed: rags, bitter little weeds sprouting in the rust, brown rained-on feedbags going to mulch. He had all these smells. He was not part of the house, and why would he be? "He never had any control over Stevia or anybody else," Jo said, spying out Susannah's mental defense of him. "Stevia tickled us until we threw up."

Then Stevia was going to have her own baby, even though she was not married, and would not agree to stay on, even until the baby's birth, and went away.

Stevia was going to stay with her sister in Georgia. She was going to have a boy. No girls for her. He would be named Steve, after herself and the dead brother for whom she had been named. She showed them a brown line going up and down from her navel, like the beam of a star. Even though Susannah knew better, knew from Stevia herself how her mother had labored ten hours to get out something even as undersized as Jo, the line made Susannah imagine a painless splitting there. Out would press the baby, Steve. A strong, grinning baby with the yellow eyes of the elf boy on the cover of the fairy tales Mrs. Bayliss had sent home with them. The same little horn nubs on either side of his head. Devil or calf, creature to be chased on his delicate little hooves, and seized by Stevia, and nursed until his mouth frothed. Or just a baby. The thought of this baby, born and named and carried around in Stevia's fat arms, would not be banished from the house, no matter how they raced and fought and teased in the hope of raising Stevia's intent pink face from her stack of maternity patterns. Their father had given her the old sewing machine, and she sat making giant gathered tops for herself out of flowered material, flouncing them up against her chest with pins in her mouth and going to look at herself, severely and respectfully, in the mirror.

The vanity case had come back out from under the bed and she had taken her egg shampoo and her jar of bobby pins off the bathroom windowsill, and packed her magazines and the framed picture she said was her boyfriend, that Susannah thought was cut out of one of the magazines.

All the last week, Susannah rummaged through drawers looking for a school picture of herself to give Stevia. At the end, with no picture to leave behind her, Stevia waved her soft plump hand at them when she left them off at Sunday school, as if it were any Sunday and she would be back in the morning.

Jo had just turned six and Susannah was nine.

Different women came in to help. Jo went to the doctor with a scabby rash on her face and neck and chest. No one knew if the rash was contagious, and eventually the doctor said it was because she was scratching at herself. But for a while, to Jo's shouts of fury and misery at bedtime, Susannah was allowed to sleep in Stevia's room. There she found the pile of their drawings, years of them, on a musty shelf in the closet. "Jo!" she yelled. She remembered this, yelling for Jo, who had not mentioned Stevia's name once since she left, or looked into her dresser drawers to see if anything remained, or even gone into her room.

During this summer Jo liked to sit in the kitchen doing nothing. She sat at the table scraping out the spaces between the little glass tiles on the salt and pepper shakers with her fingernail. The women who came in for part of the day to look after them stayed in the kitchen away from their mother and ironed, but Jo did not enter into conversation with them. The house was quiet, except for a groan now and then from the living room. At least Jo would snap at Susannah, if Susannah bothered her. At six Jo had a deep, angry voice she could summon up out of her chest when she wanted to. But when Susannah put the drawings on the table Jo bent over them with her.

Girls. Not a boy among them. There was a kind of sigh from both of them. Jo broke her silence and said in a whisper, "Stevia liked my drawings better than yours." This did not surprise Susannah because Jo was going to be an artist. She was already better than Stevia, even making fun of the black-haired girls Stevia drew, with eyelashes like ant legs and high heels on tiny, sideways feet. "Stevia! Skirts don't look like that, like triangles."

"See, those dumb clothes she made us do! And these are babyish!" Jo was suddenly furious, and began to tear up her own drawings, one by one. She flung the pieces all over the kitchen, and the woman who was ironing that day left them there so their father could see how Jo had carried on. Susannah felt a certain bitter elation while Jo was doing the tearing. But she kept her own drawings. There were smudges of Stevia's Trushay hand lotion on them. There were certain sacred noses and mouths in the margins, drawn with such careful pressure that the pencil lead still shone, and places where the paper was almost erased through, and passing back in time to the days when Stevia was newly in the house, before Jo could pick up a pencil, larger and larger faces for Susannah to copy, larger and simpler renderings of her name in Stevia's broad print. "Suzzana." In the first grade, she had taught Stevia how to spell her name.

Of her mother in the same period her memories were vivid but sparse, and not really shareable except with Jo.

There would be no one else to whom she could mention one dress of their mother's. It had a lint-filled pocket where Susannah put her hand as they sat on the couch together while her mother was giving the baby her bottle, and felt with her fingers through to her mother's thin leg, almost the same size and inertness as the banister.

Sooner or later they would be alone together, because the baby would start to cry and this would cause her mother to breathe faster and then shrink and squirm as if somebody had put a groundhog in her lap and not a baby in need of a burp. Stevia would swoop down on the dark-faced outraged baby. After a while Susannah could do it too.

Susannah did not look up at her mother's face, with the dark oily hair falling over it, the rubbed eyes and the chapped lips. Not right at it. They just sat there. She was astonished to think how many times the dress with the pocket must have been worn. In fact she thought now that her mother might have worn nothing else.

"I'm sure she wore it until it stank!" said Jo.

Had their mother always been like that? Why hadn't they asked their father? Or had he married someone who seemed no different from the women other men married? Where were the grandparents, the aunts and uncles, who should have appeared from North Carolina, so nearby, and cleared everything up?

There was only their mother, fetched from her previous life as if she had called him to come and get her. Susannah saw her father leading her mother down out of the humped Smoky Mountains. But something was not left behind.

Sometimes they had misgivings in school, away from the habit and familiarity—as expressionless, as consoling, when they burst through the screen door in the afternoon, as God—of the house. There was their mother, as she ever was. There was the kind of greeting that was hers, a look. Was there a shiver, at the sight of them? There was the hot water bottle, as ever, and why not, exactly, why not? And yet... They felt questions in themselves, but the questions, when the time came that they had pushed up far enough to be asked, seemed not to be there after all, like those mushrooms in the woods that turn to brown smoke when you step on them.

Eventually the questions were simpler, specific ones, such as where had their mother gone, the times she went away? Their father said it was not a hospital but a kind of boarding house in Maryland. You went there and people saw to whatever you needed. For a while *boarding house* gave Susannah a queasy picture of boards being used in some way that people—certain people—needed. It was not anything that hurt them; it was an involved, agonized shuffling back and forth and carrying and piling up. Boarding. How had their father decided when she ought to go, had to?

Why did he twice hire someone to do the milking, and go and get her back? It was not a subject you could pursue with a man like their father, then or later. "Don't you worry about it," he would say.

For years, Susannah and Larry took their children to the farm every weekend. There were always things for Susannah to do. When Jo came home from Chicago the first few times, she would pull Susannah away from the babies at milking time and drag her to the barn. There, while their father was hitching up the milking machines, she would storm about their mother and the way they were living, their father and Susannah and Larry, with their mother in the middle of them all like a bag of feed. With her groans! For other people, there were medicines! Hospitals!

"Well, my advice, Miss Mary Jo," their father would say from behind a cow, after letting her go on for a while, "would be, you just worry about the war." Or, "You concentrate on the show you folks are putting on out there in Chicago." He meant the Democratic convention. "Now, hospitals, and the rest of that. That isn't what you really want," he said, relenting and coming out to put his arm around Jo. "For your momma. Is it now." It was not a question. "Don't you worry about it."

Years before, somebody had worried about it. Who was it asking them questions and writing down their answers in a stuffy office in town? Who decided it was a shame they had no outings, a shame they could not swim, and bought them bathing suits and put their mother in the car with them and drove them all, with Stevia not even there, the time they went to the swimming pool?

Susannah must have been eight, the first and last time she was in the town pool. And Stevia was there when they got back after the accident, to say, "Betcha the kid that did it gets a licking," and to touch behind Susannah's ears with perfume when she had her put to bed in her figure-eight bandage.

Susannah had been idly walking on tiptoe and clapping the water, hypnotized by the spangles in the blue color all around her. Without knowing anything about pool water she had the feeling it was going to lift her. She wandered up to her neck in it, and it did begin to lift her, but then there was a shout and a slamming pain, which was the snapping of her collarbone. Everybody seemed to be screaming with her, at her, and at the boy who had cannonballed off the slide. While she herself screamed, a man carried her to her mother on a towel on the grass.

There she stopped screaming. She remembered her mother, alone, in a bathing suit with loose elastic, looking up through her hair with her bottom teeth set in the white upper lip in a terrible way. The man, who had a deep, commanding voice, said, "She'll have to go to the doctor," and her mother got up so slowly and heavily, in such confusion, holding her suit to her ribs, that

Susannah stopped crying in order to reach for her hand. She couldn't move the upper part of her body to do it. She could think just clearly enough through the pain to be sure they should never have come to a swimming pool.

Then the man fetched Jo from the wading pool and unpinned the key to their basket from Susannah's suit, and got their clothes and towels, all very quickly. The man wouldn't let Jo grab Susannah by the hand. Jo began to wail. "Stop that," the man said calmly.

He drove them to the hospital, where, he told Jo—for people knew them, they were part of the county's history—she had been born. Jo was sitting in the front, still crying, and Susannah was lying down in the back seat, partly in her mother's lap, with her feet braced in a way the man had arranged them so that she would not be jolted. Her mother was not actually holding her still, though the man had said she must. Her mother had herself backed against the door, with Susannah half propped up by the damp towels in her lap. All the way to the hospital her mother said nothing to Susannah or Jo or the man.

Susannah could remember the smell that had gotten into her new bathing suit rising off her in waves. Years later the smell of chlorine still called up the dread she had felt in the man's car and at the same time her mesmerized confidence in him.

"And while this one was being born," the man looked over his shoulder to tell Susannah, who was listening and not crying, despite the shocking pain, "a lot of people, myself included, were looking for you." And although his deep voice did not fade from memory, most of the strange day faded, to be replaced by the story of it, of the trip to the swimming pool and Susannah's broken collarbone. And she never learned to swim. Neither of them did.

Looking back, the remarkable thing seemed to be that her mother had been there at all, at a swimming pool. Who had taken them there?

LARRY KEPHART was Susannah's first boyfriend. He was a heavyset boy with sloping shoulders, as solid in body and mind in his senior year as he would be at thirty. He had a football build but he had had to drop football because his father died. Suddenly his mother and the farm were his responsibility. He worked the farm the same way he had played football, pushing and straining. He never shirked any of the things his father had put off, from fixing the augur on the old combine to lugging rocks into the fencerows. At school he slept at his desk, with his head in his arms.

That was how Susannah met him. She was helping in the clinic, actually a supply room with a cot behind the shelves, for girls with cramps, where Larry's homeroom teacher sent him to sleep at lunch time. He had the cot every day, under a window with no blinds. He slept in the hot sunlight, sweating. One day he thrashed and carried on so much in his sleep that Susannah put down her inventory pad and laid her hands firmly on his hot, tanned arms. When he sat up and made the discovery he was crying, he covered his face, and then blinked in the light to see who had hold of him, and that was the beginning.

On weekends he went to sleep at the drive-in as soon as Susannah had pulled him close to her. Sometimes right after he woke up he broke down and cried about his father. Susannah saw clearly that this boy must not wait to be comforted. She would not be class salutatorian after all. They married without graduating.

Susannah had thought she could never leave her father and sister, but she left easily, impenitently. They moved in with Larry's mother. Susannah had her one girl, Stephanie, when she was eighteen, and then her three boys, and hardly any time after this second life began—fifteen years, though it seemed more like four or five—Larry had a heart attack, just as his father had, and died.

He had it on his backhoe. Jo had won an award for her photograph of the backhoe. She had given it to Susannah and it was Susannah's right to take it off the wall and hide it on the top shelf of her dish cupboard. She was afraid to throw it away because by then she thought it might be worth money—there were books with Jo's photographs in them, and a glossy catalog of one of her shows—and she was not sure what money there was going to be.

Instead she had a fight with Jo before Larry's funeral about her insistence on carrying her camera everywhere she went. Jo had been walking around all morning with it slung on her shoulder. Was she going to take it to the cemetery? Susannah was hollow from drinking coffee and sore in the arms from grasping the receiver and listening to people tell stories of how many men in Larry's family had gone in just that way, at work. Young. Though not as young as Larry. She looked at her younger sons' bodies, already stiff and striving at nine and seven, burly in their funeral sports coats. The thirteen-year-old, the one with the secretly favored face, whom it seemed to her she had been nursing only weeks before on the art gallery steps in Chicago, was already a man. He pushed in and out of the swinging kitchen door carrying the food for later.

Susannah felt a weight on her. She sat down. It was the weight of having done a dangerous thing, in never hearkening to the stories from Larry's family, in thinking her own story—not her family's, of course, but her own—reached forward and secured Larry as it did her.

That was what she had always thought. Larry gave the story that was told about her its ending. "Yes, indeed, the little Floyd girl lived, she was found, she grew up, she married Larry Kephart."

And so . . . and so she had not seen the shape of things that Larry dragged with him, in his fast breathing and the crease between his eyes and his big restless body held back by its own muscles. And when the Vietnam War came he had been 4-F, but that was such a familiar fact in their lives that she could not remember the reason he gave. He had football injuries to his knee; she had thought it was that.

How were you to choose, out of the familiar facts, those things that were going to be the important, deadly ones? He had claimed his only problems were the knee and his bad hearing, from the deafening PTO on the secondhand bulldozer. Certainly nothing, ever, about his heart. Certainly he never frightened her.

She saw Jo and her camera. "Get that out of here!" she said in a dreadful, tight voice, like a teacher. She thought later that probably she, who was known for her good temper, had never spoken to any of her children, let alone to Jo, in just that voice.

Jo put the camera down hastily, but she recovered herself. "What did I do?" she said.

"I . . . I . . . I," said Susannah savagely, whereupon Jo backed away and shut her eyes. Tears squeezed out of them. She gave a deep sob, but Susannah had already gotten up to put her arms around her.

Jo had a very short, peeled-back haircut. It exposed her forehead with its one line and gave her big eyes a challenging look, which passed over Susannah's house as if everything in it, from the fatty pork roast in the refrigerator to Larry's caked steel-toed boots on the back porch to the children themselves, especially the stocky little boys, pointed to the thing that had happened to them. "Oh, Jo. It's OK, I'm all right," Susannah said, as if Jo were crying for her, but Jo cried on and then stopped, as if she had lost the point, and then laughed and clutched Susannah and cried again.

By the time he died, though he was only thirty-four, Larry had sold the land off his parents' farm and had his own machines and five employees, and was running a profitable operation clearing stumps and digging ponds and the foundations for the shopping centers the towns were all putting in.

Even when Larry turned out to be a success, Jo did not forgive Susannah for marrying him. His success did not matter to Jo, any more than Jo's beauty had mattered to him. "She's OK," he would say, when Susannah pushed him. "Her skin . . ." Jo had fine scars, a faint leaf pattern in the hollow of each cheek, from the rashes she had torn at with her fingernails as a child. If anything they added to the somewhat harsh beauty of her face, Susannah thought. They never kept the boys away. If there was anything at all the matter with Larry as far as Susannah was concerned, it was this inability to see what attracted men to Jo.

At first Jo was enraged at being left behind, at having to stay where she was and graduate so that she could get into art school. Then Susannah was pregnant, a worse, mysteriously worse and more serious breach.

As the children were born, Jo took for her theme the fact that Susannah, while seeming to leave, had stayed, in actuality, close by their mother. Between them, Larry and their mother, Jo said, had caused Susannah to miss everything that could have freed her, all the alterations of the sixties.

Susannah knew what that meant to Jo, that she was the same as any starch-fat war-blessing farmer's wife, such as they had never known and only Jo could think existed, even then, in a county growing and changing as theirs was. Half the farmers' wives, in the years Susannah was having her children, were just as apt to be the kind of women—young and newly arrived, with money from somewhere that they let their bearded husbands put into acreage they would attempt to farm—the kind of women who, although they canned ceremoniously all summer and tried to initiate quilting bees, tried just as hard to get reading groups going with the women in town, and gatherings to discuss the war and the changes creeping into everything.

For a while these women called Susannah, as if she were the newcomer and not they. Susannah and Larry had in fact laughed at them in much the same way Jo, away in Chicago, laughed at the country women of her imagination. Larry, who had been recruited by the state schools when he played football, called these women the scouts. "See any of the scouts at the store?" Years afterward, when she went to work in the county office building where several of them, too, had ended up, Susannah wished obscurely that she could let Larry know they were her friends.

Of course the county was different now, almost a suburb of Washington. Women had less time for thinking up things to do, a good many of them commuted the forty or fifty miles in. Only the big farms supported anybody now. The old combine Larry had repaired still sat on the lot, unsold.

While Larry was alive Susannah thought Jo's disgust with her for getting married was because Jo wished to be married herself. After Larry died she thought differently. She was no longer sure. She saw that Jo liked having boyfriends—lovers, she called them angrily if Susannah said boyfriends—but disliked and avoided men who were not her lovers.

If a man crossed the barrier of Jo's dislike, he became her lover, unless he had powerful reasons for not doing so. It had been thus since high school, when her boyfriends were boys from no particular town or farm, who lived in trailers or on roads that ended in wiregrass growing up through car chassis, where Jo herself did not know whether the thin young men drinking on porches were fathers or big brothers. Jo's boyfriends were good-looking lordly boys of no influence in school, who took shop and got kicked out or quit to join the air force. One or another of them would always be walking in the corridors with a hand low on Jo's back, and offering the other boys a secret smile Susannah hated.

"I want you to tell me right here and now why you never got pregnant in high school," Susannah said to Jo in the delivery room, groggily pressing on her own loose stomach, after she had her last boy. Larry laughed. It was when they first started letting husbands in. When the nurse saw who it was delivering she had let Jo in too. Both the nurse and the old doctor doing the delivery had been members of the search party, the nurse with the Methodist Youth Fellowship, the doctor with the Lions. The nurse said, "You can have anybody your little heart desires. I mean it. If you want Betty Ford in here, we'll give her a call."

Jo was leaning on the wall, her hair stuck to her forehead. "Hah!" she said. "You think I didn't try?"

"But Jo. What would you have done?"

"I would never have had an abortion." Jo said this shakily, sitting on the floor wiping her oily face. She had come close to fainting during the birth, and the nurse had made her sit on the floor. In the delivery room you would not have picked her for a woman who had gone into the slaughterhouse with a camera.

But she was getting her bearings now. She got up and gripped Susannah's hand. "I would have given the baby to you."

Jo was not fond of women, either, except Susannah and a few women years older than herself, art people in Chicago. She never noticed women or talked about them, except their mother.

THEIR mother did not die. Not for years. In the books and magazines Susannah read, people who had come dramatically loose from life, the regular course of life, the onward direction in which everybody was more or less heading, died. She remarked on this to herself whenever she heard one of these symmetrical accounts. They died, as often as not, of drinking, or grief, or by putting themselves in the way of accidents, or by withering away. Or in some modernized versions of these stories, they got powerful viruses or cancer.

But of the real confederation of those who turned their backs on life, it seemed to her that few withered or died. This was another kind of story, not as relished, told with a certain reproach at the inability of the characters to wind things up.

There were such people all over the countryside, like the woman with the dogs, whose husband had crossed the state line taking his tenant's daughter with him, a girl of twelve. He had been chased and sent to prison, and he had widowed his wife without ever coming back. And then to the woman's story was added the postscript of her appearance in the search party, and then the matter of her existence was closed again, though she still barged through the Safeway every few months loading a cart with hams and frozen cake.

Their mother's story had taken the place of their mother, for most people. Nevertheless certain women, such as Mrs. Bayliss and their Sunday school teachers, saw to it that their father got them to the occasional birthday party after Stevia left, in houses where they stood with their knees tight and their eyesight dim, one or the other of them the wrong age for the party because they were always invited together, among girls neither one of them played with at school.

They were sent to church camp. Teachers took them shopping.

Susannah had a friendly memory of Mrs. Grayson, who taught her in the sixth grade and was to teach Jo. Mrs. Grayson took them to Seven Corners when it was new. She was old enough to be a grandmother but she had no children. She had a chin wrinkled like a walnut and a Kleenex box in her car with a little skirt on it that seemed to Susannah the emblem of settled life. "She came into the booth with us when we tried things on. She inspected our underpants," Jo said, when Susannah reminded her of Mrs. Grayson. "Pulled on the elastic and looked in. Mine were dirty. She *told* me."

"But she was probably getting us new underpants."

"I don't care. She said, 'What a dirty little girl.' I don't know why she said it to me and not you, I was younger."

Susannah almost said, "Maybe you were dirtier," but she didn't. You could not say something like that to Jo, or not for a laugh. If you said it you would have to retrieve her; you would have to lead her by degrees, with compliments, and canceling memories, out of the fitting room where she might easily crouch forever with her back turned, stuck-out shoulder blades grubby in her undershirt, and coax her back into the light of the present.

Instead Susannah said, "You were prettier. She didn't want you to get uppity." She turned over the notion that either of the baffled children they had been could have been uppity.

Though she did remember, around the time of the Mrs. Grayson episode, being called downstairs from her own classroom to take Jo into the hallway outside third grade and reason with her. She could remember Jo's stare, magnified by the unfallen tears, her fury, mistaken by the teacher for shame. She could remember having her head pulled down sideways in Jo's thin rough fingers, her ear cupped and filled with the hot breath of Jo's curse on the school.

Their mother lived to be seventy-four, and her age resembled her youth, except that it allowed her to grow less tremulous and more remote as it shifted the whole cargo of the world gradually out of her sight and mind. But at the same time she lost control of some of her functions, she let go of pieces of self she had kept back. She lost her stillness, her vigilance, her thinness. She ate. She spread out, she lumbered restlessly through the house in her slippers, new every Christmas. She fiddled with things. She worked holes in the old couch arms and picked out the seams in her sleeves.

She grew harder to take care of, but their father did it, along with some hired help and Susannah. She had shoes left, in the closet in their father's room, but—this was what surprised Susannah, packing a bag for her, into a trance of woe such as she had not experienced in years and years—no pocketbook to take when she went into the hospital to have her gallbladder operated on and never came out.

Their father did not die either, when the burden of her had fallen away, as Susannah had secretly feared he would. It was Jo who died.

SUSANNAH got off the plane and looked for Garland. She knew very little about him but she supposed him to be an artist of one kind or another, possibly foreign. Garland was probably his last name. Jo liked to call people by their last names. Somewhere in his fifties, the age Jo liked. Probably wearing something Susannah would be able to recognize as setting him apart, something odd or foreign, like a beret.

Her feet had swollen on the plane. She took a deep breath. They had circled for an hour, and then come down a lead-colored sky in thunder and skidding sways.

"Susannah," said a Southern voice. Garland. Of course, a Southern name, she thought as she turned. A portly man in a suit, not very tall, with jowls. He grasped her hand when she put her suitcase down. "Garland Smith."

"Garland!" she said. Immediately she felt helpful. His hand was trembling. Jo had done this to the man. "I'm sorry it took so long."

"They stacked you up out there. That's my nightmare," he said. "You don't mind flying?" He picked up her suitcase. She was not used to men who said anything was their nightmare, and cast about for a reply. He walked soundlessly and she felt she was stumping along in her tight shoes.

"You'll be staying at the same place where the memorial is being held, the Dominicks'." Susannah knew she was not to stay in Jo's apartment. Tomorrow she was going there with Garland to go through things. She felt a physical resistance, a twisting in her body away from this idea.

"It's so nice of you to come get me."

"Not at all," he said with a little sideways scoop of his head. "I wanted to meet you." She didn't know whether he meant meet her plane or finally meet her. Maybe he had been thinking, before, that if he got to know her he would have another avenue to Jo. He had graying brown hair resembling her own, but thin. She wanted to say soothingly, I don't know what got her going, with you, but it wouldn't have lasted. It might have been almost, almost as bad as this anyway. Though she knew of course that nothing could match up to this.

Out in the vast parking lot of the airport it was cold, getting ready to rain. At a distance across the flat land you could see rain: a section of sky had let down a brown ramp of water that was rolling toward them. The spring wind whipped their coats. Garland didn't just open the door, he handed her into the car, the way dressed-up boys would have, years ago. Though not her. Not her: she was not to have dates, but to stand by her locker and talk to a boy who leaned against the wall because he was tired, and she was to be weak in every limb over this tiredness—the rubbed neck, the deep yawn—in one so persistent, so dogged and strong. But certainly Jo had been lowered into cars this way by her boyfriends, who were the dressers, the dancers. Jo had sunk back into a gush of skirts chosen by some Mrs. Grayson, and smiled her planning smile.

Susannah put her head back on the seat and closed her eyes. The upholstery was cracked and stiff. Garland occupied himself with the gears of the little growling car.

Jo's interest in school dances did not last. The time came when she told Susannah, "We say we're going but we don't." It was after Susannah was married and Jo was running around, racing boys in the pickup, with rolls of barbed wire gashing the salt blocks in the truck bed, doing whatever she could think up to make Susannah sorry she had left. It made Jo sick to drink, herself, but she ran with the boys who did. Every year in the spring Jo knew the boy who wound his car around a telephone pole or flipped it into the river and died. In their bedroom in Larry's mother's house Susannah would tremble to hear a siren out across the fields at night.

"It was so warm I took my dress off. In a field way up near Bluemont, know whose land? Ray said that old woman lived out there and she does. The place is a mess. He wanted me to see. He thought I'd like it."

"Why? Why would you like it?" But Susannah could see from Jo's face that she did like it.

"It was dark, and she came out with a shotgun."

"Jo! The woman with the dogs? She shoots that thing!"

"Not at us. She had it cracked over her arm just like nothing. We weren't right on her land. She came over to the fence. There I was with my dress off. I held it over me. I mean I had everything off. I don't know if she even noticed. She talked to us."

"What did she say?"

"I told her who I was. She recognized the name. She thought I was you, the search party one. She said, 'Well, you grew up, didn't you.' She said her land is posted but people hunt on it all the time. She sort of wanted us to know she was a good enough shot not to kill 'em when she shot at 'em. Ray said, 'You don't approve of hunting?' God is he stupid. She said they shot one of her dogs. She has eight left. She's not crazy," Jo said suddenly. They looked at each other. That left their mother the craziest one around.

A YOUNGISH man read a poem. Susannah realized it was a poem when it was too late to go back and recall the beginning. When he sat down a man with a long head and tinted glasses rose and spoke about Jo's work, her beauty, her openness to life, her refusal to shut out the terrible—even her welcoming of it.

What exactly was the terrible and how did he know Jo welcomed it? Had anybody said how Jo could screech in her sleep, how she could shiver in a booth in a department store? The crowd was small, Susannah thought. Well, Jo had shut out more than he thought, or tried to, and not only the terrible. But the man spoke with authority. Look at her pictures, he repeated, as if the people in the room might not have seen them. Susannah thought he might be a critic. Maybe they were all critics, not friends. She had never been sure the people around Jo in Chicago were friends. Certainly Jo did not like them. There is nothing morbid, the man said reassuringly. There is no irony, nothing we would say is ugly. Susannah let herself be soothed as he went on in this vein.

Another man stood up to speak. She knew Garland was not going to. And she had declined when he asked in the car if she wanted to. Never. Not about Jo, who was not even a grown woman, to her, let alone an artist about whom other people, who did not know her, might have opinions. An artist was what she had been when she drew pictures, when they were girls. She had been a girl.

What was Jo? She was like Larry, part of the world as it had to be, as it could not be if she were not part of it. Under her skin Susannah felt the spread of a slow, confused wrath. She had almost forgotten something: how people wanted you to lay grief aside in a year—or two or three years, the generous ones. Lay all of it aside, all the previous world. They wanted it over with. They wanted . . . And if she had forgotten that, then she must have done it, laid it aside. She must have. But it was new again as she sat there; it was always there, she thought almost with relief, ready to begin again. A woman with an alto voice was singing a song in German. The sound of the song had brought tears to Susannah's eyes, but the tears just pooled there, she did not have to fend off the quakes of crying that had overtaken her on the plane. Beside her the plump, hospitable hostess, Mrs. Dominick, whispered, "When will you come?"

"Excuse me?" Susannah said.

"It means more or less 'when will you come,' this song," Mrs. Dominick said with short puffing breaths. Asthma, Susannah decided. The woman had small old blue eyes under a layer of bright tears. Then they stood up in the big room and rock music was put on that was said to be Jo's favorite. It was turned down and then turned up again. Susannah knew from having had teenagers that it should be loud. She recognized it. No comfort in it, loud or soft, though Jo would argue that comfort was not what music was for.

Openness to life. Susannah knew what the words were meant to convey, approximately: an innocent questing, a girlish trust, along with a certain inoffensive greediness. "Openness to life!" She could hear Jo's scornful voice. You asked for it, she answered Jo. They can say whatever they want. You fixed it so people could talk any old way about you. She went on coldly in her mind in this voice. She knew that if you spoke to the dead in this way, you made a sort of puppet. A little condensed person of self-pity and shame whom you could berate and console.

Garland Smith went through the small crowd one by one, on a steady course. Almost everybody hugged him. While this was going on Susannah saw that the memorial was less for Jo than for Garland himself, that it was he, whoever he was, who had importance to the people here, and was surrounded by them in his grief because of this importance.

At home Susannah would have thought he was gay. Something about his phrases, his smooth walk. Winning the heart of a gay man would have given Jo one of her angry pleasures. It would have been worthy of some exertion, to her. But as she watched the man Susannah no longer thought so. His attention was focused on the women in the room, and theirs on him. It was the women he was talking to. If you watched for a while you saw the rueful, sweet smile, the smile of a man used to women, to having them make much of him, and make exceptions for him, a man who came to them, who accepted their help. "He's not much to look at," women she knew at work would say of a man like this. "I don't know what it is . . ." When Garland Smith bowed his head, the loose skin of his face drooped forward. He lifted his graying eyebrows helplessly so that deep wrinkles formed on the sides of his forehead.

Yet she did not doubt the sincerity of whatever he was saying. He had a handkerchief in his fist, for sweat. You can't fake sweat. He was sweating and shaking in his loose suit. Maybe he had been losing weight for his wedding. She noticed he talked for a long time to a gesturing woman with thick gray eyebrows rather like his own, and then to Mrs. Dominick, who actually reached out and with her plump thumb wiped his eyes for him.

Mrs. Dominick was an art collector. Her husband was a surgeon. Once the rows of chairs were out of the way their apartment was not much different from the houses of doctors or horse people at home, with worn Persian rugs and dusty jade plants in Chinese pots. A maid was passing out glasses of wine from a tray. If there was food Susannah couldn't see it. Glassed-in boxes with objects and scenes in them were stuck into the bookshelves. Paintings covered every wall. Susannah stopped before a small print in a corner. Mrs. Dominick came to join her as she was putting on her reading glasses and leaning to read what was written on it.

They began to walk along together, past a row of portraits in heavy frames. Susannah imagined that the subjects of these paintings would have thought twice about hanging them in their own houses. Nude and holding cats, or standing in messy bedrooms, or sitting in cars with the windows rolled up, they stared out unkindly. Walking seemed to cost Mrs. Dominick most of her breath. She had taken Susannah's arm. She looked at each painting at the same time Susannah was looking at it, and then at Susannah as if she had introduced them. "She's a hero of mine," she said.

"Which one?" said Susannah.

"The painter," said Mrs. Dominick. Despite her breathlessness she said everything easily, with no instruction in her voice. She offered the facts about her collection. It was the way you talk to children, Susannah thought, when their questions don't bother you at all. When you are happy. Mrs. Dominick was one of those here, apparently, who really did mourn Jo. For some reason she was one of them. But she lost sight of her grief in giving the name of the lengths of pipe assembled on a dais in the entrance hall—machine parts Jo must have liked—and the stroller full of rope in the study: they were installations. They were as they should be. Everything had a rightness if one paused for a long enough look.

On the plane Susannah had imagined this gathering. The women would be wearing the kind of clothes that halfway frighten you and have hair dyed red-black like Jo's. Savage gossip would be whispered. Susannah would be pointed out to men who had been Jo's lovers. Grief might or might not excuse her grown-out permanent, her feet swollen over the sides of her pumps. No one would believe Jo had been only three years younger than Susannah.

It was not like that at all. It was ordinary. Mrs. Dominick's breathing problem made little oases in the conversation, during which you did not have to do or say anything. For a while they stood together looking out at the balcony. Against the thick, brightly lighted leaves of trees in tubs, rain was coming down in big drops, separate and greenish, like something shredded, celery or fish. Susannah began to be hungry. Far down, headlights were being pulled along Lake Shore Drive, and beyond that was the dark rainy lake. On the other side of her husband, the surgeon, was saying that he was at sea with art people.

It wasn't clear who the art people were. There were a few young men with earrings and one or two bodies in very short dresses fitted like socks, but most of the guests were older people dressed just the way people would be in Virginia, and the talk seemed to be about their children's problems.

Everyone was talking in a more emotional way than she imagined they normally did. The children were in drug programs or going through divorces. Susannah thought of her own children, anxious all of them that she no longer guard them. "No one told you what to do," they would point out to her. "I guess not," she would say. They would not be able to resist saying, "Look what you did when you were our age. You got *married*." Then they would be sorry. In their minds she had gotten married because of their crazy grandmother. Simple. Escape.

Of course they could not know the thing so irresistible it parted her from everything leading up to it, from all worry, from her bedroom with Jo, from Jo. The tiny supply room at school, the sheet faintly stenciled CLINIC, the window. The high-up radiant window pumping heat across the cot at noon, when Larry Kephart woke up and she pulled him up to her by his hot arms and said to him, "Don't cry."

Standing by the window she drank more of the wine they handed her, and found she could speak comfortably with the husband, the surgeon, who did not seem to have known Jo. Or perhaps he had been one of them, too, Jo's lovers, she thought suddenly, angrily, looking at the clean gray hair behind his big earlobes and the shirt collar digging into his shaven neck. He looked considerably younger than his little elderly wife. But it did not matter, did it? Nothing at all, certainly nothing that could be said or discovered in this room, mattered where Jo was concerned. "Sad, sad," Dr. Dominick kept saying when there was a pause.

She thought of Mrs. Dominick calling her husband at work to tell him about Jo. It must seem unfair, perhaps even infuriating, after operating on people all day to be told that someone else has used this time to force the life out of herself. Has gulped all her lithium and dropped herself down, a week after the decision to get married and have children, and a day after the exuberant passing of this news to her sister and father—but the surgeon getting this call from his wife wouldn't know that, or want, in all likelihood, to know it—into the brown commercial river right in the middle of the city, in the sight of people not so far above on the bridge, where, as one couple was to tell the police, although she had been walking slowly she had done nothing to draw attention to herself, so that no one thought to grab her before she got up and over and dropped herself into a river full, as Susannah pictured it, of barges and floating trash. She could not swim. She sank. No one jumped in to save her until it was too late. No one saved her.

Some of the Dominicks' art was too large for a room with furnishings in it and occupied a wide hall. One wall held huge paintings of trees — "Prints, actually. They're colored etchings," said Mrs. Dominick — tall as trees themselves. Susannah was going to comment on their beauty but she thought better of it, after calling them paintings. On the other hand Mrs. Dominick seemed not to notice little things but to be governed, in her regard for each work, by a maternal care that it not be passed over and a confidence that the artist still inhabited it, out of sight like a shy tenant.

At the end of the hall were Jo's photographs, on a wall to themselves, on either side of an old carved door. Susannah knew that some of them were recent because there were things other than machines in them. Two even had people.

In one there was a large-bodied young woman with her arms spread out, a hand on each of two big, bomb-like old-fashioned hairdryers. Stevia. But of course it was not Stevia. It was hard to know just what Stevia would look like now, but she would be much older than this. This mischievously straight-faced fat woman was under thirty.

Stevia's son would be that age now, and more. "Ah," Susannah said. She knew why she had put on her glasses and looked so long at the little print in the corner of the living room. The title had been written in pencil at the bottom with the print number: "Man with Antlers." The man's face wore a look neither alarmed nor proud, the look of a calm beast. She thought of herself at nine, hoping all summer that Stevia's baby would have something wrong with it, something unforgivably and incurably wrong, would be *an animal.* Everybody had the same ideas, really. The artists just didn't feel ashamed of their ideas and disgusted by them.

That could be good or it could be bad.

The wine was making her mildly unsteady. She was tired from being on the plane and trying to talk to Garland in the car, and from the speeches and the loud music, and from being given no food and introduced to people who said they were glad to meet Jo's sister. Glad. Susannah felt certain she was the only one here—except maybe Mrs. Dominick, with her wall of photographs—who had found happiness in knowing Jo. She shook off dizziness and stepped firmly away from the pictures. How strange it was to think now that things done so many years ago by Jo and herself had been happiness.

She leaned against the wall to fit her fingers down the side of her shoe, and almost fell. Mrs. Dominick said, "My dear, you need a minute or two to simply lie down. You can get right back up. Come with me."

Garland met them in the living room, flushed and carrying a bottle of wine. He said her whole name, "Susannah Floyd," the way people sometimes would back home when they first ran into you on the street. He seemed to forget she had a married name. "Here you are. I never have asked how your father is."

She held up her glass. "I couldn't tell you how many I've had. Thank you. My father couldn't come. He's old, he's upset, he can't leave his cows." Words poured out of her. "He's very tired, after my mother. Anyway we had Jo's service at our church and we buried her in the cemetery." "We buried her." What strange words. Like a secret crime. We buried Jo. She would have taken a picture of the hole. Not near our mother, there wasn't a space there, and that's just as well. And for days everyone brought us food, for days—you know how they do. You're from the South. And everyone talked about Jo's birth and the search party.

"And you have children, don't you?"

Surely he knew this. "Four. Two of them are taking exams right now. They were all just home for their grandmother's funeral. My daughter—she's the one who was so close to Jo—left the next day for Indonesia. She's going to study batik." She could not stop herself from saying all this so that he could see not only why her children had not come to this memorial but that they were out in the world, like Jo, not stuck in the amber of home as Jo might have described it to him. That no matter what Jo might have said or not said, Susannah's children were people who ventured out, who were involved in art, in going to school. "Of course the younger ones were at the funeral."

Garland said, clearing his throat, "Forgive me, I didn't mean why aren't they here."

The woman he had been talking to, who had come up behind him, said, "Well, what did you mean, Garland?" She said this rather drunkenly, taking his arm, and he bent to let her down onto the couch the same way he had helped Susannah into the car. He was the bereaved, like Susannah. His hands shook. Yet he was attending to everybody. Susannah turned to speak to Mrs. Dominick so he would not think he had to attend to her.

"I don't need to lie down," she said stubbornly. "I came so I could be here."

"Just come with me. Come along." Mrs. Dominick took her arm.

There was no way to refuse. This must be what had appealed to Jo.

"That's Garland's wife," Mrs. Dominick said in the little bed-room. It was a shut-up room, with a chair, a low carved chest and a single bed in it, cool with a camphory air they had stirred to life in the dark. "His ex-wife." She meant the drunken woman with the eyebrows. She turned on a little lamp by the bed and pulled back the comforter. "This was Jo's room when she lived here, from time to time." She hoisted her shoulders and her large bust and let them down with a rasping sigh. "You know, my dear, about your sister's decision to marry Garland."

"Yes." Susannah gulped from her glass. "What happened?" She had sworn she would not ask anybody this.

"Well, my dear, your poor mother died, for one thing."

Your poor mother. It gave Susannah a little start. No one had said this, even at her mother's funeral. She said, "Actually I think Jo was more or less waiting for our mother to die."

"Well, now." Mrs. Dominick eyed her pityingly. "But these things are mysterious, aren't they? And then Garland is a man of . . . emotion. I believe the French have a word for it, ah, *l'homme* . . ." She sat down in the chair with her hand on her heart. "Oh I can't think what. Jo was not used to that, I don't think, do you?"

"I don't know." But Susannah knew everything about Jo. "Did she say much about our life?"

"Not very much at all. Oh, I don't mean . . . my dear, not the family. With *men* she wasn't used to it."

"I mean did she tell you the stories?"

"What stories are those?"

"Well, about her birth? About the search party?"

"My dear, she didn't seem to look upon the past in that way."

"What way?"

"Oh, the way we do, most of us, looking back. Oh, we regret things but we have a soft spot for ourselves and what happened to us. I do anyway."

"But she told you about our mother."

"Oh yes. But only a little."

Garland had followed them. He leaned heavily against the doorframe and rubbed his jowly face with both hands. He had taken off his tie and unbuttoned his damp collar. Mrs. Dominick settled, puffing, in the little armchair. Garland said, "May I join you?" He sat down on the bed beside Susannah and stared distractedly at her. She thought ahead, past whatever these two intended to tell her, to being able to go to sleep.

"You do look like her in certain ways," Garland said. "Doesn't she, Eugenia?"

"Well, that's a compliment," Susannah said. One of Mrs. Dominick's tears finally ran out onto the cheek, leaving a trail in the thick old-woman's powder she had on.

"Though Jo was so thin," Garland said with a bewildered sigh, and then as if Jo's thinness had been an illusion in which he had been tangled, he made a gesture toward Susannah and Mrs. Dominick, as if their proportions were reality itself. A gallant gesture. It would have blocked any reference Susannah might have made—but she was not going to do this—to differences between herself and Jo in weight, in beauty.

"A WINCH! It's a machine! Isn't it? Jo would have liked the winch," the woman with the thick eyebrows, Garland's ex-wife, called out in the middle of the story. Her name was Anne. She too was popular and important here, though Susannah did not think she was imagining that some distaste and pity attached to Anne, too. Or perhaps not. Garland seemed to rely on her in some way. Art people. But Anne was sitting on the arm of the chair stroking the hand of a thin young man sprawled there, whereas Garland sat on the bed with Susannah, in his socks, with his knees wrapped in his arms. There were seven or eight people in the room, and as many bottles on the night table. Anne's head had dropped but kept butting in Garland's direction. "Gar knows that fascination she had with machines."

"I don't remember if she liked the winch," Susannah said seriously. She felt the beginning of a pain in her chest. Heartburn. That meant nausea was on the way. She had known this and gone ahead and drunk seven or eight glasses of wine. Maybe more. "Was this after Stevia?" said Garland.

"Stevia was gone by then. Stevia," she said to the people in the bedroom, "was the girl, the woman, who took care of us. We had a—we had a disabled mother." She should have found a simple word, such as Mrs. Dominick would have found. But Mrs. Dominick had leaned back a while ago with her mouth open and her little blue eyes closed. Hours before that her husband had appeared in the light of the doorway, shaken hands all around and gone to bed.

"The things Jo said about Stevia," Garland said dreamily. His accent had deepened as the wine went lower in the bottles. It was not a Virginia accent but it was similar, she thought. Maybe North Carolina. "Now you're gonna tell me she wasn't a witch."

"Stevia?" Susannah said. "She was fat . . . maybe she teased . . . but she was . . ."

"And all those other witches and gorgons, the ones who molested her in stores and strapped her down in emergency rooms . . ."

"There was something unprotected about Jo," Mrs. Dominick said firmly, rousing from her semi-sleep.

"Well, what happened?" said Anne, with impatience. "You're winching the bull out of the creek. What happened to it?"

"Oh." Susannah had to think. "They got him out. They got him up on the wagon but his heart stopped. He died."

At the word "died," Anne gave her a sharp look. "That must have been terribly up—upsetting," said the thin young man beside Anne, with a burp, "to little girls."

"No. Well . . . not as much as you might expect. It was to my father, though. Though he wouldn't let you know. He wouldn't let on."

"I'm trying to see it. I'm trying to see you-all," cried Garland in a different voice. He wrung his hands. "You must have thought of this particular thing because it explains something about her to you."

"Do you think so?" Susannah said, ashamed now. "I think I just thought of it because of whatever it was you said, Anne, a minute ago, when you said that about Jo not being a farm girl. But she was, really. We did things on the farm when we were girls; we had chores, not just in the house, in the dairy when we were old enough. I was thinking of how we—"

"No!" Garland thundered, throwing his legs over the edge of the bed and slapping them. "I mean, *something*—!"

Susannah tried dizzily to think. There were so many stories. They had all been telling them, all night. Jo shoplifted in art school. Jo slapped somebody at an opening. She threw a camera into the toilet. She climbed out onto the girders of a huge building. These were things she had done. People in the room could attest to them, while the things Susannah could attest to were vague, they did not really have a shape or fit like the others' stories, ball into socket, with what they all knew now. It did not seem to Susannah that her own memories could be made to fit, in that way.

Memory was the opposite of the movies with their important slow motion. Everything you could bring to mind took place rather jerkily and partially. You couldn't even see the entire person. You saw or felt a limb, you *scraped* at the scene to get a face.

In her pocket, Jo had her first note from a boy. That was important, though Susannah had left it out in telling the story. "Your sweet," the note said. Jo was only nine; she seemed to be pretending more interest in the note than she felt. She had pulled it out half a dozen times, flaunting it in front of Susannah and their father, forming the two words, "Your sweet," with her lips. Jo was under a tree with her note while they were pulling the bull out of the creek. The boy who had written it did not matter to her. She did not like him. Almost certainly her heart was not racing as they dragged and hauled at the bull, the way Susannah's was, as if it would work its way out of her chest and go flopping into the water with the bull. Animals did not matter to Jo. She was not afraid of the bull, she was not afraid *for* him. It was Susannah who was literal and ordinary, even in her sadness, who stopped liking meat when she realized about Herefords, who wished for a dog. It was Susannah who sank, again and again, into self-pity. Jo didn't pity herself or anyone else.

But something mattered to her, Susannah thought. More than to me. I wasn't the one who took pictures of the slaughterhouse. Something mattered. It made Jo angry; it altered her, like the photographs she showed me where the silver had darkened and burned the paper.

No. No one ever got mad at us. No, we were not afraid. We were careful. That was all. Careful about something. It was not anything we could have described to the women who asked, Mrs. Bayliss or Mrs. Grayson, or anyone. The things that people thought should matter to us did not. We didn't care whether we went to their parties, whether we went to the swimming pool. We didn't care about our clothes or what Stevia gave us to eat.

We didn't care what anybody thought of our mother.

We only cared what *we* thought. We only cared that it was taking so long, the waiting, going on and on. We did think she was waiting, just as we were, for everything to change, as it could, as it would, if we . . . if we—but we could not pin down what it was we would have to do. We imagined her having undergone this change while we were out of the house, and waiting for us to get home from school so that she could say . . . the thing she would say to us. "Girls . . ." The way women said that, mothers. To be followed by the explanations for what had happened up until then. How everything had been for so many years, in our house, and why it had been that way. All of it.

Though eventually we did not even think that. Or I didn't.

THE bull had stumbled into the creek when the bank gave way, and broken his leg. He was not seen for days, and then they heard him. He had plowed up the creek bed trying to get out. Their father would not shoot him. He was valuable: their father gave this as his reason. The vet was there; they were going to winch the bull out. Susannah remembered the words, everybody saying them as they climbed into the pickup. Winch him out. And in fact the bull, dragged out by the heavy chain looped behind his front legs, so that they popped forward, made it onto the hay wagon and then reared up his head—as big, Susannah thought, as the tree stumps her father had been uprooting all summer with the same chain—dropped the huge head, and died. "Lungs couldn't take it," said the vet, after they felt his neck and armpit and listened and made sure he was dead. "That or the heart. We don't know how much fighting he was doing for two days." He was a heavy bull, Susannah remembered that. He weighed over a ton. She had gone up close to him once when he was in the squeeze chute getting a shot. He had rolled his globe eye with a fly in the corner of it downward and back to get a look at her, and blinked his long stiff lashes.

The vet was brushing the mud off his shirt and pants. He had his own truck parked sideways on the slope with a rifle in the rack. Susannah could see he was tired and not surprised. She felt tired too, looking at the bull's black muddy legs, and sick.

Their father turned, leaned forward and pushed on a tree with both hands. "Well, I sure thought we'd do better than this," he said. That would be the last they would hear of it. That was more than he said about most things.

But he was a man of feeling. Wasn't that what Mrs. Dominick called it? Their father was a man of feeling, and once he had wept aloud. Susannah knew this. Everybody put it in when they told the story. He wept in front of thirty men and women, when his daughter was handed up the railway embankment in triumph to him. This was fact, not legend.

Susannah had heard and sorted and judged, all her life, the stories told by people who had been in the search party, or relatives of theirs. She knew legend from fact. It was said that she had been prevented from leaving Bayliss's field, that guarded by the herd, in the same way calves are encircled and kept together, she had found the creek, drunk from it, and been shepherded away from it. It was said that the reason she was not dehydrated was that she had nursed from a Hereford mother, or eaten the wet clover, or eaten dried-up cow dung, as a child might. There was no way for anyone to know any of this.

But certain things were facts: she had been found in the middle of the herd in Bayliss's field, badly sunburned and mosquito-bitten. She had been carried back the way she must have come, across the field, the men sometimes walking backward to hail a troop of searchers farther back on the same land, who could not hear them, and down along the railroad track to the bank below her house. Several of the farmers had gotten around to combing the cinders there for signs of her. They stood up when they heard the shouts. They scrambled up the bank with her, passing her along above the brambles. Somebody went out at a run across the clover field after her father, and he came stumbling down the yard. He had on a bandana under his hat, and somebody lifted his hat and pulled the square of cloth off his head and put it in his hand for his streaming eyes.

THEY were talking about a book of Jo's photographs, a book Garland was working on. People who were his employees had made mistakes putting it together. So, Susannah thought. He was not an artist, he was some sort of a . . .

There were lost proofs of something. "Of course!" chortled Anne. "When was it otherwise?" Anne had drunk a staggering amount of wine but Susannah could see she was not confused, completely confused and sick, the way Susannah herself was.

Susannah was concentrating on staying ahead of the room's steady circling. She was in a dark lobe that expanded and contracted as if the voices in the room, slow and intermittent now, were dolefully pumping it. "In my family," she would say if things got any worse, "no one drinks. We can't, it makes us sick."

In the morning, in a few hours, she would be back in the little car on the way to Jo's apartment. It seemed less terrible than it had, to think of doing this. It seemed to have become a problem of movement, forcing movement on a body that preferred to be still. No choice. It was just heaving oneself up through waterlogged heaviness, like getting up to feed the baby, feeling along the wall to the crib, clumsy until the assault of tenderness. Only there would be drawers of underwear, letters, negatives. Jo's things. No choice. She would reach in.

The talk pulsed slowly on. Mrs. Dominick was awake again and Susannah heard her voice join in, her matter-of-fact sentences with their wheezing interruptions. She felt the voice was settling something for her but she could not make out the sense of it. She heard it the way she would hear, in bed across the room from Jo, the faraway bawl of a cow at the back of the farm. Everybody agreed with Mrs. Dominick, by the sound of it. Whatever she was saying was bringing the night to a close. Garland put his face in his hands. Susannah struggled to sit up.

She's passing out, a voice said. She knew she was not going to pass out, she was going to be sick.

In the bathroom, Garland used both hands to hold her, one on her back and the other on the old sore collarbone. Her ribs were doing the work, it seemed, opening so far they hurt her skin and shutting again to heave everything out. Garland might have been getting ready to cry one final time but the vomiting got everybody into action. Then they were gone. Mrs. Dominick said she would put tea bags on Susannah's eyes in the morning, for that was her remedy. Her faithful remedy, she said.

The bedroom had a stately, tilted spin, with a sound in it like tires rolling up on gravel. Susannah felt a momentary anticipation. Someone was coming. At length she identified the sound as rain on the window. It was raining hard now. From under the covers they had pulled over her, she tried to look through one eye without moving her head. She saw two bulky figures moving around the room, heard them whisper to each other. Garland put something on the bedside table. Her glasses. He looked down at her. From below, the lamp lit his face so that all the folds stood out, and his shadowy fixed eyes showed her herself going to sleep in the middle of the vigil she was to keep with him. I'm awake, she tried to say. He did not look good, standing there looking down at her.

Ah, she thought. Ah.

She was sailing slowly backward but her head cleared and she could see, as if from years of familiarity with his movements, the tiredness that had confused his purpose. He undid his belt to tuck his shirt in, buckled it, pressed his abdomen with both hands, and picked up two of the wine bottles. Then he put them down again and sat down in the chair beside her bed. There were faraway voices yelling. Or not voices . . . the rain.

She almost slept, but she gave a start, thinking she was falling. "It's all right," he said. To let him know she heard, she uncurled her fingers on the bed, and he put his hand in them. Without opening her eyes she weighed it in hers.

Ah. Garland.

She was carried backward again. She listened to the far-off muffled yelling. She could not open her eyes but she knew someone was coming for her, someone was in search of her.